Dedication

*For my husband Butch,
whose love and patience
provided the support and
encouragement
I needed to finish my novel.*

Survival
Climate of Fire, Book One
Shirley Bigelow DeKelver

Print ISBNs

Amazon print 9780228626503
Ingram Spark 9780228626510
Barnes & Noble 9780228626527

BWL Publishing Inc.

Books we love to write ...
Authors around the world.

http://bwlpublishing.ca

Acknowledgements

I am indebted to my friend Kay Johnston, published author, and my cousin and "almost sister" Sharon Karsten, who agreed to take on the tremendous task as my beta readers and proof-readers, and who motivated me with their valuable input and suggestions.

To my immediate and extended families, who are always willing to listen to me, encourage me, and love me unconditionally.

To my friends and members of The Shuswap Association of Writers, The Word on the Lake Writers Festival, Gracesprings Collective Inc., Writers Nook, and the Shuswap Writers Group, who provided positive reinforcement in helping me reach my goals.

My gratitude goes to Jude Pittman, Publisher of BWL Publishing Inc. and Nancy Bell, Editor, who helped me so much, as I knew "absolutely nothing" about trilogies when I stumbled across their paths. Thank you.

Author's Note

My story is, of course, fictitious, creating a background for my fictional characters, I do however, stress the devastating natural events occurring in my book are most definitely not fabricated.

Table of Contents

Chapter One

Vancouver, BC –2045 ~ The Big One

It was late January, creeping tendrils of fog wrapped around the trunks of the huge cedars and Douglas firs. A soft dusting of snow had fallen earlier in the day, and the humidity and melancholy atmosphere threatened a turn in the weather. Usually, my mom and dad worked long hours, but today they arrived home just before dinner. The strain and exhaustion masking their faces concerned me and I watched Mom as she wandered to the kitchen window and stared into the backyard. She was chewing her nails which is what she did when she was worried.

"What's wrong Mom, why are you and Dad acting so weird?"

"It is nothing Carlie, we just had a long day at work. Why don't you take Poppy outside for a run?" she suggested, turning to face me. "She's been locked up in the house all day and could use some exercise."

"Are you kidding, it's raining."

"A little rain never hurt anyone. Just take her outside please."

I stared at Mom for a moment, she was holding something back, and it made me uneasy. I got Poppy's harness and leash from the mudroom. The clinking of the dog tags alerted her sharp ears, and she barrelled down the stairs, almost knocking me over in her excitement. I struggled with her harness; she hated it when we constrained her, it was the same old rigmarole every time.

"Put on your warm jacket," Mom said. "You don't want you to catch a chill."

"Jeez Mom, I'm sixteen, I know when to put on a coat."

"Of course, you do, but I don't like the look of those black clouds, there's some nasty weather headed this way."

"Fine, I'll bundle up, but I'm already wearing my hoodie."

"Carlie, I know I'm over-protective, but you'll understand one day when you have kids of your own."

"Never going to happen," I mumbled. "I'm not ever going to get married."

Mom smiled and headed in the direction of the staircase leading to the loft. I snatched my jacket and opened the back door, grabbing Poppy's collar before she escaped. I snapped on her leash and held it tightly as I struggled with my coat.

"Don't wander off, maybe stay in the backyard, okay?"

"Mom, you're doing it again. I take Poppy out every day, what could possibly happen?"

Mom said nothing, but the troubled look on her face worried me.

"I'm going upstairs to read for a while."

"That same book you started three months ago."

"Yes, smarty-pants," she chuckled. "I will finish it ...."

"I know, I know, let me guess."

"Come hell or high water," we said in unison.

Mom shook her head, muttering something about insubordinate children.

The skies turned darker and the leaves on the trees furled inward, a sure sign the weather was changing, and not for the better. I decided to take her advice and stay in the backyard instead of taking Poppy on her usual walk around the neighbourhood. I pulled the drawstrings on my hoodie tighter.

Removing Poppy's leash, I stuffed it inside my jacket. I threw her rubber ball across the lawn, she raced after it; I laughed when her long, floppy ears bounced up and down. She brought it back, and I wrestled it from her mouth. This time I threw it as hard as I could, it bounced off the back fence and rolled to the thicket separating our lot from our neighbours. We did not allow Poppy to go there as Vancouver had a large coyote problem. They were spreading into the heavily wooded areas and becoming increasingly dangerous, attacking dogs, cats, and sometimes people.

Poppy ran across the lawn, stopped, and barked excitedly. The hawthorn tree next to where she was standing erupted, and hundreds of swallows took flight, soaring upward in a deafening, frenzied cloud.

As if on cue, the skies opened, and heavy drops of rain pounded on the ground. I stuffed my cold hands inside my pockets, trying to remember where I had left my toque, scarf, and gloves.

"Come on girl, let's go back inside, we're getting drenched."

Poppy ignored me and barked louder. Something was scaring her; I had never seen her so worked up. She growled, and before I could catch her, she bolted into the woods.

"Poppy, stop, come here right now."

I was terrified she might run into a coyote; I knew she wouldn't stand a chance if she was attacked. She seldom disobeyed me; she knew the woods were off-limits. I entered the spot where she disappeared, but she was nowhere in sight. The silence was overpowering, almost surreal. Everything felt off, and an uneasy feeling cat pawed up my spine.

The rain was relentless, and I raced down a slick, muddy animal trail, glad I was wearing my hiking boots. Without warning, the tree branches swayed as if buffeted by a heavy wind. I tumbled over a large, exposed root and landed heavily on the ground. Angrily, I stood and wiped the mud off my jeans. It was deathly still, then a low rumbling, sounding like a train, echoed through the stillness. The ground shook and pitched. Shrill warning sirens shattered the silence.

"Poppy," I screamed. There was no answering bark, and all the training and advice from my parents about earthquakes disappeared as my only focus was finding my missing dog. I prayed she had enough sense to head home.

The tremors became more violent, I wrapped my arms around the trunk of a huge cedar, lost my grip, and landed in the middle of a puddle. I struggled to stand in the slippery muck, but the tremors were too strong. I realized this earthquake was more powerful than any I had encountered in the past. I needed to find shelter, as quickly as possible.

I spotted the dark outline of the rock barrier separating our property from the neighbours. I remembered a huge hole in the wall where I used to hide when I was young, long before the woods became off-limits because of roving coyotes.

A sharp crack above my head sent me rolling aside just as a massive branch fell from the tree. I scurried on my hands and knees into the underbrush, scratching my face on a raspberry bush.

The shaking intensified, and I was relieved when I finally arrived at the barrier. I grabbed the jagged rocks for support and pulled myself upright. It had been years since I had been here, and I panicked, trying to remember where the opening was.

I spotted a cluster of bushes growing next to the wall. Could it be covering the entrance? I lurched into the undergrowth and pulled the dead branches aside. Relieved, I recognized the hole, and dived inside seconds before a huge hemlock crashed to the ground, not three centimetres from where I was standing.

I curled into a tight ball, and wrapped my arms around my head, protecting my body from falling chunks of earth and stones. The tremors seemed to go on forever, then just as quickly, they stopped.

I shook the dirt from my hair and climbed outside. Suddenly, I remembered what my parents had drilled into me about aftershocks, they often caused as much if not more damage than the earthquake itself. Almost immediately, the ground heaved and groaned, and I nose-dived back into the hole. Gigantic trees boomed as they toppled to the ground. I closed my eyes and hugged my knees tightly. My heart pounded and I found it difficult to breathe. I gasped for air, and I shook my head in denial. This couldn't be happening. Are Mom and Dad okay, what if Poppy isn't with them?

After what seemed a lifetime, the tremors subsided, and I cautiously crawled from the burrow. I stood on weak knees and forced myself to stand. I felt disoriented, not knowing what to do. In a daze, I scrambled over the fallen hemlock and gaped in shock. The intensity of the seismic waves severed and broke branches, split trunks and toppled stately pines, hemlocks, and firs. A small crevasse opened the forest floor, and rocks, mud, and huge branches were devoured by the breach.

I climbed over enormous boulders and the torn roots of fallen trees. The destruction was abysmal and I wasn't sure if I headed in the right direction. Between the trees, I glimpsed the green grass of our lawn in the distance and picked up my pace. I recognized the outline of our hawthorn tree and assumed Poppy returned to the house after the first tremor, she was terrified of earthquakes.

An earth-shattering explosion resonated nearby; the earth convulsed in agony. I flew backwards and landed in a cluster of bushes. Forcing myself to stand I stumbled toward the lawn. I froze — our house was gone! In its place was a mound of bricks, wood, and shattered glass.

In a trance I wandered over to the woodshed, which miraculously was undamaged. I spotted my toque, gloves and scarf lying on the woodpile where I had left them yesterday when I helped Dad chop firewood. I grabbed the saturated clothing and hurriedly stuffed them inside my jacket.

I headed for our demolished house. As Mom and Dad had no idea I followed Poppy into the woods, I assumed they were searching for me around the neighbourhood. They wouldn't have gone far, and I knew they would never leave without me.

But Mother Nature had more surprises in store, she was not finished yet.

I smelled gas escaping from the back of the house close to where I was standing. I raced toward the front yard. The explosion was sudden and unexpected. I heaved forward, landing on my back and banging my head on the edge of the sidewalk; then everything went black. I groaned and opened my eyes. Rolling to my knees, I struggled to stand, wincing at the painful throb on the back of my head. I gingerly reached up and touched it, and when I looked at my fingers, they were covered with blood.

I stared at the remains of our house, not accepting what was happening. Flames engulfed the rubble, turning it into a fiery inferno. I staggered back from the intense heat.

I had no idea how much time passed but I swear to this day I heard Mom whisper *'Carlie, the tsunami, run.'*

I inhaled sharply, fighting to catch my breath, realizing at that moment Mom, Dad, and Poppy had not made it out of the house in time. I fell to my knees, the tears streaming down my face, and I screamed in agony.

As before, I felt my mother's presence, and I thought of her gift, her last gesture of love to me, and a remarkable energy embraced me. I rose, and reeling unsteadily, walked through the front gate. By reflex, I turned and locked it behind me, and it was not until much later when I realized the futility of that gesture.

I wandered down the sidewalk, traumatized; the rain increased in intensity, and I shivered not only from the cold but from shock.

The pavement buckled, I glanced at the abandoned cars parked haphazardly on the street, and at the people screaming and running nowhere in panic. A power line was ripped loose, spilling sparks, writhing, and twisting like a snake. Houses located along our boulevard were consumed by flames started by ruptured gas lines. The gutters and the street were flooded with torrential rain.

I walked aimlessly, unsure of where to go, and what I needed to do. There was no doubt the magnitude of the earthquake was catastrophic, and any area within a kilometre of the ocean was the most dangerous place to be. I had no idea how long I was unconscious, but I knew a tsunami always followed an earthquake of this magnitude. It would have hit Vancouver Island less than twenty minutes after the eruption. The estimated arrival time in Vancouver would be approximately two hours, and my time was running out. I had to get to higher ground.

We lived close to the Pacific Ocean, and the highest point on Westside Vancouver was Queen Elizabeth Park, located at Little Mountain. I knew how to get there as we often went to the Bloedel Conservatory.

I ran, my head pounding, then I stopped abruptly. It was over seven kilometres to Little Mountain, and I would never make it in time if I went on foot. I spotted a bicycle leaning against a tree. I raced over to it hoping the chain was not locked; luck was with me.

Feeling dizzy, I waited to clear my head, then jumped on the bike. I tore through properties where the houses were still intact, taking as many shortcuts as I could. Cars were lined bumper-to-bumper on the thoroughfares, horns were blowing, and frantic people yelled from open windows. There was no use heading north or south as Vancouver was an island, surrounded by water, and likely most of the bridges did not survive the earthquake.

During this time of year, dusk arrived early, and it wouldn't be long before darkness cloaked the city. The headlights from the cars provided sufficient light for me to maneuver around the gridlocked vehicles. I pedalled faster, keeping away from the flooded curbs. I turned a corner and slammed on the brakes, a huge gap in the road made it impossible for the vehicles to get through, and people were abandoning their cars.

I was wasting too much time. The street sign for Cambie Street loomed out of the gloom, which l knew led directly to Queen Elizabeth Park. I made a sharp left turn and cycled harder, zigging, and zagging around stalled and abandoned cars. I wasn't the only one who had the same idea. A swarm of people surrounded me, frantically heading in the same direction.

Nausea and dizziness along with the tiredness dragging at my limbs made me realize I had a concussion, but I dared not stop. Wiping the rain from my eyes, I pulled my hoodie tighter over my forehead. I rounded a corner and swerved to the side, almost bowling into a crowd of frenzied people. They were pushing and shoving, which only slowed their progress. A roar rumbled in the distance, and I knew it wouldn't be long before the tsunami arrived. I abandoned the bike and hurled myself into the frenzied mob. I somehow found the strength to stay on my feet. A panicked boy shoved me aside; he barrelled into an elderly man and knocked him to the ground. I watched in horror as the uncontrolled mob trampled the horrified man.

The crowd raced up the path leading to the Bloedel Conservatory; I moved to the side, remembering a rocky trail looping around the park. Most people weren't aware it existed as it was narrow, rugged, and steep, but if I made the correct turns, I would get to the Conservatory in half the time. I turned left and recognized the landmarks on the path. I climbed steadily, scrambling over the rocks, ignoring the rain and my throbbing head. I was grateful for our regular family hikes to the Coast Mountains, which kept me in shape.

The darkness shrouded me, and I stumbled on the slippery rocks. I recalled the trail made a sharp turn; then I would have to climb steadily upward, and when I got to the top turn right onto a dirt path leading to the Conservatory. I spotted the lighted dome in the distance and followed the few people who had chosen to take the same route. A few of them had flashlights, and I shadowed them as we scrambled upward. Reaching the back of the Conservatory, I fell to the ground in exhaustion. The roar of the tsunami was deafening.

I heard people shouting, I walked around to the front of the Conservatory and over to the lookout, pushing my way through the hordes. A wall of water, carrying boats, cars, and struggling people, rushed toward Little Mountain. Horrified screams filled the air as hundreds of eyes riveted on the devastation below. The churning water and debris smashed into the trees surrounding the park, carrying away people who had arrived too late. The earth trembled in agony, then the tsunami receded. The silence was crushing.

Discussions regarding tsunamis and their destructive paths raced through my mind. First waves were always followed by a second, the worst was yet to come!

A small group of people, standing directly behind me, were having an animated discussion. A deep voice said. "It's over, let's go home."

I spun around, shaking my head vigorously. "You can't leave. There's another wave coming, and it will cause more damage, you must stay here."

The small group consisted of two adults and two teenagers. The man who had spoken stared at me; skepticism written across his face.

"My parents were seismologists," I continued. "And they knew a lot about earthquakes and tsunamis. You're safer if you stay here."

Then he spoke three words-three words that sanctioned their fate. "They make it?"

The look on my face was answer enough, and his words cut me like a knife. "If that was their calling, how come they didn't warn people this was coming?"

I stood frozen, unable to answer his question that I had been asking myself over and over. He turned and faced the small group. "Thanks for the warning kid, but I've made my decision, I'm taking my family home."

I watched as they walked away. The teenage boy, around my age, turned and looked directly at me. He nodded, then resignedly followed his family.

Unfortunately, they were not the only ones leaving, large groups, including adults with younger children, trailed behind them down the embankment.

I left the lookout and stumbled to the Conservatory. Ignoring the pouring rain I dropped to the ground, shivering uncontrollably. Reaching inside my jacket I grabbed my wet toque, scarf, and gloves. I pulled my toque down over my hoodie, wrapped the scarf tightly around my neck, and put on my damp gloves.

Reaching inside my jacket, I removed Poppy's leash; I wrapped it tightly around my wrist, then I pulled my toque lower and covered my eyes, masking the desolation surrounding me.

My parents' earlier behaviour now made sense; they must have known what was coming. Why hadn't we left before it was too late? The decision to remain in Vancouver had been theirs and theirs alone.

Something died inside of me that day, and it would take me a long time to find the answers to forgive them.

Chapter Two

After the tsunami, I wandered the streets like a zombie. My thoughts often returned to the day of the earthquake, remembering the intense heat of the fire as it consumed our house, with my family inside. I would wake at night, drenched in sweat, anguish engulfing me, crying uncontrollably.

The surrounding area around Queen Elizabeth Park was comprised of modular homes and rundown apartments, only a few of them were partially intact. The trees bordering the lower portion of the park sustained horrendous damage from the tsunamis, and over time the water receded, leaving twisted and skeletal bodies of the once magnificent cedars and pines.

I listened as people talked; Vancouver's entire coastline was destroyed; the houses and buildings were either burned or reduced to rubble. A large fishing boat was found as far inland as Richmond. The trees, houses, buildings, and anything located along the Fraser River were obliterated. There was nothing left outside the confines of Little Mountain.

The remaining inland districts were slowly emptying. The coldest days of winter were rapidly approaching, and soon there would be a shortage of water and food. People headed north hoping to find a better life, while the lucky few who had relatives in the Interior headed eastward.

I often thought about the families and people who survived the tsunami and chose to return to their homes, wondering if anything remained to salvage. Those who stayed at Little Mountain were the homeless or orphaned; most of them children and young adults.

At first, there was food to be found in restaurants, grocery stores, and abandoned houses, at least until it went bad. A few of the shops survived the earthquake, and it did not take long for all the supplies to disappear. I managed to salvage jeans, t-shirts, underclothes, socks, and a few warm sweaters. I found woollen pyjamas, which would come in handy in the times ahead, more than I could ever imagine. My coat and hoodie were warm enough to cope with Vancouver winters.

My greatest find was a camping store, there were so many kids inside shoving and pushing, it looked like a Black Friday sale. I was no different, and I managed to claim a sturdy backpack, a hip flask, a flashlight and batteries, and a box containing a grill with a set of tin dishes, cutlery, and matches. I spotted a lone sleeping bag on the top shelf at the back of the store. A boy around my age was standing next to me, we glanced at each other then took off. Our arms were full, and I raced after him and passed him a few centimetres from the rack. I quickly scaled the empty shelves and won the prize. He scowled, and I stood my ground. I might not be as strong, but I could run a lot faster, and he knew it. He gave me the finger, then turned and disappeared in the disorderly mob.

Finding and commandeering the supplies bolstered my confidence, I lived alone in one of the abandoned houses and survived as well as I could.

* * *

Loneliness made the days pass slowly, but I somehow managed to endure. In late August, I awoke to the sound of sporadic chopping and a high-pitched squeal outside my bedroom window. I peeked from behind the closed drapes and was surprised to see a helicopter landed in the middle of the street. Uniformed soldiers ran from house to house. It wouldn't be long before they arrived at my door.

I jumped out of bed, my heart pounding. I tore down the basement stairs and hid behind the furnace. The front door opened, and heavy footsteps thumped across the floor.

My hands were shaking, and I inhaled sharply, trying to control my panicked breathing. A woman's voice echoed through the house.

"Is there anyone here"?

I froze, not answering. A second set of footsteps joined those of the first. "Any luck Corporal?" a commanding voice asked.

"No sir, the bed has been slept in, but I don't think there's anyone here."

"You know your orders, if they don't want to be found, we leave them behind."

"Yes Sir."

"Hit the next house, we have a lot of ground to cover."

"Sir, I haven't checked downstairs yet."

"Alright Corporal, be quick about it."

I listened to the clump of heavy boots on the stairs and hunkered deeper into the shadows. A young soldier came into view. She stopped at the bottom of the steps.

"Hello, is there anyone here?" she asked again.

She must have sensed my presence, she hesitated and waited, but she had her orders. Shaking her head, she turned and walked heavily up the stairs. I heard the front door close, and my last chance for discovery disappeared.

Living like hermits for almost eight months left most of the survivors on Little Mountain distrustful, fearing strangers, trusting no one. In the beginning, I prayed someone would rescue me; I listened to the conversations of the older teenagers and gang members who expressed their hatred and distrust of anyone living "outside" Little Mountain. They blamed the Canadian military for their failure to have more rescue attempts, and as time passed their anger and hatred grew as did mine.

I wondered how my life would have changed if I had answered the soldier's calls. I grasped my personal decision to remain hidden had cost me.

I remember the day I turned seventeen, but as far as I was concerned, birthdays were irrelevant, they were events significant from a past life. There was no time to celebrate and no-one to celebrate with, it was a constant battle to exist.

The next day, while scavenging for food I spotted a cluster of boys next to an abandoned building. I hid behind a bush and unashamedly listened to their conversation.

"You hear those copters the other day?"

"Yeah, they've been around before, trying to get people to leave. No chance of that, besides, there's nothing left out there for me, I like it here."

A thin, light-haired boy nodded in agreement. "I hear they ain't coming back. That was the last rescue attempt."

"That's crap Joe, they'll be back," a greasy-looking bloke replied.

"It has been eight months since the earthquake, they're finished here. They've moved all the equipment and soldiers over to Vancouver Island, things are bad there."

"So, things are bad here too."

"It's worse there, most of the northern part of the Island is a pile of rubble, and the west coast got the brunt of the tsunami."

"What are you, a Wikipedia junky? Anything else you want to spill."

Joe had nothing more to say. He shrugged, took a half-finished cigarette from his pocket, and lit it. Inhaling deeply, he blew smoke into the air, then walked away.

"Jeez, what a jerk," the greasy guy said. "Thinks he knows everything."

Solemnly, I returned to the house, and the first thing I did was check my rations. I was out of food. I searched daily but every place was picked clean; I needed to move higher up Little Mountain and find a new retreat. I packed everything I owned, then rolled my sleeping bag tightly and tied it on the top of my backpack. The houses I passed were unliveable or damaged beyond repair. I continued my search and found a secluded root cellar dug into an embankment, concealed beneath the hanging branches of a willow tree. It was warm inside and I kept dry when it rained and my secret refuge provided safety when the ashes from the volcanos inundated the air and made it difficult to breathe. I took it as a good omen when I discovered several jars of canned fruit and tomatoes buried in the back of the cellar.

It did not take me long to realize, although it was my preference to live alone, I was easy prey. The first time I was attacked,

I did not fight back, only because I had no idea how. There were two boys and a girl, and they approached me when I tried to pass them on the street. I spent most of the day scavenging and found a small cache of food buried behind a shed, two cans of cherries, a jar of olives, and a tin of sardines.

One of the guys grabbed the cherries, and I yelled at him to give them back. His two companions hooted and stamped their feet. Then the girl stepped forward, leered, and pushed me as hard as she could. I dropped the olives and the sardines, hitting my elbows on the sidewalk when I landed. She kicked me hard and then she kicked me again. Stunned, I screamed in pain, covering my head with my arms. She looked at me in disgust as I cowered on the ground.

"Come on guys," she scowled. "This one ain't worth the trouble."

They left me bruised and battered. I lost everything I foraged; I would not eat that day. Yet that was not what I remembered about our confrontation. The girl was twice as vicious as her male companions, which made me realize, if I wanted to survive on the streets alone, I must become just like her.

I had always been a fast runner, which ability I now used to my advantage. I found a sharp pocketknife, and practiced with it, learning to defend myself if the circumstances warranted. The days passed, and I spent most of my time on the streets, foraging for food and savagely protecting what was mine.

I kept to myself, silent and sullen. I soon earned a reputation, and I had no further altercations from petty thieves and troublemakers. If anyone dared to confront me, it was they who limped away with cuts and bruises. I didn't fight pretty, but it kept me alive.

In January, I celebrated the New Year by roasting chestnuts I found on an old tree growing in the backyard of a house close by. My root cellar was warm and comfortable, hidden from wandering gangs.

I had my grill and my sleeping bag to keep me warm. I would stare into the coals, depressed and lonely, thinking about Mom, Dad, and Poppy. I would give anything to see them again, to touch them, to talk with them, but in time, I accepted it would never happen. My anger slowly dissolved when I understood their decision to stay at home rather than try to escape in our car. We wouldn't have gotten far before the earthquake struck. They decided to take their chances by being at home with their family. Unfortunately, destiny had thrown a loop in their plan.

I wondered how much longer I would be able to survive on my own. Food was scarce, the gangs were more dangerous, and it was only a matter of time before they discovered me.

Thankfully, it was a mild winter and spring arrived early. I had grown taller and was thinner. While foraging through an abandoned store one day, I noticed my reflection in the window and was astonished at the change in my appearance. My curly brown hair was long and dishevelled, my face was gaunt, and my blue eyes glared in anger.

Then I met Rusty and Eddie Coleman, identical twins, as opposite in personality as night and day. I scavenged all morning without success and wasn't in a good mood. Rounding a corner, I spotted three punks from one of the local gangs tormenting two young boys. Two of them stood to the side, while the meanest and heaviest pushed one of the boys from behind. The kid landed heavily on the gravel. He let out a wail, and unexpectedly, his brother flew at the attacker, angry as a hornet. I ignored them all, having learned the hard way not to intervene. I walked away but the cries of the injured boy unsettled me, and I stopped and turned sharply. There was nothing I hated more than cruelty, especially when mindless bullies and scumbags were tormenting little kids half their size and age.

I approached the group, and positioned myself a few centimetres back, allowing sufficient ground for me to get away if my plan did not work. One of the goons noticed me and stopped pounding on the little kid.

"You want something, girlie?" He snickered as he looked me up and down. He had to be the ugliest specimen of a human I ever met, his head shaven, his arms covered in tattoos and small cruel eyes glowering in a pasty face covered with zits. I could smell him from where I was standing. Obviously, hygiene was not a high priority on his agenda.

"Not from you, and I'm not a girlie," I answered, scowling in disgust.

"You got that right," he sneered. For some reason, his companions thought he was hilarious.

"Why don't you bugger off, and maybe you won't get hurt," I threatened.

Carlie, Carlie, what are you doing?

Zit Face stared at me as if I were insane. "Who's gonna stop me, you?"

By now I was fuming, and I know I should have walked away. "Two little kids all you can manage?" I asked quietly. I groaned inwardly, telling myself to shut up and get the hell out of there. It was then the idea came to me, I am not saying it was a good one, but it was all I had.

"How about I call the rest of my gang," I said through clenched teeth. "And we'll go neck to neck, winner takes all."

I stared insolently at Zit Face, my hand behind my back, clutching my useless pocketknife. I knew I was no match for someone his size, let alone three of them, but they did not look too clever from where I was standing.

He shuffled his feet, refusing to return my stare.

"Let's split," he said angrily. "These kids aren't worth the trouble. I'll remember you, bitch, watch your back, the next time we meet you'll be dead meat."

I watched in relief as Zit Face and his buffoons wandered off, more than likely looking for easier prey.

I was shaking from head to toe. They called my bluff, but I knew there wouldn't be a second time; they would be looking for me. I had to move on.

The boys were holding hands, and the injured one clutched a mangled teddy bear under his right arm. His brother pulled him over to where I was standing.

"Thanks for helping us. I'm Rusty and this is my brother Eddie, and that's Squishy," he said, pointing to the bear, which had seen better days. "We're twins, he doesn't talk much."

I figured they were around eight or nine years old. Both were skinny, red-haired, with freckles on their faces and arms, and they had the bluest eyes I had ever seen.

I turned and walked away.

"Hey, wait for us," Rusty called.

"Go home, Rusty."

"We don't have one, and those guys took all our stuff."

"Life is tough, Rusty. Sorry to hear about your problems, but I got my own."

"Please you got to help us," he pleaded in a quivering voice.

I stopped in my tracks, turned, and faced the two boys. "Look I'm in the same boat as you two. I was stupid enough to stop and help, and it cost me. I don't have a home either because if I stick around here, I won't last a day. And neither will you. You need to get away from here as fast as you can."

Rusty shuffled his feet, then grinned. "You can come with us, back to where we used to live. It's a bit of a walk, but it's perfect."

"Walking I can do, Rusty, and where exactly are you planning to take me? I don't know if you've noticed but the larger and tougher gangs have taken all the best real estate, so you better have a good plan."

"I do, it's back down the mountain, in a warehouse. The front is all smashed and it looks like the whole place is toast, but it's not. The roof and walls in the back are still standing, there's even a couple of windows, and there are lots of rooms."

"Then how come it hasn't been snatched by now?"

"It was for a while, but the gang living there moved away. We moved in, but we left 'cause we couldn't find any food, so we came here to look for some."

"Still doesn't work for me, Rusty. You don't leave a place sounding like that, no matter what happens."

"Well, it is right next door to a bunch of broken sewer pipes, sometimes it smells kind of gross."

"Ah-ha, the real reason." I spoke. "Sounds like heaven, Rusty. I guess we're going for a walk. And I'm Carlie."

The two boys hugged each other excitedly. I knew I would come to regret my decision, but I always was a sucker for a smooth talker with big blue eyes!

The boys followed me inside the root cellar, not leaving a lot of room to move around. I gathered my belongings and stuffed everything inside my backpack. In frustration, I handed my rolled sleeping bag to Rusty and gave Eddie the box holding my grill and dishes.

"Here, make yourselves useful and carry these."

I took one last look around; I would miss my secluded sanctuary.

Rusty reached over and tugged the bottom of my jacket. "You ain't got no gang," he mumbled. "You just pretended."

"Saved your sorry hides?"

He snickered, then turned and said to his solemn brother. "See Eddie, there's no one else here, just her. You want to know a secret?"

Eddie nodded, clutching his teddy bear tighter.

"This is a hollow, and Winnie the Pooh lived in one just like this."

Eddie's face lit up. If it worked, who was I to say anything?

"Come on boys, we need to get to Shangri-La before it gets dark."

We scrambled out of the root cellar, and I heard Eddie whisper to Rusty.

"What's a Shangla?"

Rusty shrugged, then walked away, taking the lead. Eddie and I ran to catch up. We hiked for hours, and I was thankful it was downhill. We arrived at the warehouse just before nightfall. I wasn't disappointed, it was all Rusty said it was and more. When I asked how he discovered the property, he said he and Eddie lived close by and when the gang living there left, they looked it over to see if there was anything left behind. I assumed lack of food was one of the deciding factors why the gang left.

While wandering the streets on my own, I listened to gossip about different gangs living on Little Mountain, and the most notorious and feared was the Phantoms. They had seized control of the Bloedel Conservatory, located on the highest elevation point in Vancouver, giving them the added advantage from surprise attacks. If a new member passed the qualifications he would be accepted and I shuddered to think what they might be.

The warehouse was virtually located at the bottom of Little Mountain, which increased our chances of not being discovered. It was close to the house I lived in after the earthquake. The damage in the area was appalling, the apartments and office buildings were piles of rubble, cars and buses were stacked everywhere making it hard to maneuver through the streets. The good thing about our new location was the absence of gangs; the sad thing was food was almost impossible to find. Was I taking a risk relocating here instead of heading higher up Little Mountain as I originally planned? Life had become a crapshoot, if you lost the toss, you wouldn't survive. For some reason, deciding to come to the warehouse did not feel wrong, I felt comfortable with my decision.

The building was filthy and well-used, and it had 'lots of rooms' as Rusty promised. The boys tore down the hall and stopped in front of a closed door.

"Whoa, wait a minute," I warned, as I raced after them. "Don't ever barge into a room, or a house for that matter, without checking it out first. And in your case, have someone a little older and in charge do it. Understand?"

The two boys stopped abruptly, and Eddie stared at the floor, squeezing Squishy tighter if possible. Rusty giggled and his eyes twinkled mischievously. This one I needed to watch.

I pushed the door open; there were two soiled mattresses, blankets, and clothing tossed everywhere.

"I guess this is your old bedroom."

Two heads nodded in unison.

"So, what were you doing so far from here?"

"Looking for food, but there weren't none," Rusty said.

"What about sleeping bags?"

The boys shook their heads sadly.

"Let me guess, that gang stole them."

"Yeah," Eddie murmured.

"Okay, to make this work, there's going to be a few changes made. First, you will make your beds every morning, and you will fold your clothes and pile them neatly in the corner."

Both boys groaned.

"Now, if you'll excuse me, I'm going to have a quick look at the rest of this palace before calling it a night."

I walked down the hallway and heard their footsteps behind me. I stopped at the middle door and grabbed the doorknob. Both boys gasped and stepped back. I frowned, then opened the door. I almost hurled. It was a bathroom, obviously not cleaned often, or for that matter, ever. I would have to work on that, but not right now! With no running water, at least someone was smart enough to make it into a portable toilet. I quickly slammed the door.

The next room was another bedroom, there were two larger mattresses and a smaller one leaning against the wall.

The main area was large, and luckily for us, the last tenants had left it furnished — a sagging couch, a scarred table and six wobbly chairs. A counter on the far side of the room functioned as a kitchen. There were dirty dishes piled in a corroded sink, and something vaguely resembling food had hardened in a frying pan.

"I gather when you boys lived here, washing dishes was not a high priority?"

"Don't need to wash dishes if you ain't got no food," Rusty quipped.

I nodded my head solemnly; the kid was right!

We were exhausted, and as dinner was not on the agenda, we went to bed hungry. I woke the next morning, lying on the lumpy mattress, staring at the water-stained ceiling. I tossed and turned all night and came to a decision. I tied my rolled sleeping bag to my backpack and headed for the door. I needed to get away from here, I was not prepared to take on two homeless kids; I could barely survive on my own.

I opened the door and almost collided with one of the boys. "Where are you going?" he asked in a sleepy voice.

I faced Rusty, although I wasn't entirely sure if it was him. It would not take me long to learn Eddie was the solemn twin, always clutching his teddy bear, and Rusty was the trailblazer.

"I was planning to search the surrounding buildings to see if anything were overlooked, and you two following would slow me down. The sooner you Rug Rats figure that out, the easier it will be for all of us to live under the same roof."

"Wait, we're coming."

"You're not listening, Rusty, I work on my own."

"Yeah, but you don't know where to look, I do. This is our neighbourhood; Eddie and I grew up here."

I reluctantly realized what Rusty said was true, he could save me an enormous amount of time, and he knew every nook and cranny in the area.

Resignedly, I placed my backpack on the floor. "Fine, but I'm leaving in two minutes, keep up if you can."

Rusty's eyes widened, then he turned and raced down the hall. "Eddie, get up," he yelled as he entered the room. "We got to get dressed; Carlie's leaving in two minutes."

The whining and pleading coming from their bedroom drew me down the hallway. Rusty had managed to pull Eddie out of bed, he was standing quietly with his head lowered and eyes closed while Rusty helped him put on his jeans and button the front of his shirt.

"Rusty, he needs to do that for himself," I said sternly. "He's not an invalid."

Rusty lowered his head, and I had to strain to hear what he was saying. "We were only eight when Dad died in the earthquake, then Mom got sick and died a while ago. Eddie doesn't understand what happened, he needs me, or he'll get sick just like Mom did."

It meant they had been surviving on their own for months and the only thing I could think of at that moment is they were both damn lucky to make it this far in one piece.

I turned sharply. "Come on, Rug Rats, let's go. We have lots to do today and if you can't keep up, I'm not going to wait. I'm not your babysitter, okay?"

Eddie laughed. "Rusty, she called us Rug Rats."

"Well, every gang has to have a name?" I stated.

Rusty grabbed his brother's hand and followed me to the door. I stopped abruptly, realizing my loaded backpack was lying in the hallway where I had dropped it.

"Just a sec guy," I mumbled, glancing at Rusty. "I'll be right back."

I grabbed my pack, walked into my bedroom, and emptied the contents on my mattress. I picked up my penknife and flashlight and threw them back inside the empty pack. Rusty was standing in the doorway; he said nothing as I walked past him, although I could tell from the look on his face, he knew exactly what I had been planning.

I strapped my pack on my back, grabbed two empty water containers, and opened the front door. "Okay, let's make tracks. Eddie, Squishy stays here."

I was prepared for a major eruption, but Eddie walked over to the table and sat Squishy on a chair. I imagine he knew exactly what just passed between Rusty and me. He might not have much to say, but he was as sharp as his brother.

The three of us trudged quietly down the road. We hadn't gone far when I heard Eddie whisper. "Rusty, I'm hungry."

"Eddie, be quiet."

I turned and glared at them. Eddie stopped in his tracks, screwed his eyes, tears leaking down his face. Rusty tried to console him, patting him lightly on his back.

I cursed under my breath, and reluctantly reached inside my jacket and pulled out an apple I'd been carrying around, savouring my first bite, relishing the juice dripping down my chin. Eddie's face lit up and he stopped crying.

"Here," I said crossly. "Eat this and keep quiet."

Rusty took the apple, then he raised his head and looked at me.

What is it, Rusty?" I asked. I knew immediately what he wanted. He pointed to my backpack, and I sighed.

Now there are some things I do not share with anyone: one — Poppy's leash and dog tags, two — my flashlight, and lastly — my pocketknife. I reluctantly grabbed my knife and handed it to him. "Alright, you can borrow it, but don't you *dare* lose it."

"I promise, cross my heart."

I continued walking, watching Rusty with my peripheral vision. He cut the apple into small pieces, giving them all to Eddie. I didn't interfere, what they did was their business, but the moment Rusty started whining about being hungry, I would come down on him big time.

"Hurry up Rusty," I ordered, as I stopped at a street not as congested as the ones we had just navigated. "We don't have all day. Give me back my knife?"

Silence.

"Rusty, *my* knife please."

"I lost it, I'm sorry Carlie."

"*What*," I yelled, swinging around. "You promised me you would be careful; you crossed your heart."

Startled by my anger, Rusty took a step backwards. "Jeez Carlie, relax, it's right here, I was just fooling around."

My heart was pounding as I grabbed my knife. I don't know if it would've made any difference if I had to use it, but it gave me a sense of false security.

We spent the day searching through abandoned buildings but everything was picked clean. I had the boys show me where they got their water, and they led me to a small stream flowing from a pipe several blocks away. I filled the two containers relieved I still had my brazier back at the warehouse; a person would be daft to drink water from any source without boiling it first.

We wandered down a side street, but it had nothing to offer. Just as I decided to stop for the day Rusty tugged on my jacket.

"Wait Carlie," he cried. "I just remembered; I found some stuff in that garage over there." He pointed to a collapsed building on the far side of the street. "I hid it good, maybe it's still there."

"What kind of stuff, Rusty?" I asked tiredly.

"Stuff left in the cars...pillows, blankets, flashlights, candles, comic books."

I stared at him in disbelief. "Why not speak earlier, before we climbed over every fricking car, and searched every fricking building in this fricking neighbourhood?"

"I just remembered it when I saw the sign in front of the building, it was a long time ago." His eyes filled with tears, and for a moment I thought he was going to start bawling. Eddie saw how upset I was with his brother, and he grabbed Rusty's hand, glaring at me. Who would have guessed there was grit buried deep inside Eddie waiting to surface.

"Okay, I'm sorry," I said. "I shouldn't have yelled, come on, let's go have a look."

The three of us skirted a pile of rusted cars and arrived at the entrance to the underground garage. "Rusty," I said irritably. "The whole building fell on top of it, there's no way we can get inside."

"Not from here, there's a metal door in the alley right around the corner. That's how we got in."

As we approached the corner of the building, I signalled the two boys to stay where they were, and I checked the lane before motioning them forward. We approached the door; someone had painted graffiti over it and used a heavy bludgeon to smash it open. Surprisingly, the mutilated door opened with no problem when I gave it a push.

"This way," Rusty said, pulling Eddie behind him.

I followed them up a row of stairs, then back down another, rounded corners, and just when I thought he was lost, he stopped and pointed at a wide fracture in the wall under the stairwell.

"It's in there," he whispered.

"I can't get in there, I'm too big."

"I know, but Eddie and I can."

Rusty released Eddie's hand, ran to the hole, and disappeared into the darkness. Eddie grabbed my arm tightly when he realized he was abandoned, his eyes big as saucers. I shook him off, walked over to the gap in the wall, bent over, and shouted.

"Doesn't look as if Eddie is going to join you, Rusty."

"That's okay," a voice echoed. "He doesn't like the dark. Can I borrow your flashlight?"

I must have hesitated too long because Rusty poked his head out of the hole. "I solemnly swear, with my whole body and soul, I will not lose your flashlight. I promise not to break it, crush it, or wreck it in any way. Can I have it now Carlie?"

Realizing we needed whatever he had stashed away, I reached into my backpack and grabbed my flashlight, staring at it lovingly.

"Alright, here it is," I said solemnly, handing it to him. "Just be careful with it."

"Jeez, didn't I just swear with my whole body and soul?"

I turned and stared at the far wall, trying hard not to burst out laughing. I was getting to like this kid.

Rusty was gone for ages; he finally appeared, covered in dirt and cobwebs. "It's still here Carlie, all of it, and I forgot, there's a bunch of canned food too."

"Rusty, how could you have forgotten something that important, especially when you lived right here."

"I forgot the building it was in, I looked hard, but couldn't find it again."

"Yeah, I suppose I can understand that, might as well start hauling it out."

Eddie was still standing too close to me for comfort, and he was making it worse as he was jumping up and down and bumping into me. I moved over to the entrance and took the items Rusty handed out.

There were blankets, pillows (although I don't know if I would put my head down on any of them, as they were covered in rat droppings), candles, four lighters, books and comics, paper and coloured pencils, cans of fruit, beans, and tomatoes. The pile got higher and higher, and I wondered how we were going to carry everything back to the warehouse.

Rusty climbed out. "That's all of it," he said, wiping the spider webs and grime from his hands and face.

"Rusty, you angel," I gushed, grabbing him, planting a big kiss on his cheek.

"Yuck," he sputtered, his face turning red. "Cut that out."

"Aw, you know you like it. My flashlight please."

"Yeah, about that."

"Rusty, my flashlight."

"Um, I'm sorry Carlie, I dropped it on the cement, and it broke."

"You have *got* to be kidding," I shouted. "You swore on your body and soul."

When he saw I was ready to explode, he pulled it from his jacket pocket. "I have it right here." He chuckled. "I was just kidding. Boy, you sure can't take a joke."

I grabbed the flashlight from him, but not before I noticed him smiling at Eddie. That was it, the Rug Rats conned me twice, and there wouldn't be a third time.

"Talk about insubordinate kids," I muttered under my breath. I suddenly froze, remembering the last time I heard those words. I turned abruptly and began piling the items inside my backpack, but not before I noticed the questioning look on Rusty's face.

"What's the matter, Carlie?"

"Nothing. Everyone grabs as much as you can, we must get home before dark."

I didn't say much after that, they followed me solemnly back to the warehouse, their arms loaded. As payback for scaring the hell out of me, I handed one of the water containers to Rusty to carry.

I realized I was harsh with the boys, but my memories are too personal, they are not for sharing.

Chapter Three

The weather constantly changed during the day, it was hot and stifling, and when the non-relenting sun fell at dusk, the smoke and ashes from the wildfires and volcanoes in the upper atmosphere cooled the air. At times, the clouds would darken, and the temperature would drop, followed by torrential rains, unceasing thunder, and blinding flashes of lightning. I learned the hard way to seek immediate shelter when these storms appeared.

The warehouse was solid, and we endured. At night, the salvaged blankets from Rusty's cache of supplies, and my sweater and jacket, kept the boys warm. I was thankful for my sleeping bag.

If the wind blew from the direction of the sewage pipes, we covered our noses. It was hard living in the warehouse, but the redeeming quality was we had protection from the inclement weather and the migrant gangs passing through.

Rusty's stash provided us with provisions for a while, and I rationed it closely. Unfortunately, it didn't last forever. Providing food for the three of us was a constant battle weighing heavily on my shoulders. We lost more weight, if that was possible, and shadows appeared under our eyes. I worried about the boys as they wandered listlessly around the warehouse and streets. In their present state, I wouldn't leave them alone during the day. If the warehouse were discovered; they had no means of protecting themselves. Reluctantly, I made them accompany me, although they slowed me down considerably while I searched.

While scavenging off our home base, we ran into an older dude vigorously digging a hole. Sensing he was being watched, he raised his head and looked directly at me. I started, realizing who he was. His head was still clean-shaven, unfortunately, nothing could be done about his zits and tattoos and obviously, he hadn't discovered the values of personal hygiene.

He was panting loudly, sweat pouring down his face. I pushed Rusty and Eddie behind me, gesturing them to stay put. Eddie grabbed the back of my jacket and Rusty gasped; they also remembered who he was.

"You guys live around here?" he asked.

I shrugged, discreetly saying nothing. Why was he pretending he did not recognize us?

"From the looks of it, I'd say it's been a while since you've eaten," he smirked. "Lots of food around if you know where to look."

Rusty and Eddie flinched, then ran into the open. I angrily grabbed the back of their collars. "Behind me, *now*, and don't move until I say you can."

Four blue eyes stared up at me. I hated scaring the little Rug Rats, but they had to learn to be more cautious and not trust strangers. They must have seen the hard anger in my eyes, as they guiltily returned to their positions.

"You their mother or something?" Zit Face asked as he ogled my body. The creep hadn't changed a bit.

"Yeah, I'm their mother," I answered rudely. "I was six when I had them."

He grunted, then turned his back and continued shovelling. "I've survived this long on my own. Don't look like you are doing too well though, but if you're not interested that's fine with me."

I shivered in revulsion, I would have left right then, but his offer of providing food was too tempting. I sensed Rusty and Eddie squirming behind me. They would never forgive me if we had a chance to get rations and I passed it by.

"Maybe we *can* help each other," I said. "We may be hungry, but you look like you haven't slept in a week, and those bruises on your face didn't come from walking into a door."

"Wow lady, you're a barrel of laughs. What do you have in mind? I can tell we aren't gonna be friends, but we both know it's all about survival, right?"

"You first," I responded. Over time I learned to heed my instincts and right now they were screaming at me to walk away. If it had only been me to worry about, I would have done just that.

"I know where the food caches of the old gangs who used to live here are buried; guess they had to leave in a hurry."

He smiled coldly, throwing his shovel on the ground, and climbed out of the hole.

Then he approached me, and I stiffened. Leaning over, he whispered, "Okay, it's your turn."

I forced myself not to step back, he smelled like a pigsty, but food was our utmost priority, right now we were living on bugs, dried berries, and sometimes a rat straying too close to our front door.

"We live in a warehouse," I said. "It's well hidden from intruders, furnished and has lots of room."

"All the comforts of home. Let me get this straight, I provide the grub, you provide the lodgings."

"That's my offer."

Zit Face lowered his head, and I could almost hear the wheels turning. "What about the rest of your gang, they gonna be okay with me showing up unannounced?"

To this day I had no idea why I said what I did; maybe it was intuition or self-preservation. "Our gang split up; it was too hard finding food for everyone. We're smaller now, but we have a Protector; he's away scavenging, and he should return soon. If you don't provide the promised food; he will ask you to leave. Can you live with that?"

I heard Rusty and Eddie inhale sharply, and I held my breath, expecting to be zapped by a bolt of lightning any moment for lying through my teeth.

Unfortunately, Zit Face was brighter than he looked. "You're just a bunch of misfits trying to make it on your own."

I bristled at his comment, refusing to let him provoke me. "Guess you're not any different than us," I said coldly. "What happened to your gang?"

He stared at me for the longest time. "Wait a minute," he cried, slapping his thigh. "I know you guys."

I waited, letting it sink in.

"You were the dame who screwed with my mind a while back when me and my buds were having fun with those two kids. You live here because you have nowhere else to go?"

I said nothing and looked away.

"Have your two minions follow me," he ordered smugly. "I'm almost finished digging, should be something buried here. They might as well carry it back."

I nodded.

"Oh yeah," Zit Face continued. "We weren't properly introduced, I'm Willie Arbuckle, and I'm seventeen, though I look a lot older, but probably don't give a shit about that."

"Got that right Willie."

"Carlie, he swore," Eddie whispered.

"It's okay Eddie," I answered.

Then I turned and looked at Willie. "I'm Carlie, and the young fellow over by the pit is Rusty, and as you just heard, this is Eddie."

"This is going to be a barrel of laughs." Willie chuckled, grabbed his shovel, and jumped back inside the hole.

I may have made the biggest mistake of my life, but my choices right at that moment were slim.

And that's how Willie Arbuckle joined the Rug Rats.

Chapter Four

Willie grunted when the boys told him the name of the warehouse was the Stink Hole. I don't imagine the odours emitting through the building bothered him too much, cleanliness not being one of his stronger virtues.

The first thing he tried to do was bunk with me in my bedroom. He threw himself across my mattress and gestured for me to join him.

"I don't think so, guy," I said, standing in the doorway. "You bunk down the hall."

"With Twiddle Dee and Twiddle Dum?"

"Don't call them that, you know their names."

"Wait, I get it. This is where your Protector sleeps when he returns. Nice setup."

Angrily, I threatened to toss him out. He stood, grinned as he walked past me, and then sauntered down the hallway. He grabbed Rusty's mattress and confiscated the entire back half of the room for himself. It took me a while to comfort the distraught boys. I told them they would have to sleep together on the same mattress.

"I don't want to sleep with Eddie," Rusty wailed. "He pees the bed."

They finally conceded after I hauled the smaller mattress from my room and laid it next to Eddie's. I threw in one of the bookshelves as well, suggesting it would be perfect for their comics, paper, and pencils.

Willie was unreliable, lazy, and a bully, and he had Rusty and Eddie terrorized. It didn't take him long to snatch their comics, our extra flashlights and batteries.

He harassed me continuously, asking when our AWOL Protector planned to return. I usually walked away when he brought up the subject. When that tactic stopped working, he decided our Protector died at the hands of one of the wandering gangs, and he might as well take over his position, enjoying all the extra benefits that went with it. As was my way of handling confrontation I ignored his erratic behaviour because he hadn't lied, he did have an uncanny ability to find food, and it kept us alive. The only time I intervened was when he threatened to pull Squishy's arms off. Eddie's screams and cries shook me visibly and I confronted Willie and threatened to throw him out. I was so angry I scared myself. That was when I discovered an important fact about Willie, not only was he a bully; he was also a coward.

I knew I would not be able to continue my ruse much longer, if he got belligerent, he would not leave without a fight, or for that matter, at all. He had it too good living with us, he supplied the food when available and everything else was taken care of by me and the boys.

A few days later the four of us were sitting at the table eating beans and crackers when Willie suddenly slammed his fist on the table. His plate clattered to the floor.

"You bitch," he roared, turning to face me. "You've been stringing me along the whole time."

My mind raced as I tried to think of a plausible explanation he would believe. I gestured for the boys to leave. Rusty understood my signal, he grabbed Eddie's hand and rushed in the direction of the door. I didn't want them near in case Willie got mean.

Willie raced after them, I rose quickly, knocking my chair over. I caught up to him and grabbed his arm, pulling him back.

"Leave them alone, Willie," I warned. "This is between you and me."

He was infuriated, realizing I had pulled one over on him. I feared he would use his muscle to take control. If that happened, our lives would change, and not for the better.

The boys left the warehouse, and I warned them to stay close. I told Willie to calm down, and for the longest time he glared at me, then begrudgingly returned to the table. I up righted my chair and sat across from him and explained my reason for inventing a Protector was my only means of protecting myself and the boys.

He grunted, obviously not willing to accept my explanation.

My mind raced, and I decided if that didn't work, I had to try a different guise. I would work on his egotism. Clearing my throat, I mumbled. "I'm sorry, I should have told you the truth sooner."

"You think," he said sarcastically.

"We do appreciate having you here, if we ever got in trouble with one of the gangs, they would take one look at your size and muscles and would head for the hills."

Willie nodded in agreement, then he stood and approached me. He grabbed my arms and forced me to stand. My legs tightened and I waited for his next move. I had no idea what I would do if he tried to hurt me, but I wouldn't go down without a fight.

"From now on," he sputtered, "I'm in charge. I'll continue to provide the grub; you take care of the boys and the warehouse. You got any problem with that?"

"No, that works for me," I muttered.

"Good, get the Rug Rats and tell them to keep quiet. I want to take a nap."

I realized our immediate problem was not solved, but for now it was the only solution that worked. I watched Willie constantly, always keeping my distance and a careful eye on the boys.

We needed a miracle, but they were in short supply.

Chapter Five

The next two additions to our little group we found accidentally.

I was scrounging with Rusty and Eddie, while Willie took advantage of his elevated position. He stayed at the Stink Hole, laying on the sofa reading comics. I remembered an old, rusted van in an alley we passed while out scavenging. Maybe we would find something useful; it was amazing the stuff people carried in their vehicles.

When we got to the van, I stepped on the runner board and peeked into the front window. I jumped back, almost landing on Eddie who still shadowed me like a baby chick following its mother.

"Eddie," I said in exasperation, grabbing his shoulders before he fell over.

"Did you see something, Carlie?" Rusty chuckled. He could be annoying at times, but the more I was around the little Rug Rat, the more I came to value his cheerful disposition.

"Just a pile of dust, let's check in the back. You know the routine, I go first."

I walked cautiously down the side of the van and signalled the boys to stay where they were. When I got to the back, I tried opening the door, but the handle was stuck. I jiggled it a bit and tried again. The door groaned as if in agony, then fell into a rusted pile of corroded metal on the cement.

Hearing the loud bang, the twins barrelled around the corner, exactly what they were not supposed to do.

"Stop, stay where you are, I haven't checked inside the van yet. We'll talk about this later when we get home."

The stricken look on their faces almost worked on me, but I was learning fast, especially when it involved our safety.

It was pitch black inside the van and reeked of urine and feces. I raised my flashlight, which I now kept tied to Poppy's leash around my waist, turned it on and stared in horror. Two girls, covered in filthy rags, shrank back in alarm. The younger of the two began to howl, as her companion tried in vain to silence her.

"Please, please Debbie," she pleaded. "Don't cry."

"It's okay," I said soothingly. "We're not going to hurt you. I'm Carlie, and these two funny looking guys standing behind me are Rusty and Eddie."

Rusty grinned and waved, staring in fascination. Eddie, on the other hand, immediately grabbed my jacket and hid behind my back.

"I'm Mae-Li Wong, and this is Debbie," the older girl replied.

"Hello, Mae-Li. Hello Debbie."

That was the wrong thing to say. Debbie began to wail even louder, and Mae-Li placed her hands over her ears. "Sorry, she's very loud."

"Yes, I can see that. Do you need help?"

Mae-Li nodded and threw me a couple of filthy bags. She began to crawl toward the door, which was a difficult feat as she carried a backpack with a sleeping bag tied on top. Debbie grabbed her shirt, gripped it tightly and shuffled along behind her. I knew exactly how Mae-Li felt.

I gave her a hand as she jumped spryly to the ground. Debbie was not as easy to remove. She was howling, trying to grab Mae-Li, refusing to budge.

Losing my patience, I stepped closer to the van and opened my arms to the terrified youngster. It only made matters worse, and Debbie began to shriek. I ground my teeth, trying to ignore the shrill wail emanating from her mouth, which became louder and more persistent.

"Please, let me," Mae-Li said, approaching me. "She's special."

After much cajoling, Mae-Li finally managed to get the inconsolable girl to leave the van. It wasn't until I looked at Debbie, that I understood what Mae-Li meant. Snot ran from Debbie's nose, which Mae-Li wiped on the young girl's sleeve, obviously used for that purpose more than once. Debbie had a flattened face, a short neck, and her tongue stuck out of her mouth. I remembered one of the kids in my school with the same features, and I realized she was mentally handicapped.

Mai-Li was slender, beautiful, with delicate features and long black hair tied in a braid hanging to her waist.

"Are you two alone?" I asked, scanning the area.

Mae-Li nodded, taking Debbie's hand to keep her quiet. "Our group split up, the older boys and girls merged with a larger gang and those who remained did not want Debbie. She has Downs Syndrome and needs constant care. They felt she did not contribute anything and wanted to abandon her. I left, taking her with me."

It was getting dark, but I knew there was more to Mae-Li's story than she was telling. Right now, we had to get home before the feral dogs and coyotes started hunting.

"We're headed back to our place; you're welcome to join us if you want."

Mae-Li stared into my eyes, which unsettled me for a moment.

"I have been waiting a long time for you to come," she whispered.

I must admit goosebumps rippled up my arms, but being in a hurry, there was no time to question her unexpected words.

To be honest, I was worried what Willie's reaction would be when I showed up with two more mouths to feed. As I expected, he exploded, ranted, and vowed he would leave us all to die of starvation. I let him rage, knowing full well he would never go, he had it too good living with us.

"The girls will move in with me in my room, and I'll see they keep out of your way," I snapped, looking directly into his eyes. "Don't forget, Willie, you're a guest here as well."

Willie glared at me before turning away. "They better pull their weight," he grumbled, looking in dislike at Debbie, who was walking around the room, touching everything that caught her eye.

Mae-Li noticed Willie's reaction, and she stared at him in distaste. She went and stood next to Debbie, and it was then I understood she would do everything in her power to protect the young girl.

An unlikely cluster of misfits we were, yet somehow, we managed to tolerate each other. Willie and I scrounged every day, finding enough provisions to keep us alive. At times, I caught him shoving food into his pockets, and when I confronted him, he adamantly denied my accusations. Rather than push the matter, I let it ride. I knew without his input; we wouldn't survive.

Some days later, after Debbie fell asleep, Mae-Li and I were talking quietly when she confided to me, she was seventeen years old. I was surprised as she was tiny and looked much younger. I told her to keep her age to herself as I didn't trust Willie further than I could throw him. She nodded wisely, understanding my caution.

We soon discovered Mae-Li knew how to take care of herself and Debbie. Willie grabbed a shrivelled plum Debbie was carrying around all day, which, of course, caused a deafening uproar. He mocked the screaming girl, holding the plum high above her head.

Mae-Li was sitting on the sofa, reading to the twins from one of their comics. She rose quietly, approached Willie, and before any of us knew what happened, Willie dropped like a rock. He rolled on the floor, clutching his stomach in agony.

The plum fell out of his hand and landed next to Mai-Li's foot. She calmly picked it up and handed it back to Debbie, who immediately ceased her howling.

Willie rose and glared at Mae-Li, who took a defensive stance.

"Do not threaten me, Willie," she warned. "I can, and will, hurt you."

Willie was breathing hard; I hadn't intervened, and it didn't take him long to realize he was on his own. He turned and stormed down the hallway to the boys' bedroom, slamming the door.

I had not intruded as I always made a point of staying clear of other people's quarrels and disagreements. On the bright side, I was elated to learn we had someone who was able to protect herself and her ward from Willie's bullying. It took a heavy load of responsibility off my shoulders.

I also decided I would ask Mae-Li to show me her moves. I had never seen anyone move so fast.

The first thing Mai-Li did after joining our group was to make everyone take a sponge bath, Willie included. The bathroom had a shower stall, so there was a degree of privacy. We hauled and boiled water all day, and soon we looked and smelled a whole lot better. Mai-Li had clothes and personal items in the two bags she carried when we found her, and she and Debbie shared one sleeping bag.

I washed my unruly hair, then brushed it until it dried. When I walked into the main room, everyone stopped what they were doing and stared.

"Wow, you're pretty," Rusty said.

"What?" I asked, checking to make sure my clothing covered all the right places.

"You have gold in your hair," Debbie said gleefully.

"It's brown, silly little girl," I responded.

Debbie giggled and hid her face in Mai-Li's lap.

"Carlie, it's golden brown and very beautiful, as you are," Mai-Li said quietly.

"Well, thank you." I blushed, cherishing the unexpected compliment.

After that, I often caught Willie watching me. He made me uncomfortable, and I hoped it would never get to the point where I would have to defend myself should he decide to get physical. He was not much younger than me, but in the brief time since he joined our group, he'd grown taller and heavier. His bullying worsened, and the younger kids kept out of his way. I understood he was getting back at me for not covering his back when Mae-Li attacked him, and he was still carrying a grudge from the time I conned him and his cronies when they were tormenting Rusty and Eddie. I worried at times I might have pushed too hard, but deep inside I knew he relied on us as much as we relied on him. It was a volatile relationship, but for now, it worked.

I turned eighteen, mentioning it only to Mai-Li. Divulging my age would have put me in a precarious position as far as Willie was concerned. I am sure his mentality rated all females as the weaker sex, which made him the alpha male in our group. Thus, one of the reasons I wanted Mai-Li to show me her moves.

Eddie continued to cling to me, and Debbie decided she would follow suit. My intolerance of being touched and accepting affection unsettled me and I was constantly pushing them away. I could sense Mae-Li watching, but she never mentioned my behaviour, although I knew she disapproved. I was glad to have her around, as I relied on her to watch the Rug Rats while I was scavenging for food. I no longer took the twins with me as I had done in the past; they were a lot happier staying in the warehouse playing with Mai-Li and Debbie.

One precautionary tactic I used was to ensure Willie left before me, then I would take a different route, making sure he hadn't backtracked or was following me.

Although most of my time was spent looking for food, I also spent at least an hour each day in a vacant lot I had discovered a few blocks from the Stink Hole. It was well hidden and the reason we did not come across it earlier. At one time it must have been a beautiful park, but the hot unrelenting sun and the constant downfall of ash from the volcanoes and wildfires had destroyed the vegetation, and the trees and bushes were wilted and dead. I discovered a wooden bench concealed behind a cement barrier. It was encircled by a small patch of green grass, as the building's wall provided shade from the consistent rays of the sun.

I had replaced my pocketknife with a sharper hunting knife. I had noticed it poking out of a jacket wrapped around the body in the front seat of the van where we had found Mae-Li and Debbie. I returned the next day and retrieved it, thrilled to see it was sheathed in a leather pouch. I never mentioned the dead man to the boys, although I realized they were accustomed to seeing bodies in cars and buildings.

I taught myself to use the knife as a weapon, not as a tool. I practiced diligently until I could throw it a long distance, hitting most targets I aimed at. I hid the pouch and knife in my boot and focussed on retrieving the knife quickly in case of an emergency. I often went home with cuts on my hands, and when Mae-Li asked about them, I told her it was from falling on sharp concrete while foraging in the buildings. She never said anything, although I knew I wasn't fooling her one bit.

One night after the kids were in bed, Mai-Li, Willie, and I had a long discussion about the diminishing food supply. We realized the area was picked clean, and Willie confessed he had opened all the caches. There might be enough left for a month if we cut back. Mai-Li and I looked at each other, and I bit my tongue to stop from saying something nasty. While the rest of us were barely surviving, Willie was gaining weight.

It was then I suggested we broaden our search, exploring streets and buildings higher up Little Mountain. We always made a point of avoiding those areas as it was not unusual to run across gang members, not all of them friendly. My suggestion was risky, but the more ground we covered, the better our chances would be of finding food.

I found it difficult to sleep that night. I tossed and turned, worrying I might be keeping Mai-Li awake. Debbie slept like a log, her mind free of worries.

"You must get some rest," a soft voice whispered in the darkness.

"Mai-Li, I'm sorry, I didn't mean to disturb you."

"You take on too much, worrying about everyone."

I chuckled. "Everyone except Willie."

"Perhaps, but you must broaden your search area."

"Maybe I'll find something tomorrow, it would be great if we could give the kids a treat."

"You will be successful in your search, and it will change all our lives."

Again, as had happened before, goosebumps erupted up my arms.

"Mai-Li, sometimes you scare the hell out of me when you talk like that."

"Good, at least I know you are listening. Good night, Carlie."

I turned over and snuggled inside my sleeping bag. My thoughts wandered to Mai-Li; it hadn't taken me long to realize she was not only a sensitive but also empathic. At times she said things or reacted in ways that left me troubled.

There was something else about her I could not place. She hadn't told me her whole story, but we all had secrets.

I fell into a deep sleep, not waking until the next morning when I heard Mai-Li banging pots and pans in the kitchen. I covered my head as the younger kids ran around the living room, yelling and laughing. Willie roared at them to be quiet, or they would answer to him.

I smiled, as the realization hit me solidly. This was home, and I was going to do everything in my power to keep it that way.

Chapter Six

I left early the next morning, climbing steadily up Little Mountain. I left my sleeping bag behind, and my backpack was empty except for my hip flask and half an apple. I was hoping to find something to eat during the day and return to the warehouse before dark. Willie took a different trail, and I checked often to make sure he did not follow.

I walked aimlessly, searching inside rusted vehicles, and digging through garbage. The constant threat of running into members of local gangs weighed on my shoulders, and I was exhausted, both mentally and physically. The volcanic ash and smoke from wildfires were thick as soup, and I found it difficult to breathe. Even wearing a mask, my throat was raw. I had drunk the last of my water.

The harsh rays of the sun dropped behind a crumbling building, at one time an apartment. The shadows lengthened and the wind picked up, blowing dust and grit into my eyes. I heard thunder rumbling in the distance, which as a rule was accompanied by torrential rainfalls.

A movement in the shadows made me nervous, and I worried about the feral dogs and coyotes, although I should have worried more about the two-legged kind, who were more savage than any animal I would encounter.

I was angry at my carelessness as I realized I would not make it back to the Stink Hole before nightfall. I was also aware anyone wandering the deserted streets at this time of day was either reckless or arrogant.

I suddenly remembered the cement pipes I passed earlier. They were near to my present location, I walked quickly, watching the dark, roiling clouds and the lightning strikes flashing in the distance. I sighed in relief when I recognized the construction site. I chose one of the larger pipes resting on an elevated platform, there was enough room for both me and my backpack.

My thoughts returned to the Stink Hole. Hopefully, the boys would behave, and I worried Mae-Li would have trouble managing them. I was almost positive Willie covered only a few streets each day in his search for food, and he was more than likely back at the warehouse monopolizing the couch and yelling at the kids to be quiet.

I rested my head on my pack and curled into a tight ball, trying to keep warm. I was exhausted, cold, and worried. At times like this, I tended to become despondent, thinking I reached rock bottom. Surviving in a world tossed upside down was not easy, it was near impossible. Fighting each day for every scrap of food, warm clothing, and safety was putting a strain on all of us.

I finally fell into an uneasy sleep, only to wake when the ground started to shake violently. I sat up in a panic, banging my head on the pipe. At first, I was disoriented but then I remembered where I was.

"Damn," I swore loudly, rubbing my forehead, "Can't a person get any sleep around here?" I snickered indifferently at my unshared joke. My intense fear of earthquakes and aftershocks never dissipated, and secretly I realized using humour was my way of coping.

I crawled on all fours to the entrance. It was dark as ink outside, and I rummaged in my backpack looking for my flashlight. I swore angrily, suddenly remembering it was not in my bag, I gave it to Rusty last night after listening to his whining and pleading and forgot all about it. I always found it hard to say no to the twins and this time it backfired on me.

The rain pelted down, hammering the parched earth. Weather patterns were becoming more erratic, growing in intensity and violence. We seldom got rain, but when we did it was more of a cloudburst than a shower.

Realizing the sewer pipe was the safest place to be during an earthquake, not to mention a violent rainstorm, I decided to stay where I was. My fear was not about flooding as the platform was sitting on a hill.

Being shorter and smaller had its advantages. I stood, bent over, and shuffled backwards. I heard a scraping noise outside and froze. Suddenly, a dark shadow landed heavily on top of me, and I landed hard on my back. Scratching and punching, I screamed at my attacker. "Get off me."

"Calm down," a deep voice replied. "I'm not going to hurt you."

"Then move away," I said, clenching my teeth. I reached down to my boot and found my knife. I pulled it from the sheath, and rose slowly, gripping it tightly in my shaking hand.

"Take it easy, I didn't know you were here. I'm backing up, okay? And put your little knife away, you don't want to hurt yourself."

Angrily I spun my arm around and pointed my weapon in the direction of his voice.

There was a click and a light came on, creating elongated shadows on the wall. I was holding my weapon a few centimeters from the intruder's face.

"Whoa," he said, raising his arms as if deflecting a blow. "I give up, don't shoot."

"This is a knife, you idiot, I don't have a gun." No sooner had I said those words than I realized I had just told a stranger I wasn't carrying any other weapons.

"You're a real spitfire, I like that in a girl."

I was at a loss for words, then mumbled something about being able to take care of myself.

"Good to know."

There was a moment of awkward silence then the intruder said. "Um, would you mind backing up a tad? I'm already soaked, no sense getting any wetter."

Usually, I was more vigilant around strangers, but without hesitating, I lowered the knife, hoping my trust was justified; I instinctively knew he wouldn't hurt me. There are lots of creepy people wandering the streets, especially at night, and one unwise decision could be my last.

I cautiously stepped backwards.

"Thanks, much appreciated," he said.

He was thin (but who wasn't in today's world), and around 1.9 meters in height. His hands were resting on his thighs, a duffle bag dangling from his left shoulder. He was breathing heavily from running hard to find cover from the rain. He raised his head, and I inhaled sharply. He had long dark hair tied back in a ponytail, black smouldering eyes, a chiselled chin, and broad shoulders.

"So, what's your handle?" he asked quietly, removing his wet jacket, and spreading it on the cement floor.

"My what?" I asked sharply, not understanding his question, and trying hard not to stare at his biceps.

"Your name," he asked, a half-smile on his lips, as he was undoubtedly aware I was ogling his body. "What people call you when they're yelling at you, which I imagine is often."

"Very funny. I'm Carlie.

"Carleee, anything else?"

"Fleming, but I don't suppose it matters anymore, especially nowadays. So, what's your handle?" I asked sarcastically.

"Taylor West, at your service ma'am. And it does matter to me what my name is."

I shrugged, just what I did not need, a smooth talker and a smart aleck, both of which I had no time for.

"Look, I'm sorry I scared you," he continued. "I had no idea the pipe was occupied; are you hurt?"

"I'm not scared, it's just that not every day a guy jumps on me in the dark."

Realizing what I just said, I tried to backtrack, but all I did was stutter, making it worse, and it came out sounding like a bunch of gibberish.

Carlie, stop talking, now!

"Too bad," he replied, his smile widening. "Might add some spice to your life."

I took a deep breath, refusing to let him goad me. "Look, I'm tired, I've been walking all day, and I need some sleep. You plan to leave soon."

He lowered himself to the floor, removed his bag and zipped it open. He took out a red woollen sweater and quickly put it on.

"There, that's better. And nope, I wasn't planning to leave soon. It'll rain all night, and there's room in here for the both of us. Now be a good little girl and go to sleep. Nighty night."

Using his bag as a pillow he stretched, turned on his side and closed his eyes. His legs were on top of me and before I could say anything, there was a click, and the light went out. It was going to be a long night!

Chapter Seven

The next morning, I was not surprised to see Taylor West had flown the coop.

I edged in the direction of the entrance, poked my head out and carefully scanned the area. The temperature dropped during the night, and I could see my breath. I shivered in my thin clothing, remembering my midnight visitor's warm wool sweater. I crawled out of the pipe, stretched, and headed back to the Stink Hole.

There was a long walk before me, and I allowed my thoughts to wander. I had my seclusion or as little as I could get living with five other people in a confined space. Too often, I intervened, breaking up quarrels or consoling crying kids, and with my penchant for privacy, I often wished I could pack up and leave. I never shared these thoughts with anyone, although it wouldn't surprise me a bit if Mae-Li knew exactly what I was thinking.

I almost missed the turnoff to the warehouse and heard them before I saw them. I raced to the back, ran to the door, and pulled it open. Rusty and Eddie were screaming and tearing around the room, Mae-Li was flustered, trying to settle them down, Debbie was shrieking on the floor, snot running from her nose, Willie was spread on the sofa, thoroughly enjoying the pandemonium.

I was so angry I could have spit. First, I yelled at the twins and told them to get to their room, and not to come out until they were ready to act civil. They walked down the hall, holding hands, sobbing pitifully. My heart ached for them, as they were usually well behaved. I realized they were acting up because I hadn't returned yesterday and I was without my flashlight, and with their vivid imaginations, they probably thought I was dead or eaten by coyotes.

Then I turned my attention to Debbie, and after several attempts in disengaging her from Mae-Li's waist, I suddenly had an idea. I pulled out a red rubber ball I found on my return trek and threw in my backpack. I tossed it in the air, caught it, and bounced it against the wall. Debbie immediately stopped screaming. She ran to me and squealed.

"My ball, my ball."

I gave it to her, and jumping up and down in excitement, she flung it across the room. It bounced on the floor with a thud, landing on a pile of dirty dishes sitting on the counter, shattering a plate and two mugs.

Willie howled, and it took all my composure not to sic Mai-Li on him. However, I did think it was funny, but I wasn't about to let him know that.

I realized Debbie was just copying me and unless I thought of something less harmful, we would soon run out of dishes. I spied a wooden box leaning against the far wall. I hauled it to the middle of the room and laid it sideways on the floor. I showed Debbie how to roll her new ball into the 'cave,' or 'animal house' which she thought was a better name.

After settling Debbie, I pulled Mae-Li aside and promised her I would never abandon her again, as I realized it was unfair to expect her to discipline three high-spirited kids, and one oversized delinquent, especially in such a confined space.

Then I strode over to the couch and glared down at Willie. Mae-Li quietly joined me, and the grin on Willie's face disappeared.

"Wondered where you were, Carlie," he said. "Did you run into any trouble?"

"I'm here aren't I, jerk?"

He lifted his head angrily, and jumped off the couch, his fist raised. If he weren't so essential to our survival, I would have given him the boot. Somehow, I would have found the strength. If he tried anything right now, I swore I would use my knife on him.

He may have been a coward, but he wasn't stupid. He watched Mae-Li closely, and he realized he might not come out unscathed if he took the two of us on.

81

"Jeez, what are you so mad about?" he asked lowering his arm. "I ain't done nothing."

"*Exactly*," I yelled. "Did it never occur to you to get off your ass and help around here?"

Then I turned and went to my room, slamming the door hard enough to shake the walls. I flung myself on my mattress, cursing everything and everybody — the earthquake, the tsunami, Mom, Dad, and Poppy for leaving me on my own, the continuous struggle to survive, the unplanned responsibility of three young lives, and lastly Willie, oh God, why did we have to rely so much on Willie?

Gradually I calmed down, realizing I was angry at myself. I came home empty-handed, and because of my stupidity, put myself in a dangerous position by staying on the streets after dark. Running into Taylor West was just dumb luck. It could have been someone a lot more dangerous.

I returned to the main room. Rusty and Eddie were sitting on the couch, reading comics. Rusty waved at me, and I wiggled my little finger at him, and he giggled. Mae-Li was playing on the floor with Debbie. I walked over and placed my hand on her shoulder, squeezing it. She looked up at me and nodded, accepting my unspoken apology.

Willie was nowhere around; he was probably outside pulling wings off flies. He was becoming more aggressive every day, and he seldom returned with food.

When the Rug Rats were finally in bed, I helped Mae-Li clean up. The warehouse door opened, and Willie entered, he was in a surly mood, and I could sense his eyes following me around the room. I was scared, and deep inside I knew we were headed for a confrontation.

The next morning, while sitting around the table watching three pouty faces, I suddenly had an idea. The kids had to get out and play.

"Alright," I said, trying to sound upbeat. "Everyone gets dressed, we're going on a tiger hunt. Put your survival equipment in your packs, don't forget water, get my flashlight back from Willie's stash, and let's go."

The twins cheered, Debbie clapped her hands, and Mae-Li watched me quietly. "Who did you meet when you were gone?" she asked.

I stopped in my tracks, at first not sure what to say. Knowing she wouldn't let it drop, I ignored her question.

"It is not a bad thing Carlie; it will be good for all of us."

Stuff like this always made me uncomfortable. "What makes you think I met someone?"

"Your aura is different."

"Not sure what that means Mai-Li, but maybe it changed when I got home and saved the roof from falling on everyone's heads."

"When Willie first joined us, did you not tell him we had a Protector?"

"Mae-Li, you know I said that to keep him in line. None of it was true."

She stood, calmly holding Debbie's hand, who for once was quiet. The boys were watching me like a hawk.

She knew I hated lying and would eventually work my way around to the truth. "Alright, I did meet someone," I sighed. "His name is Taylor West, and he took shelter from the storm in the same duct I was in."

I didn't elaborate on how he had landed on top of me; only so much you can say in front of two inquisitive boys.

"We barely talked, and in the morning, he was gone. I'll never see him again; he was just passing through."

"He will come," Mae-Li whispered, then went to the bedroom to pack. Debbie sat on the floor, happily rolling her ball, while the twins went to their room to get their backpacks.

I thought over what just happened. Part of me was hoping Mae-Li was right, we needed someone stronger and streetwise, who could provide us with the protection we needed as well as help us in our search for food.

I pushed my thoughts aside and restocked my backpack. "Okay everyone," I yelled. "Quit dawdling, I'm leaving in two minutes."

That threat always worked, and soon the five of us were traipsing down the street. I prayed we wouldn't run into Willie, he was mad as a wet hen when he left this morning, and I was in no mood for his antics.

The morning passed uneventfully, we had been walking and searching for almost four hours, and I knew it was all in vain. I found a few morsels, but the main provisions, or what remained, were buried in Willie's caches, and he vehemently insisted they were all empty. When I asked him where they were located, he said he forgot where most of them were. I was sure he kept the food for himself, he wasn't deprived, while the rest of us lost weight he gained.

"We're not going on a tiger hunt, are we Carlie?" Rusty asked tiredly, as he sat down beside me on a large boulder. Everyone was exhausted and hungry, so I decided it was time for a diversion.

"Not today, Rusty, I'm sorry."

He leaned against my arm, and he looked so sad.

"If we can't hunt, we might as well play. I know where there's a secret garden, and if you promise not to tell anyone where it is, I'll take you there."

Rusty raised his head, a huge grin on his face. "I promise with all my heart and all my soul...."

I grabbed him by his waist and swung him around. He laughed, and I soon realized that was an unwise thing to do. I had to swing Eddie, then Debbie, who was very solid and almost broke my back, and when Mae-Li approached me, a smile on her face, I shook my head and walked away.

When the kids saw the patch of green grass, they threw themselves on the ground. They rolled and laughed happily while Mai-Li and I sat on the wooden bench and watched. I opened my pack and took out a small bundle, placing it on my knee.

"Anyone hungry?"

"Me," the three of them yelled in unison.

I raised my hand for silence. "Well, I have one apple, two walnuts, and..."

"A partridge in a pear tree," Rusty sang in a croaky voice, causing all of us to laugh.

"Aw, too bad," I chortled. "I ate the partridge and the pear tree."

This caused even more hilarity when suddenly a voice barked. "Glad you guys are having so much fun."

We all turned as one. Willie was standing a few centimetres away, his face twisted in anger, his arm hidden behind his back. I had never seen him so furious.

"You're welcome to join us, but there's not a lot to eat."

"No thanks bitch," he hissed. "I already ate."

There was a collective gasp as Willie swung his arm around grasping a metal pipe in his fist. He moved purposely toward us, and I knew I needed to act quickly.

My first thought was for the safety of the kids. I handed the food to Mai-Li, then I rose from the bench, and left the enclosed area, walking to the open courtyard. Willie followed, slapping the pipe against his hand, and I knew I didn't have a lot of time to protect myself.

I bent over and reached for my knife hidden in my boot. When he saw the blade in my hand, he roared, ran straight for me, and shoved me as hard as he could. I fell hard, bashing the side of my face on the cement as I landed heavily. My knife flew out of my hands landing a few centimetres away. I lay stunned, struggling to catch my breath.

Willie raised the pipe above his head. I tried to stand, but my legs refused to work. I waited for the blow when suddenly I heard a scream. A small body whisked by my vision, arms waving wildly.

"Rusty, no," I yelled. "Stay back."

But my valiant hero ignored me. He flung himself on Willie, knocking the pipe out of his hand.

For a moment there was absolute silence. Willie grabbed Rusty's arm and raised his fist, but suddenly Mae-Li materialized in front of him.

"Do not touch him, Willie," she warned.

Willie hesitated, then lowered his hand. Although Mai-Li would always have the upper hand when it came to any confrontation with Willie, all it did this time was make him angrier and meaner.

"Heck, I wasn't going to hurt the little Rug Rat," he replied, releasing his grip on Rusty's arm, and pushing him away.

"And you will not threaten him again," Mae-Li commanded.

Willie looked around at the rest of our group. Debbie was crying, and surprisingly Eddie was trying to console her.

Shrugging, Willie turned and walked over to my knife. He picked it up and examined it closely. "I've been looking for a good knife, thanks, Carlie."

"Give it back Willie."

"You're not really in any position to order me around, are you?"

Mae-Li walked over and helped me up. Then she turned and faced Willie, who clasped my knife tightly. He pointed it directly at her.

"No Mae-Li," I warned. "Let him be."

"Yeah Mae-Li," Willie taunted, "You don't want me to hurt you. Who would take care of your little idiot if you weren't around?"

There was a stunned silence as everyone stared at Willie, scandalized by his hateful words.

"There's going to be a few changes," he continued. "If any of you don't like them, then you can leave. First, what I say goes. You don't do as you're told you don't eat."

No one answered. I took Rusty's hand, Mae-Li and I joined Debbie and Eddie.

"I see we have an understanding," Willie continued. "Any questions?"

"Just one," a deep voice from behind us asked. "Who put you in charge?"

Everyone spun in alarm, except me. I stood quietly, immediately recognizing who it was. I took a deep breath, then slowly turned. He was leaning casually against the side of the building. He casually strolled closer, not once taking his eyes off my knife clasped in Willie's fist. He unbuckled his backpack and lowered it to the ground. He had a leather quiver strapped diagonally across his back full of arrows and was carrying a bow. I noticed he had a holstered gun under his arm.

"You plan on using that weapon?" the stranger asked. "Your call, but I should warn you, I don't take prisoners."

Willie stepped back, realizing he had no support from any of us. Weighing his options, and finding none, he threw my knife on the ground and raised his hands in surrender.

There was a collective sigh of relief from all of us. I walked over and retrieved my dagger, returning it to the leather pouch in my boot.

Mae-Li took Debbie's hand and thanked Eddie for consoling her. Rusty and Eddie paired off as they always did. Rusty looked at me, and I nodded. When this was over, and

89

we were alone, I knew I had to make him promise to never try something that stupid ever again.

Taylor grinned as I slowly approached him. "Good to see you again, Mr. West."

"And you as well, Miss Fleming."

"Out of curiosity, how did you know about this park?"

"I've been following you."

"You've been what?" I said, raising my voice.

"Take it easy. I wanted to make sure you got home in one piece. I know a lot about the gangs in that neighbourhood, and they wouldn't have hesitated in capturing a young girl travelling on her own, especially if she looked like you, and I won't elaborate on what else they wouldn't hesitate to do."

"I'm sorry, you're right," I shivered. "Thanks for the help, I do appreciate it."

"Good to know," he answered quietly.

My face reddened, and Taylor followed me as I led him over to Mai-Li and the kids, who huddled in a cluster, as far away from Willie as possible.

"This is Taylor West; we met yesterday when I had to take cover for the night."

Mai-Li introduced herself, and I noticed Taylor's demeanour regarding her immediately changed. She pointed to the kids individually, providing their names.

Taylor shook each of their hands, and surprisingly, Debbie did not make a fuss when he reached for hers. She showed him her ball, and he admired it, understanding how important it was to her.

Now for the best part!

I led him over to where Willie was standing. I don't know what made me do it, but I couldn't resist. "Willie, this is Taylor West, our Protector, you might remember I told you about him when you joined our group."

Willie's face went white as chalk. He glared at me, then turned sharply and walked over to the far wall.

The look on Taylor's face was priceless.

"Um sorry," I muttered. "When the boys and I first met Willie, I realized he would be trouble. Unfortunately, he was indispensable because he knew where to find the buried caches of food. I invented this story about our Protector who would be returning at any time. It was the only way I could think to keep Willie in line. Guess I wasn't doing too well when you showed up?"

Taylor smiled and shook his head, obviously not upset. He studied our small group. "This is just part of your gang, right?"

"Nope, just us," Rusty replied. "We're the Rug Rats, and we live in the Stink Hole."

Taylor turned and looked at me, his eyes shining. I shuffled my foot in the dirt, my stomach tied in knots. "So, you just passing through?"

He reached over and touched my scraped face, then lifted my arms and looked at my bleeding elbows. "You need medical attention, the lot of you look like walking skeletons, although Willie doesn't look as if he's suffering too much. How am I doing so far?"

"Yup, you got it right," Rusty added.

"I don't think I have a choice, Rusty, take me to the Stink Hole."

"You better have a clothespin to put on your nose."

This caused a ripple of laughter, and I reached over and ruffled his hair. He leaned against me, and I hugged him.

"You going to join us, Willie?" Taylor asked, not turning his head. I heard Willie grunt, then footsteps as he followed us down the path.

Taylor West's addition to our group improved conditions. The first thing he did was take Willie aside for a "little chat," convincing him how wise it would be to reveal the locations of the hidden caches. Knowing Willie's nature, I was positive he kept that secret to himself as he knew full well there would be no reason to let him remain at the warehouse if he stopped contributing food.

Unfortunately, Willie also confessed the supplies were running out.

As there was no space left in the boys' room to add another person, we partitioned off a large corner of the main room and turned it into a bedroom for Taylor. At first, Willie made a lot of noise as he felt he should have the larger space, but he stopped whining when Taylor heartedly agreed to let him have the area and thanked him for taking over the position as Protector. The person closest to the door would be the first one to confront any hostile invaders and his job would be to protect the rest of us. Quickly thinking about it, Willie declined the position. It hadn't taken Taylor long to discover Willie's disposition, cowardice being his strongest flaw.

There were now three of us scavenging, myself, Willie, and Taylor, while Mae-Li stayed at the warehouse to take care of the kids. I threatened them I would take away their comics and crayons if they refused to behave. Rusty and Eddie nodded solemnly, and Debbie, in her usual manner, laughed and threw her ball at me.

The temperature was unbearable. There was a lot of ashfall from the volcano, making it difficult to breathe. Water supplies were drying up, and I worried about it incessantly. Although it would double Mai-Li's workload, we both agreed it was safer to not let the younger kids outside during the day, and after Willie, Taylor, and I returned from foraging, and it was a little cooler, we took them to the park where there was more room for them to run around. Mai-Li and I made masks for everyone. The unwritten rule was if you weren't wearing a mask you did not go outside. I marvelled at the flexibility of the kids; it did not take them long to become accustomed to the masks. We were on constant vigilance, watching for other gangs, and there were times I heard the unmistakable growl of an animal from the nearby bushes.

When necessary, Mae-Li and I remained at the warehouse to do much-needed cleaning. There was no way she could do it during the day, as watching the young people was a full-time job. On clean-up day, Taylor and Willie took over the care of the kids, and I'm sure the only reason Willie went was that Mai-Li and I threatened him with bathroom duty.

Seven people living in such a small, confined space provided little privacy. At first, I was uneasy when I bumped into Taylor and was tongue-tied when he spoke to me. I was more relaxed when the whole group was together. Willie was barely civil to me, answering my questions sharply or not at all. Mae-Li said he was jealous of Taylor, and I shivered when I thought of Willie in any way other than abhorrence. She laughed softly at my angered response.

We lived on reduced rations and Taylor dug a fire pit in the backyard to boil water, which was faster than using my stove.

The earth tremors were more frequent and more violent. The old warehouse creaked and groaned, and I wondered how long it would take for it to collapse. Eddie clung to me tighter than usual, and Rusty remained by his side (to protect him, of course). They both slept with me during those times. I understood how they felt, as I never overcame my inherent fear of earthquakes and did not have the heart to send them back to their room.

I had a terrible feeling our lives were soon to change. There was no food left in the area and searching higher on Little Mountain would be extremely dangerous, as inevitably, we would clash with the other gangs. No one in our group had any fighting experience, although I sensed Mai-Li was proficient in more than Kung Fu. And I often wondered about Taylor. He carried archery equipment and a pistol. He never talked about his past. There was something he wasn't revealing, and I hated not trusting him. My instincts weren't often wrong, but I dared not ask him.

One evening, after the younger kids had settled in their rooms, Taylor asked Willie, Mae-Li, and me to join him at the table. He stated the obvious, we could no longer remain at the warehouse.

"If we can't stay here, and we can't move higher up the mountain, what do you suggest?" I asked.

"We leave Vancouver."

The stunned looks on Mae-Li and Willie's faces mirrored mine.

"Are you crazy, man?" Willie said, raising his voice. "Where in hell would we go?"

"Just settle down," Taylor answered quietly. "I've been thinking about it and have found a way we can safely get to the outskirts of the city. Unfortunately, since Vancouver's an island, we will have no choice but to cross the Fraser at some point."

"We can't go south or west," Taylor continued. "Most of the municipalities around the Fraser River Delta have either been burned or destroyed by the tsunami. I've thought about going north, but with the mass migrations over the past ten years, there's not much left for newcomers. Heading east is our best bet."

"You're talking about going to the Interior?" Mae-Li added.

"My God Taylor," I said. "Do you know how far it is? How can the kids walk that distance?"

"We have no choice, Carlie, if we stay here, we all die of starvation, dysentery, or some other disease, unless of course, the gangs get us first. You all know it won't be long before they discover us."

"I understand, but you do realize the Interior imposed a boycott after the Depression, and it was never lifted."

"I'm quite aware of it, I was born and raised in Kelowna. But as I just mentioned, going north is out of the question. The mountains and terrain are almost impassible and would be too challenging for us, let alone the kids. A substantial portion of our travelling will be in the winter."

Then he rose and went into his makeshift bedroom, returning with a brochure in his hand. He opened it and set it on the table. It was a plan of Vancouver and its municipalities, and on the back was a map of eastern British Columbia, which showed roads, waterways, and mountain ranges.

"We'll be in for a long and strenuous trek," Mai-Li said, more to herself than to the rest of us. "Debbie will slow us down, but I think the twins have the energy and vitality to cope."

Willie slammed his fist on the table. "There's no way we can take Debbie, she has to be left behind."

The stunned silence at the table was overpowering. Taylor looked around the table but remained silent.

Mae-Li's face paled, and her eyes turned dangerously dark as she glowered at Willie. "You know my decision; I will stay here...."

"Hold it just a second," I interrupted abruptly, glaring at Willie, realizing just how far he would go to protect himself. "No one gets left behind. We are a team, small as we may be, but we all go, or we all stay."

I stood and leaned in his direction. "Suggesting that we leave Debbie on her own is borderline criminal, you know full well she is incapable of taking care of herself. You disgust me."

"Look bitch," he sneered. "You have no say in this..."

Taylor rose so quickly he knocked his chair over. He reached across the table and grabbed the top of Willie's shirt in his fist.

"Don't you ever call her that again," he snarled.

The silence in the room was overpowering. I had to intervene, the last thing we needed was for Willie and Taylor to come to blows. I cleared my throat.

"I vote we go."

"I also vote we go, as long as Debbie is included," Mae-Li added.

"You already know what my vote is," Taylor responded, as he relaxed and released Willie's shirt, picked up his fallen chair, and sat down.

We all turned as one and looked at Willie.

"I would prefer we stayed together," Taylor said as if nothing had passed between them. "But if you choose to stay, then stay."

I knew Willie wouldn't last a day alone on the streets and he knew it too.

"Since I'm outnumbered, I have no choice. I guess I'm in." He glowered.

"When do we leave?" I asked.

"I think we better start making plans tomorrow morning," Taylor replied. "We take only what we can carry. We'll fill the two larger water containers; Willie and I can each carry one."

The rest of us nodded, and the more Taylor talked the more I realized the time and thought he had put into our departure plans.

"I'm worried about the volcanoes," he continued. "We're getting a huge amount of ashfall from Mount Baker, and with the severity of the aftershocks we've been experiencing lately, there's potential for Mount Garibaldi to erupt."

"Are you kidding, Mount Baker is in Washington," Willie said, leaning back in his chair. "And Garibaldi is dormant."

Taylor pointed at Mount Baker on the map. "It's always been an active volcano, and when it erupted after the earthquake, it caused as much damage to the Lower Mainland in BC, as it did in Washington. The tsunami created gigantic mudflows and turbulent waters, which caused severe damage to the Fraser River Delta."

"So why not stay where we are?" Willie asked. "We're far enough away from the Fraser, we're safe if we stay on Little Mountain."

Taylor sighed, then shook his head. "With all the seismic activity we've been experiencing, there's every likelihood there's going to be another earthquake. If that happens there's a huge possibility Mount Garibaldi could activate, it's only eighty kilometres from downtown Vancouver. I don't plan to wait around to see if it does."

Knowing he was outnumbered Willie rose angrily, then headed to his room. He slammed the door, and I cringed. He better not wake the twins, but surprisingly, all was quiet.

"I have something to share, but it is not for Willie's ears," Mae-Li said. "My grandparents, aunts and uncles live in Blackfoot, it's an abandoned mining town just southwest of Princeton on the Similkameen River. It was taken over by the Chinese miners around 1860, and my ancestors and family have resided there ever since. My grandparents would have sent a few of their guards to Vancouver to retrieve my family after the earthquake, and they would have discovered none of them survived," she continued. "They would have returned to Blackfoot with the terrible news, and not finding my body, would not know if I was alive or dead. My grandparents and relatives would have been grief-stricken, I am their sole living heir, and they will never stop looking for me. That is why I must get there as soon as possible to let them know I did not perish in the earthquake."

Taylor and I sat quietly at the table, waiting for Mai-Li to continue.

"Debbie will be accepted as one of the family. Both of you will also be welcomed with open arms. The reason I do not wish Willie to know is he will not be allowed to stay in Blackfoot. There is no room for meanness or bigotry among my people. Once we reach the Interior, he can take his chances elsewhere."

"Wouldn't break me up," I mumbled.

"I think we better get some sleep," Taylor smiled, looking at me. "We have a lot of work to do tomorrow."

I quietly opened the bedroom door so as not to wake Debbie. I turned and looked at Taylor who was still seated at the table. He was staring at the map, absorbed in his thoughts. I prayed our decision to leave was the right one. God help us all!

Chapter Eight

When the kids woke the next morning, we told them what was decided. Rusty and Eddie were unusually quiet. I was surprised at their reaction, but then it dawned on me. They lived all their lives in this area, and their parents died here.

I walked around the table and squatted between their chairs. I talked quietly, explaining our reasons for leaving as a united group, and how we needed everyone to help.

Debbie was rolling her ball on the table, unaware of the dilemma unfolding in the room. Mai-Li and Taylor sat quietly, and Willie stared at me, a scowl across his face.

The boys raised their heads, Rusty was holding Eddie's hand, and I knew they were upset about leaving their home. They were so young, and my heart ached for them.

"Can we come back one day?" Rusty asked quietly.

"None of us can, it wouldn't be safe, we need to find a place that's not so dangerous, where there are no bad gangs, and more food and cleaner water." I answered. "Does that make sense?"

Both twins nodded, they were being so brave. A look passed between them, then they answered simultaneously. "Okay Carlie, we'll go."

The rest of the group, excluding Willie, clapped, and cheered. Debbie thought we were playing a game and cheered the loudest. Mae-Li kissed the young girl on her cheek, and I appreciated the burden she was taking on, and vowed I would help her as much as I could throughout our journey.

None of us knew Debbie's full name, when we had asked her, she told us it was 'Debbie, of course.' When we asked her how old she was, she shrugged, and did not answer. I assumed by her size, she was as old as the boys, which made her almost ten. She would always need someone to care for her, and our journey would be difficult because of her physical and mental disabilities.

Our first step was for everyone to bring their personal belongings into the larger room and lay them out. Taylor explained we would each be expected to carry his or her own pack, including their sleeping bag which would be rolled and tied on top. As the boys did not have sleeping bags, they were to take their blankets but no pillows as they would take too much room. We would try to get Debbie to carry smaller, lighter items but she would have to be watched closely, as she tended to put whatever she was carrying down and forget about them, especially if something interesting caught her eye.

I checked the articles laid on the floor. I never carried more than I needed. The trek would be strenuous, and at times we would be pushing ourselves to the limit. Taylor and Willie, along with their packs and weapons, would each carry a water container. The twins would have their packs, and Mai-Li and I would carry our provisions and share Debbie's load between us.

Taylor had his quiver, arrows and bow, and of course his gun. Willie never divulged if he was armed, and just thinking about it left me in a state of panic. My only weapon was my knife, which I kept inside my right boot. I planned to ask Taylor to teach me archery, and with the long trek in front of us, he should find time to give me a few pointers.

Mae-Li surprised me one day when I walked into the bedroom; her back was turned and she was holding a long heavy cane, thrusting the tip at an invisible opponent. Sensing I was behind her, she spun, turned the shaft sideways, and lunged at me. The cane stopped an inch from my throat. Noticing the dumbfounded look on my face, she smiled and lowered the weapon. She explained to me she was practicing Kung-Fu and offered to show me a few of her moves. I immediately agreed, and before long I was practicing as diligently as she.

Leaving Mae-Li with the kids, Taylor, Willie, and I went searching for food one last time, spending the rest of the day digging in crevices and holes. Taylor found a stash of canned beans, and I uncovered a small wooden box crammed between two boulders. I pried it open, and it was full of beef jerky. We foraged until dusk, then wearily returned to the warehouse.

This time I returned to organization and order. The twins finished packing under supervision from Mai-Li, and she convinced them what should be left behind and what should be taken.

Mae-Li produced a large tote bag, which held kitchen items such as can openers, pans, dishes, and cutlery. She was in the process of closing a long cylinder with a shoulder strap. When I looked at her questionably, she whispered in my ear "This is our toilet paper, soap, towels, and feminine supplies."

Thank goodness she was so organized.

Suddenly, I remembered what I had wanted to ask Taylor. "What about my brazier, should we take it with us? We can cook on it and boil water."

"I'm sorry Carlie, much as I would like to, it's too heavy, we'll have to use open fires."

We ate a sparse supper, and the kids were noticeably quiet. Rusty was fidgeting, which meant he was excited and eager to go. My poor Eddie was having a tough time, and when I tucked them in that night, he started to cry. I comforted him as best I could, telling him what to expect on our travels, and how exciting it would be. He eventually settled down and both boys were soon sleeping. Although I never admitted it to myself or the others, the twins were undeniably my responsibility; I swore I would watch over them and keep them safe.

I confiscated the boys' comics, crayons, pencils, and paper from Willie's stash, and was surprised to find candles, matches and a few other articles the boys and I found under the stairwell before meeting him, and which I had completely forgotten about. I stuffed the articles in the bottom of my backpack without showing them to anyone. There was no sense in having an argument with Willie on the night before we left.

Each of us, except Willie, had happy memories of the Stink Hole. Taylor's dire warnings of what we would encounter on our journey weighed heavily on all of us, and I knew deep down we couldn't stay at Little Mountain, we had no choice and were making the right decision. We would leave early in the morning; our adventure would soon begin.

Chapter Nine

In the morning it was chaos, the kids were excited and hard to control. Rusty lost his socks and shoes, and after much wailing and tears, we found them stuffed under Willie's mattress, who was standing off to the side smirking and enjoying the entire incident. It didn't take a genius to figure out who hid them.

Then Eddie panicked when he couldn't find Squishy, and after looking everywhere, I had a hunch. I unpacked his bag and there was the battered teddy bear stuffed in the bottom. I had to do some impressive talking, but I finally convinced him rather than carry Squishy all the way, his friend would be much happier sitting in his backpack with his head sticking out so he could see where we were going. Of course, I had a personal reason for this suggestion, I had no desire to backtrack to find a lost teddy bear.

Debbie sensed the restlessness in the room and ran around in circles, getting in everyone's way. Suddenly she threw her ball wildly into the air, smacking Willie on the end of his nose. Mai-Li intervened when he chased after her, warning him to back off.

Finally, everyone was ready to go. I could tell by the look on Taylor's face he disapproved the delay, but he would soon learn things never went as planned when young children were involved.

When we got outside Taylor had us form a line. He would be in the lead, then Mai-Li holding Debbie's hand, then me, with Rusty and Eddie following me holding hands, and finally Willie in the rear. He warned everyone to stay together and not lose their place in line and to remember to always keep their masks on. Everyone had a role; they were to watch the person or persons in front of them and to warn them should they drop anything.

We skirted the ruined vehicles and buildings. When we arrived at a less congested road, we used it rather than stay on the major highway. We all agreed the TransCanada was off-limits, as the abandoned or smashed cars and semis, mudslides, fractured roadway, and other debris would make it impossible to make suitable time. We kept to the side streets and walked through what was left of Burnaby, heading in the direction of New Westminster. We were aware there would be people living in some of the houses, and with the shortage of food, clothing, and weapons, we were easy targets.

After walking for a few hours, we stopped for a short break as the heat was taking its toll on everyone, and I could hear

Debbie wheezing. Taylor handed everyone a small piece of jerky and reminded us to take only one swallow of water. I noticed he was looking directly at Willie when he said it. At dusk, Taylor stopped and advised he was going to check some of the houses and find one where we might spend the night. While he was gone, we fed the kids and told them stories. Taylor soon returned, and we soundlessly followed him through the streets, watching for signs of trouble.

We walked for a short while, then he pointed to a grove of trees. An old cottage was concealed in the undergrowth and shrubbery, its walls and roof barely visible. The front door was ajar, and inside there was minor damage. We found two bedrooms. The girls claimed one and the boys headed toward the other.

After feeding the kids again and putting them to bed, Mae-Li and I went to the living room where we unwisely plunked down on a comfortable-looking sofa. Dust and ashes flew into the air, and we hacked and wheezed, glad we hadn't taken off our masks. Taylor and Willie soon joined us, and I asked Taylor about the boys. He said they fell asleep as soon as they lay down, they were both exhausted.

We sat on the carpeted floor. Taylor took out a can of brown beans from his backpack, and Mai-Li and I scrounged around in the kitchen and found a pot, a can opener, and four spoons; I lacked the energy to rummage through our packs to find ours. Although the beans were cold, they were delicious, and they soon disappeared.

While searching the house earlier, Taylor found two gunny sacks in the back pantry. As it was late September, the apples and pears would be ripe, and with any luck, we might find a few trees not picked clean. If the kids were hungry while we walked, the fruit, together with the jerky, would keep them happy until we stopped for the night.

Then Taylor laid his map on the floor. I ran my finger down his marked trail and noticed he had a second route marked.

"I know I have two routes shown," he said, as he spotted the confused look on my face. "At first, I thought we should stay in Burnaby and walk to Port Mann Bridge, but the chances the bridge survived the earthquake are negligible. Then we would have to backtrack using up valuable time."

"What about Patullo Bridge, it has the shortest crossing over the Fraser?" I asked, resting my finger on its location. "Wouldn't that be our best bet?"

"I thought the same thing, it was the first bridge on my list, and the first one I struck off. It's been under construction for many years and never completed. I don't want to take the time to walk all that way and find we can't cross it."

"There are tons of bridges," Willie interjected. "I say we take our chances and go to Port Mann?"

"We'd have to use the TransCanada, and since it was rush-hour at the time of the earthquake, I'm bloody sure the bridge, road, and bumper-to-bumper vehicles are now a pile of rubble in the Fraser. Our best chance is New Westminster," Taylor said. "There are two arms of the Fraser we must cross. At first, I thought of the CNR Bridge crossing the North Arm, and because of its height there was a good chance no damage was done by the tsunami, but it's in Richmond, which means most of the land surrounding it is either water or swampland by now. So that's off the table.

"There is a way of crossing the North Arm at Quayside," Taylor continued "There's a pedestrian/cycle bridge that will take us across the water. It is new and high enough above the Fraser and would not have suffered any damage from the flooding. When we get to the other side, we stay on the path and follow it due south until we get to the river.

"Then we must cross Annacis Channel. There is a bridge we might be able to use. It's Annacis Bridge, also called Derwent Way Bridge. I imagine with the exodus of people from the Island during the earthquake the traffic lanes were congested with vehicles, and I don't know how much damage the bridge itself sustained. The reason I'm even mentioning this as a solution is because of the railway track adjacent to the traffic lanes. I'm hoping the train traffic was more sporadic so there's a possibility the rail was clear during the earthquake. This is all speculation; I have no idea how much damage was done in that area especially to the Island. I'm gambling the west end received the brunt of the force from the tsunami."

"I still think going to Port Mann is a lot faster than this convoluted route you're suggesting," Willie interrupted sharply. "Why don't we just give it a try, it'll save us a lot of walking and a lot of time."

Taylor massaged his face, then ran his fingers through his hair. "You're right Willie, it would save us a lot of walking and a lot of time."

"So, what's the problem?"

"The problem is the entire area surrounding Port Mann is a breeding ground for gangs, lowlife, and addicts. If the bridge is open, more than likely a tariff is payable if we want to cross, and I'm not prepared to hand over everything I own, especially my weapons. If it were only the four of us, we might be able to make a run for it, but with the kids, it would be impossible. That's why I've produced this 'convoluted plan,' it's the only way we are going to get out of Vancouver."

"Thank you, Taylor," Mai-Li interrupted. "We knew when we agreed to leave there would be complications arising regarding the kids."

Taylor nodded. "Let me finish my idea, then we'll talk about it."

Mai-Li and I nodded, and the scowl on Willie's face told us exactly what he was thinking and feeling.

"When we get to the river, we should plan to stop early. While you look for a place for the night, I will go to Annacis Bridge alone as I can make better time. I need to find out what kind of shape it's in. If it's walkable, we'll cross there."

"And if the bridge is a no-go?" I whispered.

"Then we forfeit the plan, and we start looking for a boat, a rowboat, but nothing larger, and the probability is we would have to make two trips to get everyone across. We will have to carry it; we can't take a chance we'll find another one on the Island. That's where your muscle comes in Willie."

Willie grunted, his usual terse manner of communicating.

"So how much water do we have to cross if we are forced to go that route rather than the bridge?" Mai-Li asked.

"We'd have to row across the channel just upriver from the bridge, as it's the narrowest part of the waterway. Then we walk east to the far side of the Island. There's a wastewater treatment plant, which is farther south so I'm hoping we don't encounter any of the residue left from the tsunami. The last juncture will be to row across the South Arm to West Surrey."

There was silence at the table, and I bit my lower lip, trying hard not to show my anxiety. We were just beginning our journey, and already the challenges ahead of us seemed insurmountable.

"When we get to Surrey, we'll head east," Taylor finished. "Delta is probably underwater as it was mostly bogged land before the earthquake, and with the contamination of soil and water in the rivers and wells, the liquefaction, mudslides, rockslides, and flooding of the Fraser, it's a place to avoid."

"So, what happens if we can't find a boat and can't get across?" Willie asked. "Do we go back to Little Mountain?"

"We can't return, we wouldn't last a week. We try another bridge and if we can't find a safe one, then we keep walking until we do. No matter how far we go, we still need to cross the Fraser at some point, so let's try the one I've suggested first. Right now, it's our best bet."

Willie cursed under his breath, his face dark and sullen. Much as he was a pain in the ass, we still needed his muscle.

Mae-Li had been sitting quietly, listening to Taylor's every word. She cleared her throat, then leaned forward. "I think we should try the rowboat idea first rather than the bridge."

"Mai-Li," Taylor replied, hesitating before he finished his thoughts. "We'll have a tough time finding a boat anywhere in the area. I imagine most of the people living there have long since confiscated anything that floats. It's why I suggested we try both ideas, I'll check out the bridge and as a last resort Willie and Carlie can look for a boat."

"Debbie has an innate terror of heights, she might panic halfway across the bridge, and I would not be able to control her, she is very strong, especially when she is afraid."

"The tracks parallel the road, there's a cement sidewalk we can walk on instead of the tracks."

"How high is the bridge?"

"As high as most of the bridges in Vancouver, swing bridges are raised when a boat has to pass under, which means they are solid and well-built."

"Please Taylor, can we try my way first?"

Taylor remained quiet for a few minutes, nodded, then turned and looked at me and Willie. "Okay, who agrees with Mae-Li?"

I reluctantly lifted my hand, feeling like a traitor. I could tell he was surprised by my decision.

"What about you Willie?"

"Yeah, I say we try looking for a boat first, although I think both of your ideas are bullshit."

Taylor clenched his jaw, and I knew he was close to losing it. "Willie, we will never return to Little Mountain, and this is the last time I'm telling you this. If you want to go back, we will not stop you. The choice is yours."

Then Taylor rose, took the map, and refolded it. "I'm tired and I'm going to sleep. I'll see everyone in the morning."

"Night," Mai-Li and I said together.

"Willie, you sleep with Eddie," Taylor muttered. "I sleep with Rusty."

Willie followed him into the bedroom. "Hey, wait a minute, I'm not sleeping with Eddie, he pees the bed."

"Yes, I know," Taylor remarked, closing the door.

Mae-Li and I looked at each other, then we made a beeline for the bedroom. We covered our mouths with our hands, trying to muffle our laughter. The last thing we needed to do was wake up Debbie.

"You're funny," a voice said from the bed.

Oh, oh, too late. Debbie sat up, a smile on her face.

"Yes, we are Debbie," Mai-Li chuckled. "Now go back to sleep."

"Okay, Mai-Li."

We quickly undressed and jumped under the covers. I rolled over and closed my eyes, grateful we had survived our first day with no mishap.

Chapter Ten

The next morning Taylor dug through the food supply and gave each of the Rug Rats a piece of jerky, along with half an apple. He explained to them, at least three times, that it was a special treat.

I, as usual, finished packing before the others. I walked around the room, something was nagging at me, and I suddenly remembered what it was. I went to the back yard, which was overgrown with tree branches, bushes, and shrubs. I stopped and turned in a circle, realizing it must have been a beautiful garden at one time. It was then I spotted a knotty, shrivelled tree hidden in the dark shadows behind a small shed.

"Apples, big juicy apples," I yelled as I raced back to the house. "Hurry, bring the gunny sacks. And don't forget your masks."

There was a stampede to get outside, and I pointed my find to the kids.

"Okay, don't drop them or they'll bruise. Fill the sacks."

"Carlie, why don't you finish packing the boy's backpacks while I help them pick," Mae-Li suggested. "Otherwise, we'll be here all day."

She had her cane, which folded over, attached to a belt around her waist. I knew she would guard the kids with her life.

Taylor was just closing Eddie's bag, and I reached over and took Rusty's. "Hasn't he even started yet?" he grumbled, noticing his bag was empty.

"It's okay, I don't mind helping him."

"You pamper him too much Carlie. He's old enough to be more responsible, it's time he grew up."

"Let him be a little boy a while longer, I imagine our journey will take it out of him soon enough."

Taylor raised his head and stared into my eyes. My face turned red, and my heart was pounding like a drum. I heard the muffled sounds of the kids and Mai-Li talking and laughing in the backyard.

"Jeez, get a room." We spun around and faced Willie. He was sitting at the table clutching a magazine. He sneered, rose, and walked down the hall to the bedroom. Taylor did not comment, he took Rusty's backpack from me and finished packing. I stared at Willie as he retreated down the hall.

Shaking my head, I muttered. "Not surprised he didn't offer to help, but I *am* surprised he can read."

Taylor made a choking sound, trying hard not to laugh. Soon the two of us were howling so hard, everyone in the backyard came running into the house.

"What's wrong Carlie, why are you crying?" Eddie asked.

"I'm not, I'm laughing; Taylor and I are sharing a joke."

"What's the joke, what's the joke?" Rusty asked, jumping up and down in excitement.

"I can't remember," I managed to say. "By the way, how many apples did you guys pick?"

"Two whole sacks and all our pockets are full," Debbie answered.

"Wow, that's fabulous. Thanks for picking the apples."

"You're welcum, Carlie."

I grinned at Debbie, then turned to the boys. "You can pick as many as you want, but the only condition is you have to carry them yourselves."

"I think they have enough apples," Taylor interrupted. "Their pockets and jackets are stuffed."

Then he frowned and looked down at the twins. "Carlie and I just finished doing your backpacks. You had lots of time before you went to pick apples. Tomorrow, you pack your own or we leave them behind, got it?"

I noticed the looks on the boy's faces but said nothing. I understood Taylor had to lay down the law, each person had to be responsible for their backpacks.

"Would I have to leave Squishy?" a quiet voice said.

"No, of course not," I said, bending down to Eddie's height. "Squishy is one of us, we would never leave him behind. Right, Taylor?"

Taylor handed the packs to the boys. "Yeah, yeah the rabbit stays with us."

"Hey," Rusty said loudly. "Squishy is *not* a rabbit, he's a bear."

Taylor sighed, rolled his eyes, and walked over to the supplies. "Whatever," he muttered. "Come on, let's make tracks."

There was a mad rush as the kids gathered their belongings. I helped the boys put on their packs, which for some reason was always a struggle. I grabbed mine and ushered them out the door.

Mai-Li was standing at the exit, a pack dangling from her hand. "It's your turn to carry Debbie's."

"Yeah, yeah, I know."

"Willie," Taylor yelled down the hallway. "Are you coming or not?"

Willie sauntered down the hall, a piece of jerky hanging from his mouth. Taylor handed him one of the water containers. Willie stared insolently at Taylor, walked by him, and went outside. Taylor said nothing, his face rigid, and I knew he would not let it slide. Even taking one piece of jerky was stealing food from all of us. Willie was pushing his boundaries, making Taylor his enemy would not be a smart move.

"Let's go, we're already behind schedule," Taylor ordered. "Keep your masks on and stay in line."

I took my place in front of the boys, sensing Willie's eyes burrowing into my back. His hostility was worrying as it was directed at me. Did we make the right decision by asking him to join us? He was lazy and mean and never contributed unless threatened or ordered by Taylor.

I sighed, shifted my pack higher up my back, and grabbed Debbie's.

The ashfall was heavier than usual, and I worried about the young girl. The mask helped a little, yet I could hear her raspy breathing. Mae-Li was talking quietly, pointing out flowers, leaves, anything to keep her mind off the smoke. Mai-Li was a born storyteller, and she could turn her stories into magical tales. The twins perked up and kept barrelling into me when they heard her talking to Debbie. The third time this happened, I steered them in front of me and threatened if they so much as strayed off the trail, they would be back in their usual position.

The rusted vehicles and the debris from the destroyed houses, apartments, and office buildings made it hard to navigate and sometimes entire streets were impassible. We would have to backtrack and find a different route. Our progress was slow, and after four hours passed, I called Taylor and suggested we stop for a rest. The scowl on his face made me angry.

"Taylor, the kids are too young to walk this long without a break. They need water and a light snack."

Carrying my pack and Debbie's was gruelling work but I had no intention of telling him that.

He allowed ten minutes; the kids dug into their pockets and grabbed an apple. I smiled when I saw them wolfing down their fruit. A few years ago, I would have complained if my chocolate ice cream did not have whipping cream. The changes we've endured have taught us to appreciate what we had, not what we thought we were entitled to.

Soon we were on the trail again. We stopped when Taylor announced we were close to the Fraser River.

"Carlie, Willie, you two come with me. We'll look for a place to stay for the night. Mai-Li gives the kids a drink of water, but no more apples, we don't need tummy aches."

"Carlie, you head east, Willie south, and I'll see what the conditions are like west of here. You are packing?"

Both Willie and I nodded, although my "packing" was my knife. I walked for a long time and closely checked the surroundings. The houses still standing were either ransacked or destroyed. I assumed the remaining inhabitants had vacated shortly after the earthquake and those who stayed were the exploiters, fighting among themselves, forming bands who terrorized the weak and the defenceless. We knew enough to stay clear of any dwelling showing signs of habitation.

I had been walking for hours and was ready to stop for the day. I turned a corner and stopped in my tracks. In front of me was a church, half-hidden in the trees. I left the sidewalk, ran into the bushes, and quietly approached the rear of the building. I waited for a short while to make sure it was deserted, all the while picturing Taylor pacing angrily as I was late in returning.

There was a back entrance, and I turned the knob and opened the door. I was in a vestibule; the shelves had been emptied. Before me, was a second door. It opened easily and I stared in amazement at the coloured glass windows, an altar, and rows of empty pews. I slowly approached the apse and noticed a layer of dust covering the pulpit and the railings.

The church would make a perfect shelter, but why weren't there any people around? Something wasn't sitting right, and I stood still, weighing the pros and cons. I finally decided; we were in no position to be fussy.

"Hello," my voice echoed, as I walked deeper into the nave. "Is anyone here?"

It was eerily quiet, and I sensed I was alone in the church. I was excited about my find; this would make a perfect place for us to spend the night. I raced back to the group.

Before Taylor had a chance to criticize my tardiness, I told him about the church.

"Better than what I found," he said, taking me by surprise. "How about you Willie, you find anyplace better?"

Willie shrugged, which meant no. Knowing him as I did, it wouldn't surprise me if he had been napping instead of searching.

"Okay, let's go. How far away is it, Carlie?"

"Just a few blocks."

Following my earlier path, I led our group to the church. I opened the back door and told everyone to leave their packs and coats in the vestibule. Then I opened the door to the nave.

"Did you check out the rest of the place?" Taylor asked, looking around.

I shook my head and pointed to the dust on the railings and the back of the pews.

He walked over to the apse and touched the railing. Wiping the dust on his jeans, he murmured. "This is too easy. Willie comes with me."

I gently pushed the kids and Mai-Li back into the vestibule raising my finger to my lips to warn them to be quiet. "Sit down on the bench and be still," I whispered.

Taylor and Willie were gone far too long. They must have found something or someone. What if I had led everyone into danger? Mai-Li must have sensed my distress, she squeezed my arm gently. It was then we heard footsteps in the nave. Taylor and Willie were running toward us. I reached down and pulled my knife from its sheaf.

"Quick, grab your packs," I ordered. "When I say run, head for the trees."

Taylor spotted me holding my weapon, and he slowed his pace. "Wait, it's, okay?"

"Then why in hell are you two running, you scared us half to death."

Neither of them said anything, and I had an uneasy feeling. "What is it? What did you find?"

He gestured for me to join him, and I looked at Mai-Li. She had three terrified kids clutching her so tightly I wondered how she could breathe. She nodded and I entered the nave, following Taylor to the altar where Willie was standing. Whatever they had seen, it scared them both.

"You won't need your knife," Taylor whispered. I had forgotten I was still holding it.

"You want to tell me what's wrong?" I asked, replacing my dagger in its case.

"We found a backroom, it has a side entrance, which explains why the front section of the church hasn't been disturbed."

"It's bloody disgusting," Willie croaked. I heard the fear in his voice, which only added to my anxiety.

I followed Taylor down a hallway, and he stopped in front of a closed door. He pushed it open and gestured me inside. I walked past him and froze.

I gaped at a partially decomposed body tied to a chair, dressed in a black cassock, a cross hanging around its neck, with a knife buried in its chest. At first, I couldn't comprehend what I was seeing, but then it struck me like a bolt of lightning. I felt nauseous, turned, and fled the room, almost knocking Willie over, who was hovering in the hallway.

I ran into the nave, and leaned against the altar railing, trying to catch my breath. Taylor appeared beside me, a concerned look on his face. I was accustomed to seeing corpses, but it was evident the priest had been tortured and then murdered. What kind of creature would do something this vile?

"You're white as a ghost," Taylor remarked. Before I could respond, I heard a stirring and looked up and spotted the kids and Mai-Li sitting in the pews. She had given each of them an apple and a few crackers to eat. Willie was sitting in the back row, and for once he wasn't arguing or being belligerent.

"I think we need to leave this place," I whispered to Taylor.

"Yes, we do, are you okay Willie?" Taylor asked, as he headed to the exit.

Willie raised his head and as was his way of overseeing any kind of situation, shrugged, and said nothing.

The twins were watching my every move, they knew something was wrong. We followed Taylor outside, Willie caught up when he realized he was sitting alone in the pews.

"Let's find a spot to spend the night," Taylor said to me and Mai-Li. "Don't undress the kids, we need to leave this place in a hurry. As soon as it's light, we're gone."

We walked quietly down the sidewalk, heading into the trees on the far side of the boulevard. "Carlie, where are we going?" Eddie asked quietly.

"Well, we thought it might be a great idea to camp in the woods tonight, and we can watch for falling stars."

"And can we watch for comets too?" Eddie asked.

"You bet; it would be amazing if we saw one."

I turned and looked back at the church, shuddering as I remembered what was inside. I led everyone there, thinking it would be a perfect refuge for the night, and instead, we found unimaginable savagery.

It was getting dark, and Taylor turned on his flashlight. Rusty grasped my hand. I smiled as Eddie reached up and grabbed the back of my jacket, and for the first time, I didn't push him away.

Our journey had just begun, there was no life for us here, and we knew we had to leave Vancouver. Our future happiness lay elsewhere, it would be a long, difficult journey, but we would find it. I was sure of it.

Chapter Eleven

The next morning, we couldn't get away fast enough. I told Mae-Li what Willie and Taylor discovered. She was glad we decided to leave; she felt the church was a sanctuary for a holy man, not be disturbed.

By late afternoon, we arrived at an open expanse of wetland, reeking of dead foliage and acidic water. Black spruce and tamaracks covered in moss, sedges and grasses created a twisted mixture of roots, branches, and reeds.

"We must be close to the Fraser, this entire area has flooded," Taylor announced. "Keep away from the edges, there's probably quicksand in there."

I jumped back, pulling Rusty and Eddie with me.

"Are there bodies in there?" Rusty asked. I stared at him in shock. Taylor rubbed his chin, I readied myself, as he always answered truthfully. "Well, this used to be a community at one time, so I imagine there are."

Eddie grabbed the back of my jacket and hid behind my back. I turned in frustration, but the fear in his eyes stopped me. "Hey guy, there's nothing to be afraid of."

"I know," he whispered, pushing his head against my body.

"I forgot, he doesn't like talking 'bout dead people," Rusty said. "Sorry, Eddie."

"Hey, I know what we can do," I announced.

At least I had everyone's attention, all I had to do now was think of why I said that.

"I know what Carlie's thinking," Taylor said. "Let's break up into twos, and the group finding the best place to spend the night gets a special treat for supper."

I was surprised at Taylor's suggestion we stop for the night. It was late afternoon, with hours of sunlight left.

Taylor looked at me and mouthed. "No churches."

I grimaced, realizing he was only teasing, but I would always regret my unlikely choice of lodging.

The boys shouted their agreement, and of course, Debbie jumped up and down, screaming and yelling. Mai-Li grinned at her enthusiasm. I wished I had half the patience.

"And since we have an uneven number in the group," Taylor continued. "I'll head out and have a look at the bridge."

Mai-Li turned her head sharply.

"Let me explain," Taylor remarked, noticing Mai-Li's reaction. "I've been mulling it over, and after you find a place for the night, Willie and Carlie can go searching for a boat, while I look at the bridge. That way, we'll have both areas covered, we'll know if the bridge is crossable, and if we find a boat, we go that route first. Covering both options will save us time."

Mai-Li nodded, although I could tell she was troubled. I understood her uneasiness about Debbie, and although I had not voiced my concerns to Taylor, I too was anxious about the boys crossing a dangerous bridge.

Taylor grabbed his archery equipment and attached his water bottle to his belt. He must have seen the look on my face and grinned. It had not taken me long to realize facing any kind of adventure, especially if touched with a hint of danger, excited him. It worried me to death.

"I'm travelling light," he said, placing his backpack beside ours. "The less I have to carry, the faster I can get there and back."

Then he disappeared into the underbrush.

The first task on our list was finding shelter for the night. Three youths and three kids, easy enough to set up teams. Debbie started screaming when I chose her, Mai-Li took the distraught girl's hand and calmed her down. When I suggested Eddie go with Willie, he gasped and ran behind my back. By now I was ready to kill Taylor for suggesting we team up in pairs.

"It's okay Carlie," Rusty said. "I'll take Willie. Eddie doesn't like him."

"Thanks a lot, creep," Willie snapped. "Well, I don't like him either."

"Alright, we have our teams, stay in the area and away from the swamp," I said tiredly, looking directly at Willie and Rusty.

Willie smirked, then blew me a kiss. Rusty laughed, but seeing the look on my face, turned away.

"Same rules apply as always," I continued, ignoring Willie's offhand gesture. "Keep your voices down, we don't want to attract any attention. Be back in thirty minutes unless you find something sooner. Willie, make sure you're armed, and Mai-Li, keep your cane handy."

Mai-Li nodded, and pointed to her waist, her weapon securely bound.

"Oh, one more thing; would you mind feeding the kids and setting up the sleeping bags once we find a place? Willie and I want to start looking for a boat right away. It won't be long before it's dark."

"Of course," Mai-Li said.

I watched as Willie and Rusty went down a side trail. Rusty tore off ahead of him, and for a second, I almost called them back. Then I remembered Taylor's words 'It's time for both of them to grow up a little and take on more responsibility.'

Much as Taylor's words stung, I knew he was right.

I took Eddie's hand and asked him if he had any ideas where we should look. He rubbed his chin in deep concentration, then gestured north. We stayed close to the weed cover. I did not have to tell him to be quiet, it was his natural way.

Most of the houses were empty, ransacked, and damaged beyond repair. If possible, our usual practice was to take shelter inside a structure, sleeping outside was always a second alternative. Dangerous people, wild animals, erratic weather, and heavy ashfalls were just a few of the obstacles we had to confront.

We walked for half an hour, and I had a strong awareness of someone or something following us. I was thinking of turning back, hoping Willie or Mai-Li were more successful. Eddie stopped abruptly, grabbed my arm, and pointed to the right. It was an older home, in sorry shape, but at least it had a roof and unbroken windows. It looked abandoned and showed no signs of occupancy.

"Good job, Eddie. I'll bet you win the treat."

We marched back to where we had hidden our supplies. I saw a movement out of my peripheral vision and spotted Willie lying under a sweet chestnut tree, but no Rusty. I stomped heavily through the underbrush and stopped directly in front of him. He jumped up sheepishly, and when I asked him where Rusty was, pointed upwards.

Rusty was sitting on a huge branch halfway up the tree, his legs dangling over the edge. He was holding a gunny sack and was filling it with chestnuts. He reached over to a far branch, lost his balance, and grabbed the limb to keep from falling. The sack of chestnuts dropped to the ground, barely missing Willie's head.

"Hey Rusty," I said pleasantly, not wanting to startle him, although my heart was racing.

"Hi Carlie, I'm picking chestnuts. Willie said he had a hankering for them."

I bet he did.

"Since your bag is down here, and you're up there, you might as well come down. Eddie found us a place to stay for the night."

"Oh, sorry Carlie. I forgot about the contest."

"Not surprised," I muttered, as I glared at Willie.

By the time Rusty joined us on the ground, thankfully all in one piece, Mai-Li and Debbie returned. I knew climbing trees was something every boy loved, but we could not take the chance of Rusty falling and hurting himself. I told them of Eddie's discovery and asked him to lead us to the house.

The door jammed, and it took both Willie and me to push it open. We stood in a small living room, mostly furnished, everything worn and dusty. One look at the bedrooms and the obscene state they were in made us decide it was more hygienic to sleep on the living room floor. Mai-Li found a sad-looking broom, and we removed as much of the dirt and debris as possible.

We unrolled the sleeping bags and laid out Eddie's and Rusty's blankets. I placed Squishy on Eddie's side and noticed one of his arms was loose. Mai-Li carried needles and thread in her pack, and after Eddie was asleep tonight, I would operate on the teddy bear.

"I'll feed the kids," Mai-Li said. "You guys' better leave before it gets dark."

"Thanks, Mai-Li, boys, behave, and since Rusty kindly picked a bag of chestnuts, he can share them with everyone."

I grabbed an apple and a shovel, and Willie grabbed two apples, as well as a handful of crackers. I thrust the shovel at him, and he reluctantly took it, although I sensed he was angry at losing his bag of chestnuts.

We manoeuvred our way through the abandoned streets. Again, I sensed being watched; I had my knife, and Mai-Li handed me her cane just as we were leaving. Whenever I had a chance, I practiced my kicks and lunges, and although I would never have the same proficiency as her, knowing a few moves would help me if I needed protection. I knew Willie was carrying weapons and felt we should be able to protect ourselves.

On the way to the river, we searched in deserted yards and buildings, anywhere a boat might be stashed. We looked for hours, and I became increasingly discouraged.

It was then I saw a piece of wood buried in the reeds and called Willie. "Does that look like a hull of a boat?"

Willie started digging and I scraped the dirt aside with my hands. A partial frame of a boat appeared.

"Oh crap," I said as a piece of the hull snapped in my hands. It was rotted through which meant the rest of the vessel was the same. I should have known better, there was no way it would have been overlooked if it had been useable.

"Come on," Willie said curtly. "Let's try closer to the river."

The grasses and reeds bordering the river were waist high. We discovered a narrow, flattened path. Making slow time, we finally arrived at the edge of the Fraser. The bank on the far side was solid rock, which had split in half, causing a rockslide. Boulders piled high in the river made a dam creating a narrow channel where the water cascaded into deep whirlpools and eddies.

"We can't cross here, it's too dangerous," Willie announced.

"Let's check further upstream," I suggested.

"What's the use, we still don't have a boat. Come on, we better head back. Won't be long before the sun sets."

"Yeah, you're right." Hours of searching had come up empty. I hoped Taylor had better luck than us, although Mai-Li wasn't going to be happy when Willie and I returned empty-handed.

Retracing our steps, we headed down the path. The mosquitos were horrible, and I swatted at one that landed on my arm. The humidity made it difficult to breathe through my mask.

I heard a crack in the bushes, and I spun about. I hadn't been imagining it, something or someone was out there. The shadows had lengthened, and it was hard to see anything in the tall overgrown grass.

"You hear that, Willie?" I whispered.

No answer. I turned, and discovered I was alone. Where in the hell had he gone? If he was still mad about the chestnuts, this was not the least bit funny. I was on my own, with no light, and only my knife and Mai-Li's cane for protection.

I heard rustling in the tall grass, and it or they were getting closer. I reached down and pulled my knife from its sheath.

Red eyes glowed in the darkness; my heart was pounding so hard I felt light-headed. I slowly backed up, cursing Willie.

A low growl sent terror surging through my body. I remembered what Taylor told us if we ever confronted a wild animal. "Never, never run, you are prey, your only chance is to stand and fight."

Easy for him to say when he carried more weapons than GI Joe.

A large spotted animal crept out of the underbrush. I stepped back, shaking my head in astonishment, I was facing a cheetah.

The huge cat slinked slowly toward me. I realized there was no sense in running, I was facing the fastest land animal on Earth. I crouched, raised my arm, and tightly grasped my knife, realizing how useless it was against an animal this size. I prayed it would kill me quickly.

My thoughts reached out to the kids, to Mai-Li and Taylor. Who would watch out for Rusty and Eddie if anything happened to me?

It was ready to spring; I closed my eyes. Suddenly it roared in anguish. I opened my eyes and watched as it fell with a dull thud on the path a few centimetres away from where I stood, two arrows buried in its chest.

I spun around. Taylor was standing a few feet away; I ran to him, flinging my arms around his neck, sobbing uncontrollably. "I ...I thought I was going to die."

"Take it easy, you're okay," he said gently, as he put his arms around me. I stiffened, then stepped back.

I wiped the tears from my face. "Sorry, sorry.... I shouldn't have done that; I mean I shouldn't have ... I... I."

"Carlie, stop talking and take a deep breath."

I obeyed and immediately felt better. I stared at the dead animal. "Is that a... a cheetah?"

"Yes, more than likely one of the occupants from the Vancouver Zoo. During the earthquake most of the cages and paddocks were destroyed and the animals that survived escaped, I've spotted a few of them around. However, this is the first time I've seen one of the big cats."

"Should we bury it?"

"No time, if there are other creatures in the area, they'll smell the blood and will be here in a few minutes."

"Carlie, where's Willie?" Taylor asked, a frown creasing his forehead as he looked around.

I said nothing, and he gently lowered his hand and placed them on my shoulders and in a controlled voice, said. "Did you two get separated, I hope it's what you're going to say, for his sake."

I wrung my hands, not sure where to begin. Either way, Willie was in big trouble.

"I was following him down the path, he was walking so fast, I had a tough time keeping up, then I heard a loud crack coming from the underbrush. I turned to see what it was."

"And."

"I asked if he heard it, and when he didn't answer, I looked back and it was then I realized he was gone."

The expression on Taylor's face was hard. "Let's go, and don't forget your knife and Mai-Li's cane."

He walked over to the cheetah, grabbed the shafts of the arrows, and pulled them from the carcass. He rubbed the arrow points on the dried grass removing the blood then placed them back in the quiver.

I grabbed my knife and the cane, Taylor retrieved his flashlight from his jacket, then holding my hand, pulled me through the scratchy grass and reeds. He said nothing until I showed him where the house was.

Willie was sitting in an armchair munching an apple. Mai-Li was on the sofa on the far side of the room, next to where the kids were sleeping. When she saw my face streaked with tears, she came over and hugged me.

Taylor set his weapons down on the floor next to his sleeping bag. Then he walked over to Willie and grabbed the top of his tee shirt tightly in his fist. Willie struggled to get loose, his fists raised, but when he saw the look on Taylor's face, he slowly lowered them.

"You useless son of a bitch, you left her alone in the dark," Taylor shouted. "A wild cheetah attacked her, and all she had to protect herself with was her knife and Mai-Li's cane. If I hadn't shown up when I did, she would have been killed."

"I don't know what you're talking about, she was right behind me."

"Did you ever once look back to see if she was there?"

"If she can't keep up, it ain't my problem."

"Then you're admitting you left her behind?"

"I ain't her babysitter."

I had never seen Taylor so angry; he took a deep breath, looked into Willie's eyes, and snarled. "No more excuses, no more stealing, no more lies. You broke the number one rule, we always have each other's back. Pack your goddam bags and get the hell out of here."

Willie's face turned white; I must admit I agreed with Taylor's ultimatum at that moment. Willie deserved to be punted, but I also knew when Taylor calmed down, he would soon realize Willie wouldn't last a day on his own.

Taylor released Willie's shirt and pushed him back into the armchair. He walked over to where I was standing and gently stroked my face. "You okay, Carlie?"

I nodded, my face flushed a deep shade of red, I lowered my head and stared at the floor.

He squeezed my arm, then went to his sleeping bag. He removed his boots and socks, then climbed in fully clothed. He turned and faced the wall, none of us dared speak.

Willie had enough smarts to collect his sleeping bag, which was lying next to

Taylor's, and head into the adjoining room, regardless of its condition.

"Come, let's get some sleep," Mai-Li whispered.

I raised my finger to my lips, then walked over to where the kids were sleeping. Debbie was snoring lightly, holding her ball tightly in her hand, and I smoothed her hair back from her face. Rusty was mumbling something in his sleep, he always was a restless sleeper. I placed my hand on his back and he immediately settled down. Then I checked on Eddie, and I noticed Squishy had gone through surgery. Mai-Li had been busy.

She instinctively understood my feelings, touching the kids was my way of showing how thankful I was for surviving a near-death experience.

We went into the filthy kitchen and quickly changed into our PJs, then we crawled into our sleeping bags and Mai-Li blew out the lantern.

I found it hard to fall asleep, I kept reliving the scene over and over. My anger at Willie was still raw, would I ever be able to trust him again?

I also discovered how intimidating Taylor could be, especially when someone he cared for was in danger. For some reason, I felt Willie had gotten off easy.

I also realized Taylor was beginning to have feelings for me, emotions which I did not know how to return. It was then the tears started, and I wiped them angrily away.

"Thanks, Taylor," I said quietly. He didn't answer, but I did not expect him to.

I rolled over and fell asleep.

Chapter Twelve

The mood in the room next morning was strained; Willie took his food, went outside, and sat on the front stoop. Taylor refused to speak to him, and Mai-Li and I had our hands full feeding the kids and getting them ready to leave.

Eddie of course was the first to sense there was a problem. He sat close to me, clutching my jacket. Mai-Li and I decided not to say anything to the kids, if they knew about the cheetah, they would be terrified.

I asked Taylor what he had found at the bridge, as I'm sure he realized by now Willie, and I had no luck finding a boat.

"Let's finish eating. We'll get the kids to pack their stuff and we can talk."

When everyone had eaten, I told the boys we would be leaving soon and when they asked how long before we left, I told them two minutes, which always made them grin.

Taylor, Mai-Li, and I refilled our coffee cups, and I couldn't help smiling when I overheard Rusty instructing Eddie on how to roll his blanket. I insisted they tie them to the top of their backpacks in the same manner as the sleeping bags. A few days back Eddie's blanket had come untied and fallen off, and I backtracked over three kilometres to retrieve it. Willie was at the end of the line, obviously not watching the person in front of him.

"I think we can cross at the bridge," Taylor said interrupting my thoughts. "The roads are impassible, both have been severely damaged by the earthquake, and with the demolished vehicles, there's no way we can use them. The tracks are our best bet, there's a pathway we can follow, and a cement barricade on both sides, so there's no danger of falling off. However, there's one spot where the road had sustained severe damage, the fasteners on the tracks have come loose, and a few of the sleepers are broken off. There's a gap but it's not too wide, the only problem is you can see the water, which might intimidate the kids a little."

Mai-Li and I looked at each other.

"The twins should be okay," Taylor continued. "I can get them across if I carry them separately."

"Which leaves Debbie," Mai-Li said quietly. "She won't let anyone hold her but me, and I don't have the strength to jump if she's struggling in my arms. As soon as she sees the hole, she will panic."

Taylor nodded, deep in thought. "What if I just pick her up without warning and jump? It might scare her for a few seconds, but if she can see you, she should be fine?"

"I don't know Taylor. In her mind, I would be deserting her, and I would have to earn her trust all over again. Is it worth it?"

"We can't stay here. After last night, I realized why there were no people around, the heavy undergrowth bordering the river is the perfect cover for animals to hide and hunt. They know we are in the area; we need to leave right away."

"He's right, Mai-Li," I said. "The kids would be the most vulnerable, they wouldn't be able to protect themselves from a large animal."

Mai-Li nodded solemnly.

"I'll let Willie know what we have decided," I said to Taylor. "Better if you stay away from each other for a while."

Taylor scowled and continued packing.

"Should I tell him he can stay, or does he have to leave?"

Taylor raised his head and sighed heavily. "Not your problem, it's mine. Don't say anything, for now, let him stew for a while, it'll do him good."

I went outside, Willie raised his head when he heard the door opening. I sat down on the stoop next to him and told him about Taylor's findings at the bridge, and his thoughts about the larger animals. Saying nothing, he tossed his apple core in the bushes.

I knew he was waiting to hear more but I said nothing and went back inside the house, not ready to forgive him either.

It took no more than ten minutes for everyone to finish packing. It was a little farther than I expected, taking us over four hours to get to the bridge. We stood in a tight group on a small hill overlooking the devastation below.

At one time the swing bridge must have been spectacular, especially when it allowed boats to sail through. One whole side of the bridge was collapsed, and there were buses, cars, and trucks piled in the river.

"You and the boys go first," Taylor instructed, as he turned to look at me. "The path following the tracks is not very wide, so be careful. I'll bring up the rear. The gap is about halfway down. Jump across, and I'll carry the boys, one at a time."

I nodded; Rusty was almost dancing he was so excited. No problem worrying about who would go first! Eddie, on the other hand, gripped me so hard I lost feeling in my arm. I gently removed his fingers.

"Hey guy, you know I'd never let anything happen to you, and neither would Taylor."

"Eddie, do you want me to hold your hand?" Rusty offered.

I heard Willie shuffling behind me, then I heard him mutter under his breath. I ignored him, wishing he would disappear in a puff of smoke.

Taylor tousled Rusty's head. "Thanks, guy, you're a good brother, but maybe Carlie should hold Eddie's hand, and you can follow right behind them."

"Mai-Li, you'll be next, we must synchronize what we do down to the second. Have you thought about it?"

"Yes Taylor, all night long."

"Stop worrying, it'll work."

"I'll stay here with Debbie. She's going to ask where the boys are, I'll point them out to her, and have her wave to them. Then I'll bring her down the path. You'll need to make sure you're standing right next to her. She'll be distracted, that's when you will have to pick her up and jump. I'll be right behind you."

"It'll be over in a second."

"For us, but not for her. She will start screaming the minute you touch her. She will be struggling when you jump, so be aware. She's heavy and she's strong."

Taylor nodded, listening carefully.

"She will be upset and will try to get back to me. Someone should restrain her until I jump over."

"I can do that."

"There's a chance she might be upset for over an hour, she will be very angry at me, and will push me away."

"No problem, we just keep walking until she shuts up," Willie said, startling me. I had completely forgotten he was still behind us.

"Well, *you* can keep on walking if you like, Willie," I muttered. "You're good at that."

147

I had promised myself I would not say anything to him when the kids were around. But he did have a way of grinding on my nerves. His mouth twisted in anger. Taylor stiffened and Willie had enough sense to step back and leave well enough alone.

Waiting only prolonged the inevitable, so I took Eddie's hand and walked down to the tracks, warning Rusty to stay right behind me. The path was very narrow; so, I motioned to the boys to remove their backpacks. Taylor took them from me and hung them around his neck.

We arrived at the gap, and I leaned down and looked over the side.

"Little jump?" I sputtered, staring at Taylor.

"Don't worry, you'll clear it with centimetres to spare."

I swallowed, suddenly not happy about going first.

I removed my pack and laid it on the ground. I asked the boys to stand back, then I took a deep breath and ran as fast as I could. When I got to the ledge, I jumped and sailed over the gap, landing on the far side with at least four centimetres to spare.

"Show off," Taylor chuckled.

"Me next, me next," Rusty yelled. "Can I do it by myself?"

"No," I yelled. "Remember what was planned, it's just a little too wide for you to jump, maybe after you grow a little more."

"Who's first?" I asked Taylor.

"I think Eddie, then I'll come back for Rusty."

I understood Taylor's reasoning, Eddie would panic if left behind, especially if he were alone with Willie.

"Alright Eddie, this is what I am going to do. I'm going to pick you up, and I want you to wrap your arms around my chest and your legs around my waist but facing me. Then I'm going to jump over to Carlie, then come back for Rusty. Are you ready?"

"No," Eddie said in a squeaky voice. "But go ahead anyway."

Taylor grinned, stepped back, and before anyone had time to think, he was standing next to me, holding a white-faced Eddie. I took him from Taylor, and Eddie wrapped his arms around my neck.

"Be right back," Taylor said, rubbing Eddie's back. "Good job."

Eddie grinned, faced Taylor, and gave him a high five. Taylor soon returned with Rusty. I put Eddie down and had them stand away from the edge.

"Willie, do you mind?" Taylor said. "Either jump now or step back."

Willie was standing on the other side, leaning over the edge, and looking into the water. "Jeez man, I thought you said it was a breeze."

"Sorry, you're on your own, you're a little too heavy for me to carry over. You should be okay carrying your pack."

I chuckled, receiving a nasty look from Willie. He took a long run and then jumped. He landed on the edge, and Taylor grabbed him before he toppled backward into the raging river.

Willie pushed Taylor aside, and I felt the least he could have done was thank Taylor for saving his life.

"Alright, I'm going back for Debbie," Taylor said. "Carlie, I need you and the boys to stand together right here, and when you see Debbie, start waving."

Taylor jumped back, and Mai-Li and Debbie appeared over the hill.

Debbie spotted the boys and laughed. "Eddie, Rusty, it's me, Debbie."

The boys waved, and Debbie waved back eagerly. Taylor swooped down, picked her up, and jumped over the gap. As Mai-Li predicted, Debbie started screaming the moment Taylor grabbed her. He placed her on the ground; and spotting Mai-Li on the far side, Debbie ran to the edge, tears streaming down her face.

I was standing nearest to her, I grabbed her around her waist and pulled her back.

She began struggling, kicking my legs, and banging her head on my chest.

"Debbie, stop, right now," I ordered.

Wrong move. It only made things worse. She howled louder, and I had to use all my strength to restrain her. Now I understood what Mai-Li meant when she said Debbie would be out of control.

"Mai-Li," I stammered, struggling to remain upright. "You might want to get here sooner than later."

Mai-Li stepped back and jumped. Taylor yelled at her to stop, and I suddenly realized why. She was still wearing her backpack. I watched as she landed heavily on the ledge. Losing her balance, she fell backward. Taylor threw himself on the ground, reached over the edge, and grabbed her arms just as she lost her footing. He gently pulled her up, it had been too close, if she had fallen into the river, she would have drowned.

Amazingly, Debbie stopped her screaming. She threw herself on top of Mai-Li and laid her head on her chest.

Mai-Li sat up and hugged the distraught girl.

It was my fault. I told Mai-Li to jump, I should have understood she was upset about Debbie, and completely forgot she was still wearing her gear.

Taylor came and stood next to me. "I know what you're thinking and it's not your fault," he said quietly. "I'm going back for the rest of the gear; you want to give me a hand?"

"Willie," I ordered. "Keep an eye on the boys, and make sure they stay away from the edge."

I noticed the grin on Taylor's face as we turned and jumped.

Chapter Thirteen

We followed the highway. The cars and trucks stacked on top of each other, and we weaved our way between them until we reached an open field.

Mai-Li and I handed out apples and crackers to the kids. Taylor told them they could have one swallow of water each, but no more. I remembered his worry regarding the contaminated water on the Island. He took out his map and spread it open on the grass. Mai-Li, Willie, and I joined him.

"Which way do we go?" Willie asked.

"I think we'll head SE, it's not a long hike to the Fraser. While we're walking, we need to look for a boat."

"There's lots in the Marina over there. Why not take one of them? Not only are they bigger than a rowboat, but we can all fit aboard. Then we can go around the tip of the Island and head straight across to Surrey. Saves walking and running into trouble on the way."

Taylor looked at Willie in surprise. "Willie, what a great idea."

"Good job, Willie," a voice said behind us.

"Where did you come from?" I asked, looking down at Rusty. "I just saw you over there."

"We're bored," Rusty whined. "Can Willie swing us around?"

"I don't think Willie wants to play right now."

"Okay everyone," Taylor said. "We've wasted enough time; you know the drill, line up and stay close."

We headed for the marina, boats piled on top of each other, some of them buried in mud from the flooding. It would not be an easy job trying to find one intact.

"I'm going to see if there's anything we can salvage," Taylor said. "Mai-Li and Carlie, why don't you take the kids back to the park, while Willie and I have a look around? This will take a lot longer than I thought."

We herded the kids back to the open field, removed their backpacks, and told them to go play. Mai-Li and I sat on the grass and chatted. The sound of the kids giggling and yelling sounded wonderful. They had so little time for fun.

The warmth of the sun felt good on my head and shoulders, and I lay back and watched the birds eating late berries and darting among the branches. The air on the island was not polluted as in Vancouver, as there were fewer forest fires and no volcanos in the area. We insisted the kids keep their masks on as we wanted them to get used to them, as we had no idea what lay ahead.

Songbirds had been disappearing for years, and I marvelled at the increase in their numbers in rural areas, especially on the island. Was it because there was less interaction with people and the air was easier to breathe?

I closed my eyes; I awoke when my shoulder was shaken. "You dozed off," Mai-Li said. "Taylor and Willie are returning."

"It's so peaceful here, let's hope the guys have good news."

The news was not good as most of the boats were dismantled. They found a few that would have worked, but the gas tanks were empty.

"Good idea Willie, but it looks like we're walking after all," Taylor mumbled. "Get the kids ready, we need to leave."

We stayed on the path and followed it around the abandoned buildings. Taylor stopped when the path split in two directions.

"Rusty, can I borrow your compass?" Taylor asked.

"Yup," Rusty said as he ran to the front of the line.

"Thanks, bud. I think we should walk due east until we get to the river. Rusty, you want to watch the compass and make sure we're going in the right direction?"

Rusty nodded eagerly.

"Make sure we are always headed east, if not let me know, okay?"

I was glad Taylor was giving Rusty something to keep him occupied. It was the perfect pastime for an over-active boy.

Rusty returned to his place in line, placed the compass around his neck, and said to Eddie. "You want to help me with the compass?"

Eddie nodded, but not as heartily as his brother. Rusty took Eddie's hand, and they were ready to go.

We hadn't walked far when Mai-Li pointed. "Look, aren't those boathouses?"

There were two rows of buildings, and on each door was a symbol of a sailboat.

"Yeah, they are," Taylor said. "Come on Willie, the rest of you stay here behind those willows. Don't move until we return."

Willie joined Taylor, and I was happy he was being so cooperative. I suppose he was trying to make amends after the cheetah fiasco and wanted to stay in Taylor's good graces. Taylor still hadn't said anything to Willie about letting him stay with the group.

This time the guys were gone a little longer, and I began to fret. What if something happened? Anything or anybody could be inside those buildings.

After what seemed an eternity, we heard the guys returning down the path. They were talking animatedly, which was a good sign.

"Good news everyone, Willie found a boat."

"Good job Willie," the twins said simultaneously as they joined the guys on the sidewalk. I couldn't help myself; I chuckled but stopped when I saw the anger in Willie's eyes. No joking with him, I swear, sometimes it was like being around a cranky old bear.

"Unfortunately, there's not enough room for all of us, so we'll have to make two trips. But first, we hike to the South Arm, I think it's around nine kilometres from here. And Willie and I will be carrying the boat."

We followed Taylor and Willie to the boathouse. They led us inside one of the buildings and again I was angry at the destruction and graffiti that greeted us everywhere we went. I spotted a battered rowboat in the back storage room. It had certainly seen better days.

"Any oars?" I asked.

Taylor nodded and pointed to the rafters above our heads.

"You think they're, okay?"

Taylor stepped back, took a few steps, and jumped. He grabbed hold of the rafters swung his feet up and wrapped his legs around them. Then he grasped the oars, tossing them down. It took him three seconds to release his hold and land agilely on the floor in front of me.

"Good job Taylor," I teased. I raised my hand for a high five, but he frowned his 'wasting time' face and joined Willie at the boat.

Willie retrieved the oars and was examining them closely. "They're in decent shape. I studied the boat; there's some damage in the hull, which needs patching and one of the seat's broken, so someone will have to sit on the bottom, maybe one of the kids. Otherwise, it should be good to go."

Taylor moved over to the rowboat and flipped it over. There was a hole about the size of a fist.

"Damn," Taylor said angrily. "Now we know why the boat is still here."

"I can fix it," Willie said, shrugging his shoulder.

Taylor stared at Willie, a surprised look on his face.

"My old man fished for a living. I grew up around boats. Shouldn't take much to fill in the hole."

Taylor gestured for Willie to grab the rear end of the boat and they carried it outside. "What do you need, Willie?" Taylor asked.

"If we can find some wood, I can trim it to size, and pound it into the hole. Just temporary, but good enough for what we need."

"Okay everyone, Willie needs wood. Spread out."

Mai-Li and Debbie went one way, Rusty joined Taylor and disappeared around the corner, and Eddie and I headed over to a dilapidated shed near a small group of trees. The shed was empty, everything stripped bare. We returned to the boathouse; Mai-Li was carrying a pile of wood, which she threw on the ground in front of Willie. He chose a few pieces and placed them next to the boat. By now Taylor and Rusty had returned empty-handed.

"I'm going to need your knife, Carlie," Willie said. "To pare down the wood."

I must have hesitated too long. "Unless you have an axe in your backpack?" he asked sarcastically.

"I do," Taylor said. He retrieved his pack from the pile, dug through the contents and pulled it out.

"Wow," I said. "What else do you have in there?"

"You'd be surprised," Taylor said. "My dad trained me well; never go anywhere without the essential items: an axe, knife, flint, rope, and of course, my weapons."

Willie took the axe and started chopping the wood. I was sitting with the kids and Mai-Li next to the door when I suddenly realized how late it was.

"It's getting dark guys, and the boat won't be ready for a while. We should stay overnight in the boathouse and Mai-Li, and I will get supper started."

Taylor rose, stretched, and looked around. "Haven't seen any trouble so far. I guess it's safe to stay. We might as well set up camp. You'll be what, another hour Willie."

"'Bout two," Willie replied not lifting his head. He was measuring and hacking the wood, and it was the first time I had seen him take interest in something other than reading comics and eating food.

Mai-Li walked over to Willie and watched what he was doing. "You seem to know a lot about the framework of a boat, Willie?" she commented.

"First thing my old man taught me, if you can't repair a boat, you don't deserve one."

"Sounds like good advice to me."

"One day I was to inherit his fishing boat, it was a nice vessel. We kept it clean and in decent shape."

Mai-Li nodded. "I imagine living so close to shore, most of the boats and houses were destroyed by the tsunami."

Willie stopped chopping, then he looked away, his gaze settling on the bordering trees. "I was out with a few of my buds near Little Mountain when the earthquake hit. Dad was out fishing, he drowned in the tsunami."

Mai-Li placed her hand lightly on Willie's shoulder. "What about your mother?"

"Ma left us when I was about ten, so hey, I might not be an orphan after all," he answered bitterly.

"I'm sorry, Willie."

At this point, Taylor stepped in and took the wood from Willie. "Hey man, this should work perfectly."

Willie's eyes refocused, and Taylor handed the wood back to him.

Mai-Li and I fetched the packs, then headed inside. There was no trouble finding a place to set up, as anything of value was long gone. The kids knew the routine so well, they finished before Mai-Li and I had started. I opened my pack and dug out a pile of comics and a pack of cards.

"Whoa," said Rusty. "Are those our comics?"

I nodded and handed them to him. "You kids have been so good; you deserve a treat. Mai-Li and I are going to start supper while you sit quietly."

"Thanks, Carlie," Debbie grinned.

"You're welcum," I replied. Debbie giggled, then covered her mouth with her hand.

"That's the first time I've heard Willie talk about his family," I said solemnly, turning to face Mai-Li.

"Some people have difficulty talking about personal tragedy, especially when they have lost someone close."

I shrugged, then changing the subject, I murmured. "This is as good a time as any to take stock of our food and supplies. How about I do that, and you put together something for supper."

"Carlie, you can't ignore your sorrow and grief forever, you must face them one day."

"Not today, okay?" I said in a harsh whisper.

"Of course, are you cooking or taking inventory?"

160

I raised my eyebrow, saying nothing.

"Anything to get out of cooking," Mai-Li chuckled.

It was peaceful inside the boathouse, the boys were reading quietly, Debbie got tired of looking at the pictures, so she took her ball and threw it against the wall. I emptied the supply bag and laid the food on the floor. If we were careful, we had enough left for four days. By then, we should be out of Vancouver and heading east. We needed to find uncontaminated water; it would take a few hours to boil enough to fill the two canisters. Our apples were disappearing quickly, and only six cans of beans remained. We would have to do some scavenging tomorrow, or when we got to Surrey.

The door opened and Willie and Taylor entered. Taylor noticed what I was doing, and he wandered over.

"Are we going sailing tomorrow?" Mai-Li asked.

"Aye Captain," Taylor responded. "Bright and early, before the sun gets up."

The kids groaned, and I knew exactly how they felt.

"Time to start foraging again?' Taylor asked. "What are we low on?"

Mai-Li had everything set out for supper, so I suggested we eat first, then we could check through the provisions. She gave Willie and Taylor extra crackers, then poured about a quarter cup of water into their mugs and shook the jug to indicate it was almost empty.

"Yeah," said Taylor. "No water until we get off the Island. Remember I told you kids about the bad water here, so no drinking and no touching anything liquid."

We let the kids play a little longer, then announced it was bedtime. I took Eddie outside to pee. He'd been doing so well since our journey began but sometimes, he slipped. I never punished him and chastised anyone who teased him.

The kids were soon asleep, and we talked about our dwindling food supply.

"When we're back on the trail," Taylor said, "Carlie, why don't you do some scavenging, within shouting distance, please? It's around nine kilometres to reach the river. We'll have to stop and rest a few times. The boat is heavy, and it looks as if we are in for another sweltering day."

"Mai-Li," I offered, "If you want a change of pace, I'd be happy to watch the kids if you want to do the scavenging."

Mai-Li shook her head. I knew she hated foraging with a passion.

"Then it's settled," Taylor stated. "Thanks for setting up our sleeping bags, ladies."

Mai-Li and I found a secluded corner to change into our PJs. I pulled a pile of clothing from my backpack, sniffed them, and wrinkled my nose. "We need to do some serious laundry, Mai-Li. I don't want to even think what the boy's backpacks smell like."

"I was considering the same thing. Taylor doesn't want us to touch the water on the island, so as soon as we get to Surrey, we should find a secluded place by the river. We'll do some much-needed cleaning which would be a suitable time for everyone to take a bath."

Mai-Li blew out the lantern, and I lay in my sleeping bag, wondering what lay ahead. Today had been traumatic for the kids. So far, we had been lucky, and I prayed it would stay that way.

Chapter Fourteen

The next morning, we were up early, the sun just breaking over the top of the mountain. The kids were hungry, and we gave them our usual fare, half an apple, and two crackers.

Taylor pulled me over to the side and asked if I would lead the group, and he and Willie would bring up the rear. I invited Rusty to monitor the compass again, and make sure we were always heading east. He nodded happily, and Debbie and Eddie touched the compass in awe.

Taylor and Willie flipped the boat, then they threw their packs and the water jugs inside.

Unfortunately, we had a minor distraction; when Debbie realized the lineup had changed, she refused to move. Screaming and crying, she clung to Mai-Li, who sat her down on the ground and explained why our routine changed. Taylor sat impatiently on a rock, and Willie paced angrily.

About ten minutes later, Mai-Li stood and informed us we could now leave. We took our new positions, and I reminded Rusty to always watch the direction on the compass, and if he got tired of doing it, Eddie would like a turn. Eddie's eyes grew wide as saucers, and I told him I would be happy to give him a hand, I thought it would help bolster his confidence. He thought for a few moments, then nodded.

We walked past abandoned office buildings, apartments and fast-food outlets, there were no signs of people anywhere and the whole island seemed deserted.

The going was slow, the boat solidly built, and the guys needed to stop periodically to rest. As Taylor predicted, the hot sun was brutal, adding to our thirst and sapping our energy. I was worried about the kids, they stumbled often.

When the sun was at its highest, we stopped and gave crackers to the kids, with one small sip of water. I suggested this might be a good place to search for food. I would take Eddie with me, and Mai-Li could take the lead with Debbie, while Rusty monitored his compass. We would catch up with them later, hopefully with good news.

"Better plan than stopping," Taylor said. "Just don't wander far. Every ten minutes I'm going to yell, and I want you to answer, and I'll whistle to let you know I'd heard you. We're only assuming the Island's deserted we don't know for sure."

I nodded, took Eddie's hand, and headed on the way to an apartment development on the far side of the field. If any food were left, it would be there.

We walked for ten minutes, then I heard my name being called. I shouted back, waiting for Taylor's whistle. My thoughts at the time were if anyone were still on the Island, it wouldn't take them long to discover us. I suppose Taylor worried more about us getting lost or injured than confronting anyone.

We arrived at the apartment complex; one of them was in better condition than the rest. I decided to have a look inside. I pushed open the front door, climbed six steps, and stopped in front of Apartment A. I reached down and retrieved my knife, turned the knob, and opened the door. I signalled for Eddie to follow, and we walked down the corridor and into the kitchen. The place was trashed, and anything of value was long gone. I opened every cupboard, but they were all empty. We quickly left and hit the second apartment, and by the time we arrived at the top floor, I was frustrated and exhausted. It was then I remembered Taylor's signal. I swung around and stared at Eddie, who solemnly shook his head, knowing I was in big trouble.

"We have to go, Taylor will be fuming," I said.

Eddie, who was always a stickler for obeying rules, surprised me by asking. "Let's check the last apartment, please Carlie, it has an E on it for Eddie."

I hesitated for a second, and realizing I was in trouble regardless, nodded at Eddie to go ahead.

We entered the suite, observing our usual procedure, and just as I decided it was time to leave, I noticed a trapdoor built in the back of one of the cupboards. At first, I couldn't get it to budge, but after a few tries, it swung open, and Eddie and I stared in shock. It was full of food.

We began emptying the hidden cache. "Wait a minute Eddie, let's get the others. We won't be able to carry all of this by ourselves."

We tore down the stairwell. I called for Taylor, and he answered immediately.

"Taylor, we're over here," I yelled.

It took the group five minutes to reach us, and Eddie was so excited he couldn't wait to tell the good news. "There's tons and tons of food, come on, come on." Everyone, except Taylor, raced after Eddie to the stairs. Taylor was angry and I knew he had been worried sick about us when we did not answer his signals.

"I'm sorry," I said. "We started looking through the apartments, and I suddenly realized we missed your call. I almost walked away but Eddie wanted to check out the last one."

Taylor raised his eyebrows, knowing Eddie as well as I did.

"Honest, I gave him the choice. He surprised me too; he said he wanted to look inside because the 'E' on the door was for Eddie."

No response.

"I know I screwed up. But there are cans of soup, peaches, beans, tuna, salmon, and boxes of pasta, rice, cookies, and a lot more. I don't think anyone has lived in the apartment for a long time, so we wouldn't be stealing from them."

"Carlie," he said tersely. "We can't ignore our safety, food is important, but protecting each other comes first."

"I know security is a top priority, but so is food. I can't stand looking at the kids. They've been losing weight and are so listless all the time, for God's sake they had a cracker and a sip of water for their breakfast and lunch. It was a miracle we found the cache of food. Just this one time, can you forgive me?"

Tayler sighed and ran his fingers through his hair. "This time, Carlie, but never again. I don't want the others thinking it's okay to break the rules if something better comes along."

"I understand."

"Come on we better join the others; Willie's probably found a can opener and half the food will be gone before we get there."

I led him to the apartment, and we could hear laughter and excited voices.

"Taylor quick come see," Eddie said when he saw us at the door.

After emptying the cubbyhole, everyone stood quietly, unable to believe their eyes.

"Let's get this stuff downstairs. Willie and I will get the boat and bring it here. We'll fill our backpacks and throw the rest in the boat to carry. It should take about two hours to get to the river, we'll stop for the night, start a fire, and have a feast with Oreos for dessert."

He lifted a bag of Oreos over his head, and the three kids jumped up and down in excitement.

We hauled the food down the stairs, Willie and Taylor carried the loaded boat. It was a long, tiring hike, but soon we were standing by the river's edge.

"Keep back from the water, Rusty," Mai-Li warned. "The river is running high; we don't want you falling in."

Taylor and Willie stared at the churning water. "Now what?" Taylor asked to no one in particular.

I stared at the eddies. I tried not to show my disappointment, wondering if we came all this way for nothing?

"What's wrong?" Willie asked.

Taylor pointed to the river.

"Not so bad, all we have to do is paddle harder."

"You think?" Taylor replied cynically.

"I've rowed in a lot worse than this. I got good at reading currents and flows."

"Willie, you're not shitting me, are you?"

Eddie's eyes grew big and before he could say anything about profanity, I steered him and Rusty in the direction of the backpacks. "Come on kids, we should set up camp. Let's find a good spot, I don't know about you, but I'm starving."

"Find an open, cleared area, away from the trees and bushes. We'll start a campfire, we need to be extra diligent, it wouldn't take much to start a fire," Taylor said.

The guys stayed by the river talking, and Mai-Li and I found an area that would work perfectly. They soon joined us, each of them carrying pots and pans filled with water, which Taylor placed next to the campfire.

It turned out to be a fun night. We were comfortable there were no people around. We heated a few cans of beans, and everyone got half a bowl. I opened a box of Oreos and gave everyone two. After we had eaten, the kids put on a play for us, singing, and dancing wildly. I laughed so hard my sides ached. I looked up and noticed Taylor watching me, a warm smile on his face. I blushed, and awkwardly turned my head, but not before I saw the irritation printed on Willie's face.

We settled the kids down for the night, then we sat in our sleeping bags, staring hypnotically into the crackling flames.

"Willie feels he can get us safely across the river, since I don't have his rowing skills, I'll go across on the first trip with Mai-Li, Debbie, and Eddie and I'll stay with them while Willie comes back for Carlie and Rusty. We'll be in Surrey, and I have no idea who or what we will confront."

"Once we get to the other side," I interrupted. "Mai-Li and I want to find a place by the river, preferably secluded. We need to do laundry and take baths."

Tayler nodded, but again I noted the frustration crossing his face. I decided to not let his moods bother me. There would be delays, it is what it is!

"Are you worried about violence?" Mai-Li asked, sensing the tension between me and Taylor. "Isn't Surrey far enough away from the damage caused by the earthquake?"

Taylor picked up a rock and tossed it in the air, catching it as it came down. "Vancouver Island and most of Vancouver City rated as high hazard zones, which is why there was so much damage caused by the earthquake. Surrey is one of the low-lying areas and is heavily susceptible to liquefaction from the flooding caused by the tsunami, which absorbs building foundations just like quicksand. Unfortunately, most of the structures will be inhabitable."

Mai-Li nodded, listening closely to Taylor.

"As for residents," Taylor continued, "I suspect most of them have moved on. The inflated prices of homes and the constant threat of fires forced hundreds of thousands to head north as there's a better chance to find work and affordable housing. I know a lot of them tried to go east, but we're all aware the inhabitants of the Okanagan boycotted transients and outsiders as the diminishing supply of water turned their fertile fields into parched wastelands and they were struggling to grow enough produce to feed their own. The ban is quite stringent, and should you leave, you're not allowed to return."

"Why did you leave Kelowna in the first place?" I asked.

"For those who didn't own land and were not able to grow food, they really had no choice. The recession made it impossible to find work, there just weren't enough jobs to go around. People were struggling to survive, there was no money to buy canoes, boats, or anything to do with recreation; we were forced to shut down our store. We left the Interior, knowing full well we would not be able to return. We hoped to find something in Vancouver, not realizing it was in worse condition than Kelowna."

"So why are we headed to the Interior, why not settle here?" Willie asked.

"If I thought for a moment," Taylor responded. "There was something available, I would have suggested we settle in Surrey, or Langley, or any of the outlying municipalities. But there's no liveable housing, no work, no food. Having to worry about our well-being all the time from thieves, violent gangs, or whatever else is living there, is no way to live. We must leave Vancouver and find a place where we can set down roots, not just for ourselves, but for the kids."

For a short while, there was silence.

"Maybe one day Vancouver will rebuild, but that's far in the future, Willie, probably long after our time," Taylor replied.

"I think we need to walk east across upper Surrey," Taylor continued, as he tossed the stone into the tall grass. "But we'll keep away from Port Mann Bridge. We'll eventually arrive at the TransCanada, then we'll cross it, and return to the Fraser River. We'll follow the path of the river, and I'm hoping if we boil the water, it will be drinkable. I'm not sure how far upstream the flooding went, but we'll soon find out."

"You plan to pass through, or close, to Mission and Chilliwack?" I asked.

"Then let's stop at one of them," Willie interrupted. "And see if we can get some help?"

"It's been over a year and a half since the earthquake, and I imagine those places saturated with refugees from Vancouver. I don't see them welcoming us with open arms. Of course, as I've said all along, any one of us can leave whenever he or she wants. I'm willing to take my chances in the Interior," Taylor said, looking at Willie. "The choice is yours."

"The boys and I are in for the duration," I pronounced.

Mai-Li nodded. "As are Debbie and me."

Taylor leaned back on his elbows, then looked at Willie. "The two of us can go into Chilliwack and see what the situation is like, but we are not staying long."

Willie shrugged, I never could figure out if he were in agreement or not.

"Taylor, I know it's a lot to ask, but the boys need sleeping bags," I muttered. "When the weather turns, their thin blankets won't be warm enough."

Taylor looked directly into my eyes, then said quietly. "I'll see what I can do, no promises though."

"Thanks," I said, lowering my face.

"I'm hitting the sack, we have a long day ahead of us tomorrow," Taylor said.

He rose and poured the water from the pots over the fire, feeling the embers and ashes to make sure they were cold. I raised my head and looked into his eyes as he passed me on his way to his sleeping bag. My heart was racing, and I took a deep breath.

I got into my sleeping bag, and as was my routine, I mulled over the events of the day. I scolded myself for behaving like a giggly schoolchild every time Taylor looked at me. I needed to stay focused, I would not let it happen again.

The next phase of our trip would be to leave Vancouver and head for the mountains, and hopefully find shelter before the snow started.

For some reason, I felt as if everything was moving in fast motion. I had been born and raised in Vancouver and leaving it would be difficult.

I closed my eyes and dreamt of sleeping bags, assorted colours, and varied sizes. Just as I drifted off, I consciously realized I had exceedingly boring dreams for an eighteen-year-old girl!

Chapter Fifteen

Taylor had a fire going, and his map spread across his lap when I opened my eyes. He heard my movements, and without lifting his head, said quietly. "I'll wake the kids and you can wake Willie."

I snorted, unzipped my sleeping bag, and stretched my arms. It's amazing how well a person can sleep when they have food in their stomach.

"Sure, if you promise to get the boys dressed, and help them fold their blankets and pack their bags."

"You wish."

"You started this. All I need is a long stick to jab Willie, then my job's done. Is it a deal?"

"Sorry I mentioned it," Taylor mumbled. "I'll take Willie."

"Hey, I'm awake you idiots, quit talking about me." Willie crawled out of his sleeping bag, grumbling under his breath.

"Just joking man." Taylor chuckled. Willie scoffed, then wandered into the underbrush.

"I guess I better get the kids up," I sighed heavily secretly hoping Taylor would give me a hand. He ignored me and continued examining his map.

The morning routine took a good hour; two grumpy boys, Debbie full of energy, and throwing her ball at anyone close enough to catch it. Mai-Li finally got the kids rounded up and I promised to make a special breakfast if they packed their bags.

After thinking about it for a few minutes, and about how much I hated cooking, I grabbed two cans of peaches. "Better yet, let's have crackers and peaches. There's enough liquid to help quench our thirst, at least until we get across the river."

"And enough sugar to turn the kids into maniacs," Willie interrupted.

"But think of all the energy they'll have."

No one complained about their breakfast, and soon we were ready to go. We hauled our packs down to the water. The waves were lapping against the side of the boat.

"The first load will be more crowded, so we'll take a third of our bags and supplies, and the rest we'll bring over in the second trip," Willie said. "The current will get stronger before I can turn in the right direction to row over to the far side. Just remember, stay as still as you can, we don't want to capsize the boat."

Taylor and Willie pulled the boat closer to shore, and Mai-Li got in first, and of course, Debbie was right behind her. Eddie was grasping my hand tightly, and I knew he was scared.

"Alright, you're next Eddie," Willie said.

"Don't worry," I said, rubbing his back. "It'll be fun, and Rusty and I will join you in no time at all."

I walked him down to the boat, but he pulled back. "Don't worry, I'll be right behind you," Taylor said, as he approached the boat with his arms full of packs and supplies. "You can sit on the bottom between my feet. We need someone to watch the hole Willie fixed, just in case it leaks."

Eddie looked at me, then back at Taylor. I nodded and he raised his arms for Taylor to lift him into the boat.

When everyone settled, I helped Willie push the boat into the water. He jumped in, sat down on the thwart, grabbed the oars, and began rowing. The water caught the vessel and pulled it downstream; Willie soon had it under control.

Everything he said about his rowing abilities was true. Was I wrong, was there a chance Willie was finally growing up and pulling his weight?

Rusty and I sat on the riverbank, enjoying the cool shade. All of a sudden, we heard a high-pitched shriek. We raced down to the water's edge. At first, I couldn't see what was wrong; suddenly, a dark head appeared, then a second one.

"Oh, dear God," I whispered, realizing it was Mai-Li and Debbie. All I could reason was Debbie must have panicked, as Mai-Li worried might happen, and fallen overboard. Mai-Li would have jumped in to save her; now they were both pulled downstream by the current.

Debbie was struggling so hard, she pulled Mai-Li under. I covered my mouth with my closed fist, praying silently. Rusty started to cry, and I held him close, telling him Taylor and Willie would save them.

Again, their heads broke through the surface of the water. Debbie was screaming and kicking but Mai-Li kept her hold on the young girl. I knew there was nothing she could do to calm her down, she needed to concentrate on keeping their heads above water. I spotted enormous boulders directly in front of them, but it would be futile to try and warn her as she would never hear me over the roar of the rapids. Willie got her attention and pointed at the rocks. Mai-Li kicked her legs as hard as she could and headed for the river's edge toward a huge cedar lying partially in the water. When she was close, she lunged and grabbed a large branch. She said something to Debbie, and the young girl nodded and wrapped her arms around Mai-Li's waist.

Willie was concentrating on the flow of the current, as the whirlpools threatened to pull him downstream. My eyes riveted on Taylor's face, which was tense with fear. Eddie had his arms wrapped around his neck, making it difficult for Taylor to see what was happening.

The boat slowly approached the tree, Taylor leaned over and whispered in Eddie's ear, then jumped overboard. He swam hard, fighting the current. At last, he reached the cedar. He reached out to grab Debbie, who immediately started screaming. He spoke to the young girl, and she reluctantly let go of Mai-Li's neck, allowing Taylor to swim her back to the boat. Willie reached over and grabbed her, then placed her down next to Eddie. Taylor took a deep breath, then swam back to Mai-Li. He placed his arm around her waist, and she slumped in exhaustion against his body. He struggled against the current, and when he arrived at the boat, he lifted Mai-Li into the boat and climbed in behind her.

Taylor sat in Mai-Li's old position and held Debbie tightly, while Mai-Li sat in the front of the boat with Eddie sitting between her legs. If Debbie acted up again, she would have to contend with Taylor, who was strong enough to keep her under control.

When everyone was safely aboard, Willie used his strength to get the boat turned and pointed in the right direction.

Their progress was slow, while Willie laboured safely through the heavy currents. Taylor shifted places with him and took over the rowing. Willie was exhausted, he lowered his head between his legs. Debbie reached up and patted his face.

Soon they arrived at the far side, and Mai-Li and Eddie jumped out. The rest of the group followed, and Willie lifted Debbie out of the boat and placed her on the ground.

Taylor and Mai-Li unloaded the boat. When they finished, Taylor waved his arms to get our attention and raised his index finger. I nodded, and Rusty uttered. "He means it will be one hour before Willie comes back to get us, right?"

I nodded. "Yes, they all need to rest a bit, so we might as well relax."

We lay in the cool grass. The warmth of the sun and the chirping of grasshoppers were soothing, and my thoughts wandered in circles. I realized how lucky we were in getting Mai-Li and Debbie safely out of the river, it could have just as easily ended in disaster. I looked down at Rusty. He was sound asleep, his head resting against my arm.

We had just begun our journey, and I knew there would be other risks we would have to face. The three younger children were more susceptible and needed watching constantly. There were times I wished we'd never agreed to leave Little Mountain, although I never voiced my opinions to Taylor. Yet, deep in my heart, I knew without a doubt leaving was our only alternative.

I raised my head and spotted the boat dipping through the waves. I shook Rusty awake, and he sat up and waved to Willie, who waved back.

When Willie arrived, he jumped ashore; I handed him a box of cheese crackers. He opened it and grabbed a handful. I handed two to Rusty and took two for myself.

"That was too close," I exclaimed. "If it hadn't been for your rowing skills things might have turned out differently. Thanks, Willie."

Willie shrugged, as was his way. "I've been through worse," he said. "The earthquake caused a lot of rock and mudslides which created piles of debris in the water. That's why there are so many narrow channels, which in turn created rapids and eddies. Taylor made a wise decision, not only is this the safest place to cross, but the landing on the other side is also flat."

I nodded in agreement. "I'm going to pack our bags and gear in the boat, while you rest. How are Mai-Li and Debbie doing, by the way?"

"Good thing Taylor was holding Debbie, there was no way Mai-Li had any strength left to restrain her if she freaked out again."

"I thought that would happen, Debbie is having a hard time on this trip."

"You know, I still don't understand why we brought her along. She's going to hold us up all the way, we should try and find someone who will take her for now; you know when we stop at Chilliwack."

So much for thinking Willie would ever change. I couldn't believe what he just said.

I carried a pile of bags and equipment to the boat, choking back my anger.

Rusty knew I was ready to explode, he jumped in and sat down on the seat.

"Willie," I said turning slowly to face him. "We could never do anything like that to Debbie. She wouldn't last a day with someone else. Mai-Li has committed herself to her safety and well-being, and I pity anyone who gets in her way. You should know what I'm talking about."

"Yeah, Mai-Li may be quiet, but she's quite the fighter," Willie muttered.

"She is, so I would suggest you keep your thoughts about Debbie to yourself. You about ready to go?"

"We'll launch the boat together. Rusty, you're hanging on tightly?"

"Yup," Rusty said, as he leaned over the edge and watched the water flow past.

"Good," I said. "Now sit down on the bottom of the boat and grab the edge of the seat."

On a count of three Willie and I pushed the boat into the water, just as I was ready to jump aboard, I slipped in the mud. I felt Willie's hands around my waist, he lifted me and placed me inside the boat. He held me far too long, I quickly pulled away, thanking him for his assistance. He continued to stare at me, which creeped me out.

We sailed downstream, and for a few minutes, the ride was bumpy as Willie steered the boat through the rapids and vortexes. Just when I was thinking we missed the landing spot, I noticed Taylor and Eddie standing on a rocky embankment. Willie rowed in their direction, and Taylor ran into the water and grabbed the bow of the boat. Rusty jumped out and ran to his brother. The boys spotted Mai-Li and Debbie standing near the trees, and they raced over to them. Mai-Li laughed at something Eddie said, then she told them to play in the sand, while she helped to unload the supplies.

When the boat was empty, Willie reached up to help me out. I stiffened, then leaped out before he could touch me. Taylor noticed my reaction but said nothing.

I was grateful Willie was pulling his weight, but I was also nervous about his behaviour around me. He knew Taylor was interested in me although I hadn't encouraged him in any way. Just when I was starting to believe Willie was changing, he had to make a stupid remark about Debbie. The last straw was when he tried to come on to me.

As we no longer needed the boat, everyone had to carry the extra weight of the food, but there were no complaints. Taylor knew Mai-Li and I would be looking for a suitable spot to do laundry and take baths.

After walking for a few hours, he pointed to an alcove in the trees. It was perfect and we soon had the sleeping bags and the boys' blankets laid out for an airing. We threw the dirty clothes into a huge pile.

Taylor started a fire, while Willie filled the metal water containers, then placed them over the flames. Waiting for the water to boil, Mai-Li decided we would have tuna on crackers, and cookies again for dessert.

After we ate, we sent the kids to play, warning them to stay close. I confiscated the huge cooking pot Taylor always carried and filled it with hot water. Mai-Li retrieved the soap, and we soon had an assembly line going. I scrubbed the clothes and handed them to Mai-Li who wrung them out, who in turn handed them to Taylor who spread them on top of bushes and hung them on tree branches to dry. Willie was given the option to help with the laundry or watch the kids, and surprisingly he chose the latter. Of course, I couldn't relax for a minute, I listened anxiously, expecting to hear a splash as one of the kids fell into the river.

It was a long and tiresome chore, but we finally finished. I was sweating and my shirt clung to my chest. What I would give for a tall glass of iced water right now. I lifted my head and stared into Taylor's eyes; he had been watching me. I took a deep breath, smiled, then lowered my head.

Mai-Li had noticed the interchange between us and chuckled.

"Don't say one word," I whispered in her ear.

"About what?"

I raised my eyebrows, collapsing on the grass. Mai-Li lay back and reached over and picked a wilted daisy. Then she grinned, pulled off the petals one by one and mouthed. "He loves me, he loves me not, he loves..."

"Mai-Li," I said. "You are so bad."

"Bad about what?" Taylor asked, joining us on the grass. My face turned a deep shade of red, and I looked away.

"Nothing," I answered.

For the longest time, I sat in awkward silence. Taylor was watching me, and I knew he was enjoying my discomfort far too much. I jumped up, and as I walked away, he said quietly. "Did I win?"

I stopped and turned slowly. "I guess you're going to have to wait to find out."

For the first time since knowing Taylor, he was at a loss for words.

Mai-Li threw the flower away then stood and wiped the dirt from her jeans. She looked down at Taylor. "We all need baths; do you think the water is safe?"

I stopped walking, waiting to hear his reply. Water was always one of our worries, and we needed to always be attentive to its use.

"It should be okay," he answered. "It's flowing swiftly, there was no algae along the banks."

"I'm more worried about the kids," Mai-li persisted. "If they drink any of the water, we can't take a chance they come down with something. I have no idea how much water

Debbie swallowed when we fell into the river. That goes for me as well."

"You're right, that's a good point. Why don't we give the kids sponge baths, and the rest of us can swim if we choose, just be extra careful."

I waited for Mai-Li to catch up with me, then I joined her near the sleeping bags. She pulled clothes from Debbie's backpack, and I dug through the twin's packs and found something for them to wear.

We headed in the direction of the shrieks, hoping there were no broken bones or injuries. We both stopped in our tracks and gasped, Willie was clasping Rusty's arms and was swinging him high above his head. When he saw us, he dropped Rusty, who nose-dived into the ground. I raced over to Rusty, grabbed him tightly, and asked if he was okay.

"Carlie, let me go," he said indignantly. "We were dive-bombing, you wrecked it."

"I... I'm sorry, I thought you had hurt yourself."

I dusted off his clothes (and all I could think about was more dirty laundry), then he pulled away from me and walked over to Willie, who patted his shoulder and gave him a high five. There are times the male species drives me batty; I'll don't think I'll ever understand them!

I turned to Mai-Li and sighed. "I'm getting too old for this. You break the news to them; I don't have the energy."

Mai-Li chuckled. "Okay kids, its bath time, let's go. Oh, I forgot to ask," she said turning to look at me. "How did it go with Taylor?"

"Thanks to you, I'm sleeping with my eyes open tonight," I replied.

Mai-Li laughed, and the kids followed her to the edge of the river. "Alright, out of your clothes, then into the water, but no deeper than your ankles."

Debbie immediately began disrobing, but the twins stared at us in horror.

"What?" I asked.

"You can't see us naked," Rusty said. "You're girls."

Eddie nodded solemnly, obviously in agreement with his brother.

"Taylor," I yelled. "We need you down here."

Taylor strolled over. "Boys," I said, as I faced the twins.

Rusty was peeved at me; so, Eddie spoke in his place. "Carlie has to leave because we need to get baths, and she can't see us with no clothes on."

The look on Taylor's face was priceless. Regaining his composure, he turned and faced me and Mai-Li. "I'm sorry ladies, you'll have to leave; this is the men's bathing area. There's another alcove right around the corner. You can go there."

He winked at me, then turned to face the boys.

"Let's get this show on the road," he said. "You too, Willie."

Then Taylor started removing his clothes, and Mai-Li and I grabbed Debbie and her discarded clothes and made a beeline for the adjacent nook.

My face flushed and Mai-Li chuckled, I ignored her. She was enjoying herself at my expense far too much.

We stripped to our underwear, then we took Debbie's hands and led her down to the water. When she realized what we were up to, she stopped in her tracks and pulled back. Mai-Li talked to her quietly, explaining we were going to have a bath, all three of us together. Understandably, Debbie's narrow escape from drowning was still heavy on her mind, and she wanted nothing to do with the river ever again.

"Look Debbie," I said. "I'm going into the water, and you'll see how safe it is, okay?"

I walked in up to my waist, then dived, remembering to keep my mouth closed. It felt marvellous, I resurfaced then waved to Debbie, and she waved back. Still, a no-go, water was off-limits.

"You go first Carlie," Mai-Li said. "Then I'll take my bath while you watch Debbie."

I nodded in agreement and dove again. I had grown up around the Pacific Ocean and was in my element. I realized I had swum out past the cover of the recess. Willie was standing in the water, watching me. Taylor appeared and spoke to him, and Willie swam back to shore. Taylor waved and I returned the gesture, suddenly realizing he was able to see me from my waist up. I gasped and dived, and when my lungs were ready to burst, I came up for air. I swam back to shore. Mai-Li had managed to get Debbie wet enough to sponge bath her and had wrapped a towel around her. She grinned, took the soap, and dived into the cool water.

The last thing I wanted was to get involved in was a male testosterone war.

Chapter Sixteen

The next few days were uneventful, we followed Taylor's planned route. The water was drinkable after we boiled it, and we always made sure the containers were full.

We made a point of avoiding people, often hiding behind bushes, rocks, or trees. The kids learned quickly and obeyed our instructions and warnings without hesitation. We managed to find deserted houses or buildings to sleep in during the night and didn't start any fires to announce our presence.

Eventually, we arrived at the outskirts of Chilliwack. I knew Taylor wanted to keep moving, but Willie reminded him of his earlier promise. We passed a cement barrier behind one of the older abandoned buildings and Debbie pointed to a big hole in the wall, which after close examination, revealed a space large enough to hold all of us. We shuffled the kids inside, warning them to keep their voices low.

Taylor and Willie took only their water flasks and flashlights, and I noticed Willie had his gun tucked inside his jeans. Taylor reached over and removed it, then placed it in the holster under Willie's arm, gesturing for him to cover the weapon with his jacket.

"I don't know how long we're going to be gone," Taylor said to the rest of us, "But do not come out until we are back. Use your flashlights when it gets dark and be careful the light isn't seen. Carlie, I'm leaving my gun."

I stepped back, shaking my head. "I've never fired a gun; I wouldn't know how to use it."

Taylor shook his head, then looked over to Mai-Li, who nodded and took the weapon. "The first thing I am going to do after we get away from civilization," he said, turning to face me. "Is gives you shooting lessons."

"I don't like guns; my dad wouldn't allow them in our house."

"Well, things are different now, Carlie."

Then he joined Willie outside. The kids poked their heads around the cement entrance and waved until they disappeared behind a hill.

There was enough daylight for us to prepare a cold supper, and everyone had a drink of water. After tucking in the kids, we entertained them by telling fantasy stories, which of course was Mai-Li's forte. I sang quietly to them, and soon they were sleeping.

"How long do you think the guys are going to be?" I whispered. "I don't know what they expect to find, they have no money and nothing to trade."

Mai-Li nodded. "Do not worry about Taylor, he can take care of himself. It's Willie I would worry about."

I chuckled as Mai-Li leaned back against the wall. She said quietly. "You must be careful of Willie, and always make sure Taylor is around."

"I know. At times, I'm comfortable around him, then he does something stupid like touching me, or saying things he shouldn't."

Mai-Li nodded, then slid inside her sleeping bag. "Willie has always had feelings for you, and continuously being overshadowed by Taylor makes him, at times, unpredictable."

"I know, he tried being assertive when I got on the boat, but I pushed him away. Then after we crossed the river, and I was getting out, he tried again. He backed off when he noticed Taylor watching us."

"I sensed something was wrong. Have you talked to Taylor about it?"

"Why would I talk to Taylor?"

Mai-Li smiled but said nothing.

"No really, why?" I persisted.

"It's very obvious he has strong feelings for you, Carlie, but your aversion to intimacy is so evident, you keep pushing him away."

My face burned red with embarrassment. I leaned against the cement wall, hurt by Mai-Li's words.

"You need to decide soon, if you do not, you will lose him. Taylor is a good man and will always protect those he loves."

My silence was my answer. Mai-Li sighed, then closed her eyes.

The sun gradually set, and I welcomed the darkness. I thought of Taylor, and what he meant to our group. We all relied on his wisdom and leadership.

My mind was spinning. No matter how much I tried to ignore Mai-Li's awareness of the situation, I confessed to myself I did care for Taylor but was nervous and awkward when I was alone with him. I rolled over to my bag, crawled in, and was soon fast asleep.

I don't know how long I slept when I woke to shuffling sounds outside. I shook Mai-Li awake, and she was out of her bag and standing at the entrance before I realized she had moved; she held Taylor's gun in her hand, as her cane was far too long to open in our confined space.

"Damn you, Willie, you almost got us killed," we heard Taylor say.

"That asshole was asking for it."

"I told you not to cause any trouble, we're strangers there, and the last thing we needed was to be noticed, showing you were armed just provoked them more."

"That asshole ..."

"Shut up, Willie. No more. We need to wake the girls and the kids and get out of here. I'm damn sure there's a lynch mob looking for us."

"We're right here, Taylor," Mai-Li whispered. "We'll rouse the kids and get them dressed."

It was not easy trying to wake three exhausted children in such cramped quarters. I had no time to ask Taylor what Willie had done, but I was sure we would hear the story when the time was right.

We used Rusty's compass and managed to walk for a few kilometres. We heard no sounds of pursuit. The moon was full and provided sufficient light to travel without using our flashlights and giving our whereabouts away. We arrived at a paved road. There were no vehicles in sight, and we spotted a garage on the far side. We approached cautiously, hesitating before we opened the creaky door. Abandoned and by the look of it, for a long time. Thankfully, there was enough space for everyone. I took Eddie outside for a pee, and when we returned there was a surprise waiting.

Two new sleeping bags were laying on the floor, and Rusty was inside one of them. "Eddie, quick come see what Taylor got us."

Eddie was gone in a flash, and it took us a while to get the boys settled in their new beds. The adventures of the night and the unexpected midnight hike had worn them out, and soon they were both asleep.

In the excitement of our rapid departure, I hadn't noticed Taylor was carrying extra supplies.

"Taylor, thank you," I said, smiling happily. "I know how hard it must have been to find them."

Taylor smiled, closed his eyes, and fell asleep.

The rays from the sun woke us early. It was sweltering in the garage, and I knew we were in for another long, muggy day. I showed the boys how to roll their sleeping bags properly, and how to tie them to the top of their backpacks. They would soon become accustomed to the extra weight. I, however, had to add the weight of their blankets to my pack.

We ate a cold breakfast washed down with water, then set out. All of us walked in moody silence, the kids quiet and exhausted from lack of sleep, Taylor mad at Willie for causing a disturbance in Chilliwack, and Mai-Li and I because everyone else was on edge.

Although I had no idea what Willie said or did in Chilliwack, I was angry at him for putting all our lives in peril. I also noticed he was sporting a black eye, his arms covered with scratches and bruises.

That night, we found a secluded field. The kids dragged their feet and could barely keep their eyes open. Mai-Li and I decided to give them a special treat for supper. We opened a large can of Spaghetti-o, which they wolfed down. The cookies were almost gone, and they soon finished them. We didn't have to tell them to go to bed, they went on their own.

The rest of us sat around the campfire. The tension between Taylor and Willie was still evident. I stared at the ground and watched an ant struggle with a cookie crumb. I cleared my throat. "You guys want to tell us what happened?"

There was silence, and I looked at Willie. He was staring into the flames, his face sullen and angry. Taylor was staring at the map.

"First of all," Taylor said, raising his head." Willie and I disagreed, call it a guy thing, and leave it at that. And secondly, we need to make some decisions on where we should head next."

"A guy thing?" I asked derisively, staring first at Taylor, then Willie. "He almost started a riot in a strange city, and it was a guy thing?"

I turned and stared into the flames, frustrated with both Taylor and Willie. One minute they were at each other's throats, the next they were buddies. "Men, I'll never understand them," I muttered.

Taylor chuckled and turned back to his map, tracing the path of the Fraser that headed inland. Then he traced his finger on a spot away from the river.

"I thought we had decided to follow the river," Mai-Li said to Taylor. "That way we would have a steady supply of water."

"Yes, I know," Taylor replied. "It worked for a while. Going into Chilliwack was a good move, we got to find out what the conditions were like. It was disorderly, there was no police protection, and it came down to survival of the fittest. Most of the businesses closed or shut down, and I imagine the earthquake and tsunami just made things worse. It's a new World, and we must learn to change with it, or we won't survive."

"What do you mean?" I asked, raising my head.

"People will have to learn to be self-sufficient, to return to the land if they want to subsist. Mother Nature has been sending us a message for a long time and we have not been listening."

"What about earthquakes and tsunamis, man can't control them."

"True, but we have studied them. Take your mom and dad, for example, both were seismologists and were quite aware of the astronomical destruction they would inflict on Vancouver, not to mention the devastating damage caused by aftershocks. It comes down to educating the people, preparing them for unexpected disasters."

When Taylor saw the look on my face, he leaned over and touched my arm.

"I'm not putting any blame on them, but these matters need to be addressed."

"I know what you're saying, I've been asking myself the same questions over and over since the earthquake. Why hadn't my parents acted earlier, why did they wait until it was too late?"

"Just because they were seismologists doesn't mean they neglected their responsibilities, caught off guard as were millions of others. You mentioned they got home early that day; I believe to be with you when the earthquake struck. There was nothing they could have done."

My stomach tightened in knots, and I realized everything Taylor said was true. I lowered my head and stared at the embers.

"Okay, let's get back to now. Besides the sleeping bags for the boys, I also found two tents, a larger one for the ladies and the kids, and a smaller one for me and Willie. People are selling whatever they own, and I managed to get everything for a fair price. If it were just the four of us, we would be able to take advantage of following the river, but that's not feasible with the kids. We need to head inland, away from populated areas."

"We saw kids the same age as the twins in Chilliwack," Willie mentioned abruptly.

"Did you not see how they were living? They were on their own, trying to survive on the streets. Most of them won't make it to their teens."

"What are you suggesting?" Mai-Li asked Taylor.

"East, to the Fraser Valley."

Mai-Li started to speak, but Taylor kept talking. "Wait a minute, let me finish. I know there are mountains, but there are streams we can follow, which lead to lakes, providing fresh water from the glacier melts."

Mai-Li lowered her head and closed her eyes. "It's early October, winter is not far off."

"Yes, and you will recall we discussed this exact issue before we left Vancouver. If it snows early, we will have to look for an abandoned cabin or a cave and stay until spring. Then we can turn north proceeding to the Okanagan-Similkameen region."

"I thought we were going to Kelowna?" Willie questioned.

Taylor glanced at Mai-Li. "I doubt if we could even get into Kelowna, you know about the ban on itinerants in the Interior, and our small group doesn't have a lot to offer. We would just be more mouths to feed."

"Then why north?"

"The towns are smaller, and people are more conducive to helping strangers," Mai-Li added, looking away.

"Kelowna is too far away, Willie," Taylor said. "For now, we'll follow the river, keeping away from populated areas. We'll go as far as Hope, then turn east to the Fraser Valley. We'll be in the mountains by then."

Willie looked at each of us in turn. I'm quite sure he was mulling over the reason for our change of destination.

"Fine," he said. "Let's give it a try, but only if you promise if it doesn't work, we change directions and head to Penticton or someplace else."

"Okay, Willie," Taylor said. "I think that's fair. Everyone else agrees?"

Both Mai-Li and I nodded in agreement.

We had no choice, we had to make it work!

Chapter Seventeen

We walked for several days, avoiding houses and their occupants. Without a doubt, if they came across us, we would have nothing left. The stress was hard on all of us, and I could see it taking a toll on the kids.

Some days we ate standing up, not resting until we found safe shelter for the night. No fire was started, and no one complained about eating cold beans or peaches.

The terrain was changing, the hills were steeper, and it wasn't unusual to pass hectares of blackened tree trunks burned by a wildfire. The weather changed, there were more clouds, rain showers, and heavy mists cloaking the hills.

Late one afternoon, Taylor stopped at the edge of a thicket and motioned us to set down our loads. The kids flung themselves on the ground, and I handed each of them a cracker.

"Hope is just around the corner," he said. "I have a little money to get a few things; we need batteries for the flashlights, and I imagine the girls need a few personal items."

We 'girls' nodded, and Taylor grinned. "Anyone else needs anything?"

"A pack of cigarettes would be nice," Willie suggested. "And I suppose a case of beer is off the table?"

"Got that right, Willie, the money is for emergencies and essentials only. All we need is to get caught in a wildfire started by a cigarette butt."

Willie shrugged, then walked over and stood next to Taylor.

"Oops, sorry guy," Taylor said, "This time Carlie is coming with me; you stay here and watch over Mai-Li and the kids."

Willie grunted, then kicked at a clump of dirt. At times, he reminded me of a petulant young boy.

"It's not I don't enjoy your company," Taylor said. "But unless you can find the 'personal items' the ladies require....?"

The unfinished sentence was all Willie needed to step back. "Fine, I'll stay here, just don't take forever, okay?"

"Aw, the first time the old lady and I get a chance for a night out, and the kids complain."

Mai-Li giggled, covering her mouth. I looked over at the kids, Rusty was grinning, not missing a word of our conversation. At times, he seemed older and more mature for his age.

Taylor strapped on his backpack and reached for his bow and arrows. I knew he had his gun, and my knife was always nearby. "See if you can find a place to camp for the night, might as well set up the tents."

"And don't forget to feed the kids," Rusty piped in. I laughed and Taylor gave him a thumbs up.

I grabbed my backpack, and Taylor said. "Leave it here, you won't need it. I have all the supplies we need in mine." He handed me our two empty gunny sacks and I followed him down a steep slope, remembering Rusty's parting words. I grinned; how dull our journey would be without him.

We spotted an animal trail and followed it until we came across a gurgling stream. The setting was beautiful, Pacific willows, alders, and Douglas maples grew along the bank. "This would be a perfect place to camp for the night," I murmured.

Taylor nodded and kept walking. "This is the same stream where Mai-Li and Willie will be setting up the tents, the scenery should be similar."

We walked for over an hour and eventually arrived at the outskirts of Hope. We stood behind a huge Lodgepole pine as we surveyed the town.

"What do you think?" I asked. "Do we go any farther?"

"We don't look too menacing; I think we'll be okay."

"Now I understand why you left Willie behind."

"I'm sure you don't," Taylor whispered in my ear. "But someday you will."

I jerked and stepped back. Taylor winked and walked away.

At one time Hope must have been a thriving town, but now it was struggling like most small settlements. It took us fifteen minutes to reach the downtown core. We strolled down the sidewalk and looked through the window of a store that sold everything from hardware to food. A hanging sign read "Hope Mercantile."

We entered and walked up and down the aisles, Taylor found a box of batteries, so I left him and went in search of the items Mai-Li, and I needed. I found what I was looking for and joined him at the clothes bins.

"Socks got holes in them?" he asked. I grabbed his arm and steered him over to the children's section.

"Ah," he remarked. "Okay, what are the boys short of?"

"Socks and underclothes."

"And Debbie?"

"The same, I guess."

We chose several items for the kids, then added the same for the rest of us. We walked over to the cashier. An older man stood behind the counter; I was aware he was watching us closely; his eyes continually following our movements. I don't imagine a lot of strangers came into town carrying a bow and a leather quiver full of arrows.

"You good with that thing?" he asked, pointing at Taylor's bow.

"Yes, sir," Taylor replied. "My dad and I did a lot of camping and hunting when I was younger, and I soon discovered I preferred archery to gunfire."

The man nodded, then waited while we laid our items on the counter. I noticed Taylor had added a bag of ground coffee and a box of chocolate mix. He signalled me to wait, then returned shortly and placed a brown bag on the counter.

"That it?" the man asked.

Taylor nodded, and the man totalled our purchases. Taylor paid him, and the storekeeper stuffed everything into the two gunny sacks. "Any place around here good to eat?" Taylor asked.

"Well, there's a hot dog stand at the end of the street."

Taylor shook his head. "Then there's Grace's Diner, tasty food, and only half a block north, then right on Fraser Way. You can't miss it."

"Thanks that sounds better."

"Might as well leave your stuff here, you can pick it up on your way out of town. You can leave your archery equipment as well."

"Thanks, I'll leave the purchases, but I'll take my weapons with me. I'd feel naked without them."

The storekeeper raised his thumb in acknowledgement and turned to help another customer. I stopped Taylor outside the store. "How can you afford all that stuff – and I know you did not buy the sleeping bags and two tents while you were in Chilliwack for a song?"

Taylor pulled me away from the door and led me around the side of the building. He reached inside his jacket and handed me a leather wallet. I looked inside and gasped. "This is full of money. OMG, did you rob a bank?"

"My dad and I never believed in banks, and we both worked. When he didn't come home after the earthquake, I cleaned out our safe and left. Now let's go, I'm starving. Of course, this is between you and me, Willie doesn't need to know."

"Wouldn't have it any other way," I whispered.

The aroma emitting from Grace's Diner was heavenly. Taylor opened the door, and we found a booth in the far corner. I noticed several of the men seated at different booths looked closely at Taylor as we walked past.

A matronly woman came to our table. "No menus folks, just what's written on the board over there?"

"Oh, is it your special for the day?" I asked.

"Every day, sweetie." She laughed.

Taylor watched me closely. My stomach tightened, and I took a deep breath.

"Two specials," he said to the waiter. "And coffee for now."

"Taylor," I hissed. "We can't afford a ...."

"This is my treat, and you know I can afford it," he interrupted. "Besides, you deserve a hot meal, it's not easy taking care of twins."

"Twins!" the server exclaimed, shaking her head in amazement. "Honey, you look like a kid in high school, not a mother of twins."

"Well, they are a little older now, they're almost ten." I could dish it out just as well as Taylor.

"Ten!"

I nodded tiredly, and she reached over and patted my shoulder. "Honey, you deserve to be pampered, you enjoy your meal."

Then she turned, walked behind the counter, and pushed open a two-way swinging door. "Two specials Barry, for this nice young man and his tired wife in the corner booth."

My face flushed in embarrassment, Taylor smiled, and I kicked his shin under the table. I swore everyone in the place was listening to everything we said. A few of them, especially the women, were smiling and nodding. There were no secrets in Hope.

Assuming our server was the infamous Grace, I thanked her when she brought over two steaming cups of coffee. I almost kissed her when she reached inside her apron pocket and dropped two sugar cubes on the saucer. I lifted the cup to my nose, inhaled deeply, and took a sip. Nothing tasted as good.

"Stop that," I said to Taylor, as I lowered my cup.

"What?"

"Staring at me, I don't like it."

"Sorry, I can't help myself."

"You are such a pain."

"I know, I know I am."

I decided I was getting nowhere in a hurry, so I concentrated on my coffee. When the meal arrived, I couldn't believe my eyes; three pieces of fried chicken, mashed potatoes and gravy, a hot buttered roll, carrots, and peas, and for dessert a huge piece of apple pie.

I ate one piece of chicken, then wrapped the other two in my napkin.

"You're taking those back to the boys, aren't you?" Taylor asked.

I was too busy shovelling the rest of the food into my mouth to answer him.

"You might as well take these as well," he said as he handed me his napkin, wrapped around two pieces of chicken. Now we had one piece for each kid and one for Mai-Li.

"Oh, oh, what about Willie?"

"Don't worry, I bought him a treat from the store."

We finished eating, and I laid my head back on the booth and sighed.

We paid the friendly waiter, and I noticed Taylor gave her a two-dollar tip. She walked us to the door, then she handed me a small box. I thanked her, and the rest of the people in the diner waved goodbye.

When we were outside on the street, I opened the lid, it was full of sugar cubes. I showed them to Taylor.

"The people here are so friendly."

Taylor nodded. "Let's get the gunny sacks and head back to camp. We have an early rising ahead of us tomorrow morning."

"Thanks for the meal, Taylor, it was marvellous."

He reached down and took my hand. I pulled away, pretending to swat at a mosquito. I know I wasn't fooling him, but he said nothing. When he retrieved his purchases from the store, he handed me one of the gunny sacks, which I tossed over my shoulder. Adjusting the strap of the quiver, he reached down and picked up the second sack.

I knew Taylor was waiting for me to make the first move, but I was not sure if it would ever happen. Every time I thought about the two of us being together, I froze. I was in no condition to become serious with anyone, not when I couldn't control my own emotions.

The hike was uneventful. We arrived at the camp, and I was happy to see they set up camp close to the brook. The kids played by the water; their laughter sounded delightful.

I unpacked and distributed our purchases. Mai-Li noticed the bag of ground coffee and looked at Taylor.

"This water is a lot better to drink, so I figured a hot cup of coffee in the morning would be a nice treat instead of boiled water all the time."

Then I showed Mai-Li the chicken, and when Willie saw there wasn't one for him, he scowled. Taylor reached into his pocket. "Here guy, this is for you. Wasn't too sure what you preferred so I bought you a selection?"

Willie opened the bag and sounded like a kid opening presents at Christmas. "Wow, chocolate bars."

"You might not want the kids to know what you got, could start a riot."

"Oh," I said to Mai-Li and handed her the box of sugar cubes along with the chicken. "I'm thinking we can give these to the kids, as a treat. They don't get a lot of sugar in their diet, so it won't hurt them."

Then I helped Mai-Li make supper and called the kids over. They were so excited when they received the fried chicken. I warned them about the bones, and it didn't take long for everything to disappear.

After they ate, we let the kids go back to the stream to play. Mai-Li and I wanted to sort through the new clothes, and she was pleased when she saw the socks and underwear for Debbie.

The tents were set up with the sleeping bags inside. Darkness came earlier when the sun settled behind the mountains. We called the kids over, got them into their pyjamas, read them a bedtime story, and settled them for the night.

The trees protected us from the elements, the rain had lessened, and a fine mist began to fall. Mai-Li and I just finished washing the dishes and cleaning up when Taylor returned and sat down by the fire.

"Before we call it a night, I think we need to discuss the next step of our journey."

"Oh, oh," Willie said. "Where are you taking us now Taylor?"

Taylor opened the map. "I managed to talk to the owner of the mercantile store while Carlie was doing her shopping. I told him where we headed and I asked him about the conditions of the highways. He suggested we take the Coquihalla. The only other operable solution was the Crowsnest Highway, although he said there were numerous rockslides and mudslides along the route, especially with the intermittent tremors occurring. Few people travelled anymore, just local traffic and delivery trucks. I told him we were walking; he was shocked, more than surprised. He said far too many people were getting robbed, even killed, so I immediately erased both highways from our list."

"I thought you had originally decided to stay away from the roads," Mai-Li said. "Why the sudden change of interest?"

"True, but we still have a long way to go, and I wanted to see if the inland highways might be safer to use. I guessed wrong, it's the same everywhere we go."

The four of us sat quietly, absorbing Taylor's words.

"Have a look at the map," he continued. "And see what I've marked off. With the Fraser River flooding, most of the land north of Hope turned into swampland and is impossible to get through. It means we head due east, cross over the highway, and in the direction of the mountains, putting on as many kilometres as we can before it starts snowing. Any questions so far?"

"How far have we come so far?" Mai-Li asked. "And how far do we have to go?"

I was so glad she asked, as I was thinking the same thing myself.

"Well, you know it's around three hundred kilometres directly to Princeton from Vancouver by the highway. However, we have and will have to take a lot of detours."

"Which are?" I asked.

"For one, we took an indirect route to get out of Vancouver by crossing the Fraser River. That was the only way we could travel if we wanted to stay safe. It did, unfortunately, add on more walking. I know it's hard on the kids, but so far, all three of them have been doing well."

"Okay, so the highways are off the table. What's our alternative?"

"If we go north, we'll end up in the Wastelands, but I'm hoping to avoid that area."

"What are the Wastelands like?" Mai-Li asked.

"Entire forests have burned down, and with the rising temperatures, barren regions and deserts are appearing in places that used to be green and fertile. While living on Little Mountain, I heard talk about the Wastelands, and how hard it is to survive, although some of the gang members have relocated there.

I raised my head and looked at Taylor. He kept his eyes on the map, not returning my stare. His words sounded forced, there was something he wasn't telling us.

Taylor slowly folded his map. He stretched and went to the little tent. I walked over to the stream and filled the kettle and a pot with water and doused the flames.

Later, when all was quiet, I thought of what lay ahead with a sense of foreboding. If I started to doubt Taylor, we would never make it to our destination. We relied on him, and we had a long way to go, yet I feared the worst part of our journey was still ahead.

Chapter Eighteen

We walked east and eventually arrived at the interchange of the Coquihalla Highway. We crossed the road with no problem, as traffic was light. As the storekeeper told Taylor, with the cost of fuel and oil, and the threat of constant violence, people stayed close to home.

Taylor was right in his suspicions regarding the landscape. The earthquake caused a massive rockslide, and half the mountain collapsed. We crawled over sharp boulders and deep gullies. Each day was harder than the one before. There were times we pushed ourselves to the limit, hiking over twelve hours, trying to put as many kilometres behind us as possible.

It was especially hard on the kids. I worried about the twins and their lack of energy. Mai-Li spent half her time coercing Debbie to keep walking as she exhibited a tendency when she was tired to plunk on the ground.

Willie voiced his displeasure as often as possible; we ignored his constant bellyaching. At times, I caught Taylor clenching his fists. I understood his frustration as Willie had the same effect on me, but the last thing we needed was for everyone to start bickering among themselves.

On the fourth or fifth day, I can't remember as I lost count, we stopped early and set up camp. Taylor started a fire, and as we had a few apples left, he showed the kids how to bake them on the end of a stick. It was a great diversion until Debbie burned her tongue and started screaming. Mai-Li spent a long time calming her down, and it was then I noticed how tired she looked. There were times I tried to help her with Debbie, but it only made matters worse. The burden of caring for a child with disabilities was enormous and I respected Mai-Li so much for her dedication.

We fed the kids, then got them into their pyjamas. Eddie fell asleep standing up; I tucked him into his sleeping bag and kissed the top of his head.

Mai-Li and I joined Willie and Taylor at the fire pit. I stared into the flames, my mind far away. Suddenly Willie poked a stick into the coals, causing sparks to flare upward.

"Hey man," Taylor said sharply. "You want to tell the whole world we're here?"

"We haven't seen a living soul in days, and who'd be interested in a pack of misfits like us?" Willie shot back.

"Someone who has nothing. We have supplies, clothing, food, and weapons, and there are a lot of people out there who would kill for that stuff."

"Sorry, I forgot."

"We can't forget, we have to make sure we are always on alert."

Taylor ran his fingers through his hair. Then he angrily kicked at a rock encircling the fire pit. "This isn't working, we're way behind schedule."

"I told you when we first started our journey the kids would have difficulty keeping up to your pace; climbing over huge rocks and deep gullies is one of those times. I'm afraid one of them is going to fall and hurt themselves," I remarked.

"I understand, but if we don't move faster and make a better time we're going to be stranded in the middle of nowhere when it starts snowing. We absolutely must get to the mountains and find some kind of shelter."

"Like in a cave or a hole in the ground," Willie snorted.

A dark expression masked Taylor's face. He turned and glared at Willie. "I believe we gave you the choice of coming or staying behind, so keep your mouth shut and your thoughts to yourself."

Willie jumped up angrily, spilling his coffee down his shirt and jeans. "Christ, look what you made me do."

Taylor rose menacingly and took a step toward Willie. I grabbed his arm and pulled him back. "Taylor, settle down, we can't start bickering among ourselves."

At this point, Mai-Li intervened. "Stop it. You cackle like crows, throw insults at each other, and get nothing solved. We must all pitch in and help, which means you as well Willie."

"I wish to hell I'd never agreed to come on this stupid trip, we were a lot better off at Little Mountain."

Anger filled me so suddenly that I had to take a deep breath. "We will never turn back, we have no choice, we continue, and we'll make it, all of us."

I turned and looked at Taylor. "We need to change our plans; I think we should head north to the Wastelands. We'll save ourselves some time."

Taylor rubbed his face with his hands, and I could sense his hesitancy. "Conditions can be brutal, worse than what we're facing now."

"How long to the mountains from here?"

"At this pace, about two weeks."

"And from the Wastelands?"

"Well, counting the two days to get there, it will be another week before we reach the Foothills."

"Then we save ourselves five days of walking, isn't it worth the risk?"

"Carlie, I've heard nothing good about the Wastelands. One of the guys belonging to a gang at Little Mountain mentioned it to me, he spent some time there and was never so glad to return. There's no water, no cover from the relentless rays of the sun, and there are gangs out there that would take everything we own, including two young women."

"Then we'll travel at night and rest during the day. If we run into any of them, we fight. We are not completely defenceless."

Taylor shook his head. "We can't travel at night. There are too many animals prowling around, safer to walk during the day. Willie and Mai-Li, what are your thoughts."

Willie stood close to the flames, trying to dry his clothes. "Let's try it. I'm all for saving time."

"Mai-Li?" Taylor asked.

"I know we can't go back." She looked down at her lap, then slowly raised her head. "The Wastelands, we must make it to the mountains before it starts snowing. I can feel the change in the weather, the days are getting colder and it's getting dark earlier."

"Well, I'm outnumbered," Taylor muttered. "The Wastelands it is."

We started early the next morning, eating a cold breakfast. Mai-Li and I started rationing the food again, so all everyone got was an apple and a granola bar.

We hadn't gone far before Rusty stopped abruptly. "Hey, you guys, we're going the wrong way."

"How do you know Rusty?" Mai-Li asked.

"I just know."

'Well, you're right," I said proudly. "We've changed directions, we're headed north. Good job, Rusty, you figured it out all by yourself."

Eddie, who was following close behind me, smacked the top of his forehead. "People, puleeese, he used his compass."

Everyone burst out laughing, and I must admit it felt good.

"What did we do?" Rusty asked.

I ruffled his hair. "Nothing, boys, just be yourselves, and don't ever change."

The second day was a repeat of the first, and later around the campfire, Taylor announced we would arrive at the Wastelands the following morning. He reminded us of although travel was faster in the Wastelands, the kids must keep as quiet as possible as sound travels a long way in the desert. I was both excited and apprehensive about what lay ahead.

Everyone woke early, yet it still took another two hours before we left the rocky terrain behind. We stopped and stared in silence. It had to be the most inhospitable place I'd ever seen in my life, barren hilly slopes, kilometres of crabgrass, thistles, and ragweed.

"With deforestation, rising temperatures, and wildfires," Taylor said, "Thousands of hectares of forested land have disappeared; erosion and drought finished the job."

His next words made me shiver. "Man's legacy to the World, and now the planet is fighting back."

As usual, Eddie was directly behind me, clutching my jacket. Over time, I became so used to him shadowing me, that I sometimes forgot he was there.

"Are you angry, Taylor?" Eddie asked as he peeked around my arm.

"Heck no," Taylor said, as he looked down at Eddie. "We finally made it to the Wastelands. No more crawling over sharp rocks, or climbing down gullies, much better, right?"

Eddie nodded shyly.

"Okay, everyone. I want to try and get in a few kilometres before we stop for lunch. We'll have to look hard to find a place to pitch the tents tonight. What's the first rule, Rusty?"

"Always look for a place having lots of protection."

"Right on, who's next?"

Eddie raised his hand, then he quickly answered. "Everyone helps to set up camp, nobody can be a lazy bum."

"You got that right buddy, good job boys."

"Me, me," a loud voice interrupted.

"Wait a minute, we almost forgot Debbie. Okay, what's the third rule?"

Debbie grinned happily, then she grabbed Mai-Li's arm and clutched it tightly.

"Debbie," Mai-Li asked, looking at the young girl.

"No throwing my ball inside the tent."

"Super Debbie, that's a good rule to remember."

"Hey, that's not one of the rules," Rusty sputtered. "She just made it up."

"It's Debbie's rule, to her it's important. Remember, everyone treated the same?"

"Sorry."

I reached over and squeezed Rusty's shoulder, then pointed north.

We walked for almost three hours. There was an immediate temperature difference. The sun shone relentlessly in a cloudless sky. We stopped for a break, and Mai-Li distributed the rationed water and a light snack of apples and jerky. "That's the last of the jerky," she announced.

When our break was over, the boys removed their coats and put them in their backpacks, but not before I made them dig for their caps. "Wear them all the time, you can take them off when you go to bed. And guard your coats with your lives. You'll need them when it starts getting colder."

I watched as the twins ran to catch up with the others, Squishy's head bouncing up and down with every step Eddie took.

"What I would give for some sunscreen right now," I muttered.

We plodded until sunset, then Willie stopped and pointed in the distance. "Looks like an outcropping, we might find some shelter there."

"Good job Willie," Rusty said. Willie, as usual, grunted, turned, and walked away.

It took about half an hour to reach the projection, and after Willie and Taylor checked the area, we found a recess in the ledge that would work perfectly. Soon we had the tents pitched, and Mai-Li had beans heating on the coals. She also made a pot of coffee and hot chocolate for the kids.

The kids joked and laughed while they ate, and we let them sit around the fire. I dug out one of the comics I had in my pack and read to them.

I'm quite sure Willie was listening, although he had read it a hundred times.

We trudged until sunset the next day, and the farther north we went the hotter it became. I dared not complain about the conditions as I was the one who wanted to change course. I often sensed Taylor watching me, and the frown on his face was enough to deter any conversation.

That evening, Taylor stopped and announced, "I'm going to look at the hills over there, I hope to find a place for the night. Remember, no tents and no fires from now on."

"I get not having a fire, but what's wrong with pitching the tents?" I asked, noticing the unhappy look on the kids' faces.

"We might have to leave in a hurry, and we can't afford to lose them."

I noticed Taylor had his bow and arrows with him, and I spotted his gun tucked under his shirt.

"You want me to come too?" Willie asked.

"I plan on running, if you can keep up, be my guest."

Mai-Li and I turned and looked at Willie. "On second thought," he said. "I'll stay here and guard the women and kids."

We looked at each other and rolled our eyes.

Taylor noticed our reaction, grinned, and left.

We sat down on the ground. Mai-Li was having trouble keeping Debbie awake. The twins were leaning against me, their eyelids drooping.

"It's okay Mai-Li," I said. "Taylor will be gone a while, let the kids sleep. There's enough of us to take turns carrying Debbie if we must."

"Don't expect any help from me," Willie blurted, "I got enough to carry."

Mai-Li said nothing. Willie was who he was, and we were slowly beginning to accept his place in our small troupe. He and Taylor carried their supplies, the tents, the larger water containers, as well as the bulk of the food.

Taylor returned about an hour later, flushed from the heat, sweat pouring down his face, and breathing heavily. He must have run the entire distance.

"I found a warren in one of the embankments used by an animal at one time, but it'll work."

I woke the boys and Mai-Li managed to get Debbie to open her eyes. The kids tripped over their feet as we headed for the den, I was so proud of all three of them. The heat sapped their energy, and I watched Debbie as she pluckily kept up with the boys. We followed Taylor, and he finally motioned us to stop.

He pointed to a hole dug into the side of the bank. Rusty looked inside and shook his head. "Oh, oh, you forgot something, Taylor."

"What's that?"

"There's not enough room for everybody."

"That's because you kids get to sleep inside. The rest of us will sleep outside."

"Cool," Rusty and Eddie said at the same time.

"Wow," Eddie said to Debbie. "We get to sleep inside an animal house."

Debbie nodded happily, if Eddie was happy, so was she.

"Let's have a bite to eat first. Afterward, Carlie, you, and Mai-Li can set up your sleeping bags."

Mai-Li opened two cans of beans and counted six apples from our rapidly dwindling supply. "Dinner is served."

We ate directly from the cans as our water was for drinking only, not for washing dishes. Although the apples were slowly drying up, they still had a sharp tangy taste and not wasted.

I took a quick peek inside the warren. It was small and smelled musty. The kids' sleeping bags would take most of the room, but they would be warm and comfortable.

Taylor waved his hand to get everyone's attention. "Before we call it a night, I want to go over a few ground rules. No fires, at any time, we can't take a chance of someone seeing the smoke, and of course, the ground is so dry, one spark is all it would take to start a fire. No tents until we reach the treeline. If we're discovered, we'll have to make a run for it, and we can't leave them behind. I can't stress enough their importance. It might be our only shelter for a while, so we must guard them fiercely. We sleep with our bags packed all the time. Unfortunately, we are going to have to go on water rations."

The group stood solemnly; their eyes riveted on Taylor's face. "Now, the next thing I want to talk about is really important," he said looking sternly at Rusty, Eddie, and Debbie.

I did not want to hear what he had to say.

"If for any reason me, Willie, Carlie, and Mai-Li leave you alone for a while do *not* come out of the animal house. We will return as soon as we can, we might be gone for hours. Understand."

I started to say something, but Taylor shook his head. "Carlie, I knew you would be the one who would disapprove, but if you take the time to think it over, you'll know it's the only solution."

"I'll take care of Eddie and Debbie," Rusty said.

"I knew I could count on you, guy," Taylor replied, as he reached over and squeezed his shoulder.

"It's 'cause the bad guys might come, right?" Eddie said quietly.

"That's right, and you must not be found as the gangs are not nice, so, you need to be extra quiet when we're gone."

The brothers nodded solemnly, and Debbie copied them.

"Carlie, can you read us a story?" Debbie asked.

Realizing I was in no shape to do anything, Mai-Li pointed to the burrow. "Let's make your beds first."

We lugged the sleeping bags inside and soon had them set up.

"Let them sleep in their clothes," Taylor said. "It's probably a good habit for all of us to get into as long as we are in the Wastelands."

In no time the three kids were inside (but not before each of them needed to climb out and have a pee...Debbie twice). Exhausted, and lacking the energy to dig for a book from my pack, and as lights were taboo, I made something up. There must have been magic in my words, or the story was so boring, as they were asleep in a few minutes. To this day, I have no idea what it was about.

I dug my sleeping bag from my pack and set it close to the entrance of the warren. I started to untie my bootlaces when Taylor interrupted. "Sorry Carlie, starting tonight, we start guard duty, two at a time. Willie and Mai-Li, Carlie, and me. Who wants the first shift?"

I sighed, bent over, and retied my laces. "We'll go first," Mai-Li said. I noticed the annoyed look on Willie's face. "Taylor ran for well over an hour in the heat of the day to find us this spot, he needs to rest."

I understood why Taylor paired Mai-Li with Willie as she had more common sense in her little pinky than Willie did in his whole body. Of course, fearing Mai-Li's martial arts abilities was a huge deterrent.

For some reason, I had never told anyone that Mai-Li had been teaching me Kung-Fu and I had picked up some wicked moves.

Hopefully, I would not have to rely on them in the future.

Chapter Nineteen

Taylor was soon asleep, and I tossed and turned, wondering if I had made a mistake in suggesting we come to the Wastelands. But was it any worse than hauling the kids over huge rocks, and dark crevices?

I finally dozed off only to awaken a few hours later by Mai-Li returning from her watch. I yawned, peeked into the warren to make sure the kids were asleep, then joined Taylor. He and I decided to head in different directions, reminding each other to stay in hearing distance.

I walked for a while, then remembered a hill we had passed earlier. When I got there, I lay back in the dried grass, staring at the star-lit sky. The occasional scuffling of a small animal disturbed the solitude. I closed my eyes, savouring the quietness.

My thoughts returned to a time when I had no worries and fears. I felt a sharp pain in my chest and took a long slow breath. The anguish of losing my parents and Poppy was lessening, and I was slowly coming to terms with my loss.

I heard footsteps behind me, and I reached down and pulled my knife from my boot.

"You can put it away, Carlie," a deep voice said. "It's just me."

"Good God Taylor! You scared the hell out of me," I said sharply as I sat up.

"Didn't mean to."

"Were you following me?"

"No, just out for a quiet walk in the moonlight."

"You're so full of it."

Taylor grinned, and I returned to my former position. Sometimes he was so annoying, he drove me crazy. "I'm quite capable of being by myself, I don't need a bodyguard."

I raised my head and stared at his silhouette, sensing him more than seeing him. He lowered himself to the ground, sitting so close I felt the warmth of his body. Then he leaned over and whispered in my ear.

"Good to know."

I found it hard to breathe. I quickly sat up and cleared my throat. "We better get back, it's past our return time, and if Mai-Li wakes and finds we haven't returned, she might worry."

"She'll be okay; of course, Willie is a different matter, especially if he thinks we're together."

I looked at him in surprise, then I laughed quietly.

"Never heard you laugh before," he murmured. "I like it. You need to do it more often."

"Stop it," I said. "Or I'm going to leave."

"Okay, what do you want to talk about, world economics or maybe the weather?"

"Tell me about yourself, where you lived, and grew up."

"Always nice when a pretty lady wants to hear about my personal life."

"Jeez Taylor, just answer me, and stop being a jerk."

"I was born in Kelowna, which you already know," he said in a monotone. "Dad owned a camping and hunting store. My Mom died when I was ten."

As was my fault, I found it hard to offer sympathy when hearing of someone else's loss. So of course, I changed the topic, bringing up something completely irrelevant. "Did you do a lot of camping with your dad?"

"Camping, hunting, fishing, skiing, hiking, mountain climbing, you name it, I've done it."

"I know you and your dad moved to Vancouver to find work; you told us that earlier."

"True, and that, my dear, is the biggest mistake my dad ever made in his life. He figured he would have a better chance finding work in Vancouver."

"What happened?" I asked, knowing full well what his answer would be.

"No work, inflation, a mad exodus of people leaving the city, moving to better climes, looking for the proverbial pot of gold at the end of the rainbow. We managed to rent a run-down condominium in Burnaby, and took whatever job came along."

"I'm sorry Taylor."

"Well, it's a story often told. Dad found a job doing landscaping at Stanley Park. He never came home after the earthquake. I sat on the doorstep, waiting for him to return, but I knew inside I would never see him again, so after a month, I packed my gear and left."

I stared at the ground, saying nothing. He must think I'm the most cold-hearted person he's ever met when I offered no consolation.

"How did you end up at Little Mountain?" I asked.

"As you know, Burnaby sustained a lot of damage because of the earthquake. People started leaving, food was scarce, and it became increasingly dangerous to walk the streets, especially if you were alone. I listened to the gossip about the survivors, and Little Mountain came up in their conversations, stories of undemolished houses to crash in, lots of food. So, I packed my belongings, left Burnaby, and headed north. At first, I lived comfortably on my own. Then the food was all gone, water was at a premium, and it turned more depressing each day."

I nodded, my memories stirring. I had been there, and I knew what he went through.

"And there were the constant altercations with gangs," he continued. "I finally got so tired of looking behind my back everywhere I went, I joined one and things improved a little."

I nodded but said nothing.

Taylor turned and looked at me. "My life briefly. Now, it's your turn."

I hesitated, not sure if I wanted to dig up unwanted memories. I never talked about it with anyone, and I struggled with the words.

"I was born in Vancouver and both my parents were seismologists and worked as researchers at the University."

"Yes, I know, did you live your whole life in Vancouver?"

"On Marine Drive, a few blocks from the Pacific."

"I knew where Marine Drive was. Pretty fancy digs, you must have loved living so close to the ocean."

"I used to, before the earthquake and tsunami."

Taylor shrugged, picked up a rock, and tossed it aside. He wiped his hands across his jeans then stared at me and spoke. "We all grew up knowing Vancouver is located on the fault line of two plates, the Cascadia Subduction Fault and the San Andreas Plate, and the possibility of both Plates erupting at the same was always a conceivable event, which could increase the magnitude of an earthquake to as high as 9.2 on the Richter scale. That, unfortunately, is exactly what happened and why there was so much damage."

"The aftershocks and tsunamis were more violent than the earthquake," I mumbled, recalling the devastation at Little Mountain.

"Can't blame Mother Nature, kiddo."

"I don't," I whispered. "At first, I blamed my parents."

Taylor gave me a penetrating look but said nothing.

"Both Mom and Dad were home when the earthquake hit," I continued.

"And you blamed them, why would you do that?"

"They must have known it was coming but never said a word," I answered angrily.

"We discussed this before. Realizing they had only one choice, they chose to be home with their daughter. Where are they now?"

I stared into the darkness, not wanting to continue, not sure if I could continue. The moon appeared from behind low-lying clouds, and I was able to see Taylor's face. "They were in our house when the gas line exploded."

"Oh Carlie, I'm so sorry."

"I had taken Poppy, our cocker spaniel, outside for a walk, and she ran into the woods; she sensed the earthquake and panicked. I went after her, but I lost her. I found shelter when the tremors started. Then I heard a loud explosion, then a shattering crash, and I rushed back to the house. It was a pile of rubble, and I couldn't find my parents or Poppy anywhere. That's when the second blast happened."

Taylor reached over and pulled me into his arms. He smelled like smoke and sweat, which I found soothing. I looked into his eyes. He touched my cheek, then kissed me gently and pulled me closer. My heart raced, and excitement rushed through my body. I moaned softly, and I wrapped my arms around his neck. I passionately returned his kiss. He placed his hand inside my shirt, I froze and pulled back sharply.

"What's wrong?"

"Nothing."

"I know you're attracted to me, and you know how I feel about you."

"We have no time for this, Taylor. We must concentrate on getting everyone safely to the Interior."

Taylor frowned and then sighed heavily. He removed my arms gently, then pushed me away. For the longest time, he stared into the darkness. "It's just an excuse. You're scared about getting too close to anyone."

"What's that supposed to mean?" I asked harshly.

"I see how you push the kids away when they try to touch or play with you. Mai-Li notices it too."

I inhaled sharply.

"And no, nothing was said to me," Taylor continued. "I have eyes too. I know you've suffered Carlie, but all of us have. You can't let it consume you, otherwise, you will never find contentment or happiness."

"I don't want to talk about it, okay?"

"Your wish is my command."

If I hadn't been so shaky, I would have punched him. Angrily, I rose and headed back to camp. It wasn't until I reached the warren, I realized Taylor was not behind me.

It took me a long time to fall asleep, hurt by Taylor's words, or his insight. I woke the next morning exhausted and grumpy. Taylor joked with the kids, helped Mai-Li with Debbie's pack, and not once looked in my direction.

If this was how I wanted it to be, why did I feel so angry, so rejected? At times, my feelings festered inside, and often I dreamt I was in a dark abyss, frantically trying to claw my way out.

Carlie, you can't have it both ways. You've made your choice, now live with it!

Chapter Twenty

We broke camp early, hoping to get in a few kilometres before the sun got too hot. The starkness of the land was depressing. Gale-force winds blew and I yelled at the kids to pull up their masks. Dirt and debris lifted upwards, making it difficult to breathe.

Eddie pulled my shirt, and I turned and looked at him. "Carlie there's a top spinning over there in the desert."

"Taylor," I yelled. "There's a whirlwind headed in this direction."

Taylor grabbed his binoculars, he said nothing for the longest time, then he raised his finger and pointed in the distance. "See that ridge over there, it will give us a little protection, stay together, don't get separated."

That worked for about one minute. I turned to check on the boys, and they had disappeared. Frantically, I called their names, I heard a muffled sound, but I couldn't detect what direction it came from.

"Both of you stop," I yelled. "Keep talking and I'll head toward your voices."

But there was no answer.

"Rusty, Eddie," I shouted. "Answer me."

"I have them, Carlie," Willie's voice broke through my rising panic. "Keep talking, and we'll find you."

I shouted as loud as I could. My voice was raspy, and I coughed when I breathed dirt and sand into my nose.

The boys hurtled themselves at me, and it took all my strength to stand upright. Willie was right behind them, and the four of us formed a tight circle, saying nothing. The twins were crying, their faces streaked with dirt.

I mouthed a grateful thank you to Willie.

"Grab onto my coat," I ordered. "Let's get out of here."

"But Taylor said to stay in line," Eddie hiccupped between sobs.

"Sometimes plans have to be changed."

Without warning, the wind shifted, and we spotted the rest of the group not far ahead. They must have heard our calls and had wisely stopped.

It felt as if we were in a vacuum, the air was intensely hot, and everyone was sweating heavily. Mai-Li pointed in the distance; lightning bolts struck the dry ground, and I noticed dark clouds and rising smoke.

Taylor raised his binoculars, then recoiled. The anxious look on his face sent a shiver of fear down my spine. Mai-Li looked at him oddly but said nothing.

Taylor gestured for Willie and me to join him. Mai-Li bunched the kids together, ordering them to hold hands and stay close.

"I don't want to scare the kids any more than they are," he whispered. "Keep your voices low?"

"The kids, what about me?" I laughed nervously.

"Sorry, just thinking aloud. We need to find shelter, in a hurry."

"It's a grass fire, isn't it?" Willie asked.

"Partially. The smoke and ashes we walked through for days are from different fires burning randomly, started from the gasses discharged from the swamps bordering the Wastelands."

"I'm not liking where you're going with this Taylor," I muttered.

"The small fires eventually form into one large fire, which draws in the surrounding air, creating an inflammable air pocket of oxygen. The pocket increases combustion and the production of heat. The fire stays stationary, and it can't spread outward."

"But you're not finished yet, right?" I asked as the terror inside of me increased with each word he spoke.

Taylor looked over to Mai-Li and the kids, who were taking turns gazing through the binoculars.

"Stationary fire creating air pockets," I replied, urging him to continue.

"Right. Gusty winds develop around and in front of the fire and can change direction erratically."

"But lightning is usually followed by rain," Willie said.

"Not in this case. The lightning generated by the fire occurs ahead of it, which also applies to the winds."

"Then why are we still walking in this direction, shouldn't we be walking *away* from the fire?" I asked.

"We'd never outrun it, there's no place to take shelter behind us, and we have no idea which way the wind is blowing. The fire could change directions anytime."

"Man, what a load of shit," Willie swore.

Taylor glared at him, then said in a muffled, urgent voice. "I know you're afraid, both of you, and so am I. But right now, we need to pull together if we are going to make it through what's ahead."

I looked at Willie, then he nodded.

"Good. Now there's a deep ravine close to here, and if I remember correctly, a creek runs through it. The banks are steep, and it's our only hope to find shelter."

"And if we don't?" I asked.

"We will," he retorted, then he left and returned to his backpack. Mai-Li handed him the binoculars, and we lined up, ready to go. She turned and stared at me, and I realized she wanted to know what Taylor had just told me and Willie. I shook my head and pointed to the kids. She nodded and took

Debbie's hand. I decided it wouldn't hurt to break the line for once. I held out my hands and Rusty and Eddie each grabbed one. I should have known they sensed something was up, but from the look on my face, they were smart enough not to ask.

The smoke got heavier, I took shallow breaths and told the boys to do the same. I heard Debbie coughing and saw Mai-Li lean over to adjust her face mask.

I could feel the panic rising in my chest, and forced it down, jabbering nonsense to the boys. They watched me like hawks, all the while keeping up with Taylor's pace.

We reached the top of a hill and stopped in stunned silence. In the distance, the fire was moving ravenously in our direction, devouring everything in its path. I looked at Taylor, he studied the landscape in every direction, then took out his map.

"Pay close attention. We're going to run, fast. There's a deep gully up ahead, and we must get there before the fire does."

The twins gaped in horror at the engulfing flames and billowing black smoke. I knelt and held them tightly. "Listen to me, you must do everything Taylor asks. We need to run and run hard."

The boys nodded, Taylor checked to ensure his bow was secure, then started down the hill, directly into the approaching inferno.

"Man, he's crazy?" Willie mumbled numbly.

"Be quiet Willie," I said harshly. "Taylor is our only hope, so just follow his lead, okay? Unless you'd rather stay here?"

It must have been the unexpected vehemence in my voice, but Willie turned to follow Taylor.

"Nope," I said grabbing his shirt sleeve. "Behind us, you need to help anyone who falls or lags."

I was waiting for one of his colourful expletives but instead, he said, "For you babe, anything."

I ignored him. Eddie gave Willie an angry look, then grabbed my hand. I followed Mai-Li and Debbie, holding tightly to the boys.

The closer we got to the fire, the more intense the heat. The kids walked quickly, struggling to keep up and rapidly tiring. I noticed Mai-Li faltering a few times, coercing Debbie to stay on her feet. I reached over and took her pack, wrapping the strap around my neck, and letting the bag dangle behind me. She thanked me quietly, and picked up Debbie in her arms, running to keep up with Taylor.

Just when I thought all was lost, Taylor veered to the left, away from the conflagration, and headed straight to a hedge of sagebrush.

Mai-Li was breathing heavily, and she wavered with every step she took. Debbie was far too heavy for her to carry. Without warning, she fell over a clump of dirt, dropping the panic-stricken girl, who immediately let out a wail as loud as the roar of the fire.

Willie shot past us, helped Mai-Li to stand, and gathered Debbie in his arms. When Debbie realized he was not Mai-Li she began struggling, kicking, and screaming.

Mai-Li grabbed Debbie's hands tightly, looked into her eyes, and shouted. *"Debbie, be quiet and do as you're told, now."*

Debbie's eyes got as round as saucers, but she stopped and took hold of Willie's neck. I felt sorry for the young girl, knowing she didn't understand what was happening. Mai-Li never raised her voice, but I knew she realized it was the only way she and Debbie were going to get through this alive.

We ran like the wind, getting closer to the undergrowth. The boys were breathing haggardly, but they never faltered. The avalanche of flames roared robustly, attacking everything in its path.

Taylor quickened his pace, then he ploughed through the sagebrush, using his knife to hack a path through the shrubs. I looked down at the twins, their faces flushed, sweat pouring into their eyes.

Taylor stopped abruptly and Mai-Li and Willie almost ploughed into him. The boys and I arrived a few seconds later, breathing hoarsely. We were standing on the edge of a deep gorge. Below, a creek flowed sluggishly around stones and through the sagebrush.

"We have to climb down to the bottom, when we get there look for shelter, a hole, an animal house," he said looking directly at the kids. "Even an overhang, anything that will protect us."

"Do we just jump down?" Rusty asked.

I grabbed his arm tightly, and I'm sure he got the message.

"We're going to pretend we're mountain climbers, and tie ropes around our waists. Grab hold of any rocks, grass, whatever you find on your way down, to stop from falling."

Taylor was pulling a rope from his bag, then said without turning around. "And no Rusty, you can't go first."

It was then Taylor noticed Willie carrying Debbie. He smiled but said nothing.

"I'll go first," I offered, although my heart was beating like a drum.

Taylor nodded, removed the two backpacks I had been carrying, then tied the rope around my waist, all the time looking into my eyes and smiling. He led me to the ledge, and I lay face down on the ground, then eased my body over the side, trying to find a foothold. At first, my boots slid on gravel and sand, then suddenly I found a jutting rock. Taylor lowered the rope, and I scrambled down, jumped the last few centimetres, and looked up. Eddie was just above my head, swinging in the air, I reached up and grabbed his legs. Taylor pulled up the ropes. Rusty was next, but he climbed down so quickly, that he put the rest of us to shame.

"Good job, boys," I said softly, more to myself than them.

The next to come was Willie, with Debbie clasping his neck so tightly his face was turning blue; both ropes were tied around his waist, and Taylor and Mai-Li were above, holding the other ends, tightening their grip when Willie lost control.

Without warning the water container hanging around Willie's neck snapped loose. He cursed, and reached out to grab it, but missed. It flew past my face missing me by centimetres. Hitting a large rock, it smashed open, and the water spewed out, rapidly absorbed by the parched earth.

Debbie panicked when she heard the crash of the container, and that was when she realized she was dangling in the air. Her flailing caused the ropes to swing, and Willie struggled to keep a tight hold. Mai-Li yelled at her from above, ordering her to behave and be still. Debbie immediately obeyed.

We were taking too much time, the fire was steadily approaching, and the roar of the flames was deafening. Taylor and Mai-Li were right in its path.

I pulled the boys over and told them to start looking for a hiding place but not to wander far. If they found anything they were to yell as loud as they could.

A few seconds later, Willie was standing next to me. I grabbed Debbie from him, and she threw her arms around my neck. Willie untied the ropes and Taylor pulled them up.

"Everyone starts looking, we can get down on our own," Taylor shouted from above.

I headed in the boy's direction, and Debbie grabbed my hand. Willie went upstream to search. I hadn't gone far when Taylor and Mai-Li arrived. Debbie began struggling and I released her hand as she raced back to Mai-Li. Taylor gestured for me to keep looking.

The air got hotter, and burnt debris and ash fell from the sky. An ember landed on my arm, and I brushed it off, watching a blister form.

Is this how it would end, burned alive in some God-forgotten Wasteland by a raging inferno? It was all my fault. I was the one who wanted to try an easier route.

"Animal house, Eddie, come quick. Animal house."

Was that Debbie calling?

The boys and I raced in the direction of her voice. Mai-Li was nowhere in sight, and Debbie was clapping and jumping up and down. She pointed at the embankment.

Taylor and Willie weren't far behind. Mai-Li poked her head out of a huge, dark hole. "Have a look Taylor, this should work. Bring your flashlight."

Taylor dug it out of his backpack. He climbed the incline and joined Mai-Li. They both disappeared into the shadows.

"Alright everyone, start piling in, and don't forget your bags and supplies, no second trips," Taylor ordered, his voice echoing from inside the hole.

I grabbed Debbie's hand and helped her climb the steep slope. The boys followed and I yelled to Rusty who had forgotten his pack; it was lying at the bottom of the gully. He ran down the slope, a cascade of rocks following in his path. He tore up the incline, passing Eddie, then me and Debbie, and disappeared inside the cave. When we arrived, I released Debbie's hand, and she chased after the boys. I bent over to enter when suddenly Willie was behind me, he put his hands around my waist and spoke. "Need any help."

I froze, and turned my head, not wanting to make a scene, especially in front of Taylor.

"I am perfectly capable of climbing into a cave by myself. But thanks for the offer, Willie. Now let go of my waist."

"You got it, babe."

I twisted sharply and went inside, bumping hard against Taylor. He was standing at the entrance glaring, and he stiffened when Willie walked past, a grin on his face.

Then without warning a blast of heat surged into the tunnel, I gasped as my body hurled against Taylor. I fell to the ground, struggling to catch my breath. For once I was glad, I had my backpack strapped on, as it took the brunt of the sweltering gust.

Taylor grabbed my hand, pulled me up, and dragged me down the passageway. The beam from his flashlight flickered against the sides of the tunnel, our bodies making elongated shadows.

The passageway opened into a small den. Mai-Li and the kids were on the far side. Willie was sitting behind them, his back resting against the dirt wall.

Taylor faced me and asked in a raspy voice. "Carlie, did you get burned?"

I shook my head slowly. "I'm okay."

He let out his breath, the boys were staring at us with wide terrified eyes.

"Mai-Li, thanks for finding this shelter, it's perfect," I blurted, releasing Taylor's hand, and walking over to the group.

"Not me, it was Debbie."

All eyes slowly turned and looked at Debbie, who was unaware she was the centre of focus.

"Debbie," I said. "Did you find this cave all by yourself?"

"Carlie, it's not a cave it's an animal house."

We all laughed. We certainly needed the distraction.

"Listen everyone," Taylor interrupted. "Shortly, the fire will reach the gorge, I'm relying on the sagebrush to slow the flames. When that happens, there's going to be a roar, and it's going to get a lot hotter in here. Hand me your face masks and I'm going to pour a little water on each of them. Put them on right away, then use your sleeping bag to cover your head and body."

No sooner had Taylor returned the masks, than we heard a rumble. The roof of the cave shook, and clumps of dirt fell on our heads. The kids screamed, and Mai-Li, Taylor, and I each grabbed one.

"Your masks and covers everyone," Taylor yelled over the roar.

We threw the bags over our heads and waited. As Taylor predicted, a surge of scorching air gusted into the warren, and I felt the heat on my arms and head. Eddie was practically sitting in my lap his arms clasped around my neck so tight I choked. As quickly as the noise started, it stopped.

"Everyone stays put," Taylor said in a muffled voice from under his cover. "There might be a second surge."

We waited for ten minutes, sweating profusely. There were no more heat gusts, and the rumbling gradually tapered. Taylor gave us the okay.

"Why was the fire growling?" Eddie asked.

"It was the noise of the animals running from the flames."

The kids stared at Taylor; their mouths open in shock.

"I'm sure they're okay, they can find shelter in this ravine just like we did," he said quickly, looking directly at me and Mai-Li. "Is anyone hungry?"

Of course, the kids and Willie raised their hands.

"We might as well have something to eat, but we're down to one water container, so only one sip each. We'll spend the night here, then have a look at the damage tomorrow."

"I've never seen a wildfire move so fast," I said." It was like a dragon, roaring and breathing fire."

"It wasn't a wildfire."

Taylor rose, took a deep breath, turned, and stared down the passage. "I've never seen one before, but I've heard and read about them, gale winds heading for the fire not away from it, lightning strikes, and intense heat. It was not a wildfire."

"What was it then?"

"A firestorm, Carlie, it was a firestorm, and we are damn lucky we survived."

The next morning, I joined Taylor and Mai-Li outside. Willie was still asleep, and the kids were just beginning to stir.

Tendrils of flames had made their way into the gulch, and large patches of scorched bear grass and reeds covered the ground. Taylor walked over to the stream, and a small trickle flowed around clusters of silverweed and cacti.

"This is Peers Creek, and from my map, it looks like a secondary stream. This is nothing but a trickle. I was hoping there would be enough water to fill our container," he said, more to himself than us. He ran his fingers through his hair, then kicked at a clump of dirt.

I placed my hand on his shoulder. He shrugged it off, and for the first time since I had known him, I noticed defeat in his eyes. The thought troubled me; we had come to rely so much on his strength.

"Is there enough water to fill our kettle?" I asked.

"It would take forever, Carlie, we'd be here all day."

"Water is much more important than missing one day of travel."

A wind blew into the ravine, blowing ashes in our direction. I rubbed my eyes, then wiped the soot off my forehead with the back of my hand.

"It's all my fault we ended up here," I stammered. "I'm the one who wanted to take an easier route, and I put all of us in danger."

"You're talking nonsense," Taylor said.

"I'm not," I replied. "Through this entire trip, you've made nothing but intelligent decisions, we wouldn't have made it this far without your leadership. I'm not surprised at all you're having a meltdown."

"I'm not having a meltdown," Taylor snapped. "I'm just tired, I didn't sleep well last night."

Typical male response.

He turned and faced me, took my arms, and wrapped them around his neck. My face reddened, and I gently pulled away. Mai-Li had a smile on her face, and to pay her back, I told her she would oversee boiling the water.

We went inside the cave and got the kids dressed and fed. We told them we would be staying here for the day, and they could do whatever they wanted. Then I remembered the ashes and soot, and no water for washing clothes.

"Wait, change of plans."

Three gloomy faces stared back at me. I went to my backpack and took out our supply of colouring books, crayons, cards, and comic books. They were showing evidence of over-use, the pages were torn and greasy and the cards furled in the corners.

"Okay, change of plans. It's not nice outside, and probably not very safe either. So, today is going to be an indoor day."

Then Mai-Li and I, and Willie, once we explained to him the cards and comics were for the kids, not him, went outside to help Taylor.

At first, our task seemed impossible. It took over an hour to fill half a cup. I was beginning to regret my impulsive suggestion.

"The water must be coming from somewhere. Something is blocking it," Mai-Li said.

Taylor jumped up and kissed her forehead. "Thank goodness one of us is using her head. I'm going to have a look around."

"I'll come with you," Willie offered.

"I'd rather you stayed here."

"You want me to babysit them?"

"No, I want you to protect them. Keep your gun handy, and don't let anyone wander off."

"You honestly think there are gangs around when everything in sight is burned to a crisp?"

"No, but I've been thinking about the den. There's a water supply close by, this gorge is protected from the weather, and the den is a perfect hideout for predators. There's a likelihood whatever was living in there might return."

"There's no way it would have survived."

"A big enough animal could have outrun the fire or jumped across the ravine, whatever lives in the cave is headed back this way."

"What kind of animal could have outrun that fire?" I asked.

"I have no idea; it could be anything. We need to be prepared."

"You're thinking of the cheetah."

"Not necessarily, although it might be one of the escaped Zoo animals. It's not that far from Vancouver for a large animal to travel."

Taylor went inside the den and returned with his bow and arrows. "I don't plan to go far. I'll be back shortly."

I grinned when he disappeared around a bend and noticed the immediate change in his attitude. When Taylor felt he was needed or realized an adventure awaited ahead, his mood immediately changed for the better.

Willie went inside and returned shortly, his gun under his shirt.

We began ladling water into the kettle, Mai-Li would boil it, then put it in the sole canister, which was almost empty. We soon got into a rhythm, Willie and I bailed, and Mai-Li would check on the kids. I suggested we let them come outside for a while.

The kids were happy to get out. The air was thick and smoky. They were wearing their masks, which did not seem to bother them at all. I hated mine, and there were times I wished I could be as flexible, or better yet just toss it away.

I called for a break and went inside and brought out cookies. Mai-Li poured half a cup of water, and we all shared it.

"The water tastes like smoke," Eddie commented.

"I imagine it does, the ground and plants around the stream were burned by the fire, so we will probably be tasting smoke for a while, at least until we get away from the Wastelands," I stated.

"Carlie," Rusty asked. "How long will it be before we get to the Interior?"

"A long time, after leaving here, we will be climbing a few mountains. By then it will be snowing, so we will be looking for a cabin or someplace to spend the winter."

"Can we make snowmen?"

"Or a fort?" Eddie added.

"Yeah, a fort," Debbie shouted.

"You can do both."

I wiped my hands across my jeans, then picked up the cup and headed back to the stream. "Now remember, stay close by so we can see you guys at all times."

Willie and I continued our tedious chore, and Mai-Li warned the kids at least ten times to keep away from the fire and the boiling water. The canister slowly filled, but we still had a long way to go.

"Where's Taylor?" Debbie asked, suddenly realizing he was missing.

I looked at Mai-Li and Willie. "He went for a walk, but he'll be back soon."

"Is he looking for the bad guys?" Eddie said. I decided I would have a little talk with him when we were alone, as he seemed to have a fixation bad guys were waiting around every corner to pounce on us.

"Eddie," Rusty replied. "You don't look for bad guys, you run away from bad guys, right, Carlie?"

Well, that just made my future talk with Eddie a little tougher. "Taylor's checking out the stream to see if something is obstructing the ...." I started to explain, but the three kids disappeared before I finished my sentence. Bad guys were cool, obstructions, not so much.

The heat and heavy smoke from the firestorm were overpowering, and I felt a headache starting. Mai-Li suggested we go inside for a lunch break. We sipped water and ate a granola bar, and the difference in the temperature in the den from the outside air was pleasant. After we ate, and after a lot of complaining, the kids settled down for a short nap. The excitement and energy expended the day before, the heat and lack of food, left them exhausted, and in five minutes they were fast asleep.

The rest of us went back outside, and I reminded Willie to take his gun as I noticed he took it off when we came inside.

"It's like a furnace out here," he said. "It was burning my skin."

"Then cover it with a towel, and place it next to the fire," Mai-Li suggested. "Just make sure you can get to it in a hurry if the need arises."

I'm sure Willie was counting on having a nap with the kids, and to be honest, I would love to have joined them.

We continued for another hour, and by now I was starting to worry about Taylor. He must have run into trouble.

Just when I was going to suggest one of us go look for him, he appeared around the bend, sweat pouring down his face, his hair glued to his face. He waved at us, then sat down next to me. He removed his mask, then his quiver, and laid his bow on the ground. I gave him a quarter of a cup of water. He drank it all, licking the drops condensed on the side of the cup.

"You hungry?" I asked.

"No, I took a granola bar with me. Where are the Rug Rats?"

I pointed at the den. "Tuckered out and sound asleep."

"So," Willie prodded. "Did you find anything?"

"The remains of a deer close to the stream. It fell into the ravine and triggered a rockslide, which blocked the flow of the water. We can salvage most of the meat, and the dirt and rocks can be moved. Unfortunately, it's not a one-man job."

Before I could volunteer, Taylor looked at Mai-Li. "I'm wondering if you wouldn't mind joining me, I've seen you wield a knife back at the warehouse, and I need your talent. Sorry, Willie, you need to stay here, and Carlie, you might as well continue bailing water, we're going to need as much as we can collect."

None of us was happy with our allocated task, yet we recognized the wisdom of Taylor's thinking.

"Grab the gunny sacks Mai-Li, we'll need them to haul the meat. The sooner we leave, the sooner we'll get back. When Debbie wakes and finds you gone there's going to be an uproar."

"I'll watch her," Willie volunteered. "She'll listen to me."

Three shocked faces stared at Willie. Changing the topic, I asked Taylor. "And we'll be out of here tomorrow?"

"That's my plan."

I stared at the ground.

"I thought you'd be happy to get out of here."

"I am but imagine what the kids are going to see when we climb out of the ravine tomorrow. There must have been a lot of animals that perished."

"Carlie, we can't hide them from everything."

"You're right, forget what I said."

"No, I understand your concern. I'll look at the map tonight, maybe we can find a different route than the one the fire took. The mountain range runs along the eastern edge of the Wasteland, so we might be able to reach it from a different direction."

"Thanks, Taylor, sorry I make things so difficult at times."

"Yeah well, you're worth it."

My face flushed in embarrassment, Mai-Li tittered and covered her mouth, and Willie grunted and went inside the den. Things were back to normal.

Chapter Twenty-One

Mai-Li and Taylor left, and I returned to bailing. Willie hadn't made an appearance, and I had no intention of chasing after him. It took him another ten minutes to join me; saying nothing, he took the scoop from me and took over the bailing. I checked our wood supply and walked around the area, gathering what survived the fire. We discovered it was easier to let the fire go out, refill the kettle, then restart it again.

I heard shouting coming from the cave. I went inside to see what the ruckus was about. Rusty and Eddie were at loggerheads, which didn't happen often.

"Hey, hey what's the problem boys?"

"Nothing," Rusty said.

"Well, something must be wrong, otherwise Eddie wouldn't be crying."

"He's a crybaby."

"Now that's not true, he never cries unless something bad happens. Come on Rusty out with it," I asked firmly.

"I didn't do nothing."

"Rusty, I've discovered in my ripe old age, that if someone automatically defends himself, it usually means he has something to hide."

Rusty stubbornly looked away and refused to answer. I turned to Eddie, and he looked up at me. I knew I wouldn't get anything from him either, they never tattled on each other.

"Well, I guess it's over then?"

"Rusty was bad," Debbie muttered.

"He was?"

Debbie nodded, looked over at Rusty, and then stared at the floor.

"Okay, if no one is talking then I think it's time everyone come outside for a while. Taylor and Mai-Li have gone for a while..."

Realizing what I had just said, I waited for the inevitable. Debbie jumped up, began wailing, and ran for the exit. "Mai-Li, Mai-Li."

"Debbie, wait." I yelled, tearing down the tunnel after her. The boys followed on my heels, and we all arrived at the exit at the same time.

I grabbed Debbie's arms and looked into her eyes. "She's helping Taylor with the water, and will be back soon, okay? You can sit with me if you like."

Debbie breathed decply and looked at the boys. She shook her head. "No, I want Mai-Li, I don't want Rusty and Eddie to be mad anymore."

"I know, but they won't tell me what's going on, so why don't we pretend they aren't here."

Debbie looked at me for the longest time, then nodded. When we arrived at the bottom of the hill, she plopped on the ground next to me and began gathering rocks.

I looked up and realized the boys hadn't moved from their position. Something was wrong, and I suddenly realized what it was.

"Eddie, where's Squishy?" I said, looking up.

Rusty's face paled, he looked at his brother, then back at me. Suddenly he crumpled and ran down the incline.

"I'm sorry, Carlie, I'm sorry, I never meant to hurt Squishy."

"Rusty what did you do?"

"Eddie was making fun of me, so I threw Squishy in the air. He disappeared."

"Things don't just disappear Rusty. What happened to Squishy?"

"No, Carlie," Eddie said quietly as he sidled down the hill. "It's true. Rusty made Squishy disappear, just like magic."

I turned and looked at Debbie. "Is this true?"

Debbie nodded and splayed her fingers. "Poof," she said seriously.

Willie burst out laughing, then he choked and started coughing. Rusty ran over to him and pounded his back. "You okay, Willie?"

Willie pushed Rusty's hand away and returned to his bailing.

"I'm sorry, Carlie," Rusty said, as he returned to where I was sitting. "Squishy disappeared, I must be magic."

Surprisingly, the kids amused Willie. It was not like him at all, as he usually spent most of his time ignoring them. What was he up to.... whoa wait a minute.

I swung around sharply and faced Willie. "What did you do with Squishy?"

"Me, what would I want with a dirty stuffed toy?"

"I don't know, why don't you tell me."

"Look, I had nothing to do with any of this, okay? Besides, I've been out here all the time."

I thought over what he said. "You were in the cave for a short time after Taylor and Mai-Li left, you had lots of time to hide Squishy somewhere."

"I'm getting sick and tired of everyone blaming me for whatever happens. I was reading one of the comics, okay?"

I raised my hands in defeat. I did have a habit of immediately blaming Willie for everything. Of course, I was usually right. But this time, he sounded sincere, so I was back to square one.

"Okay, I'm sorry, I shouldn't have blamed it on you."

Willie shrugged.

"I'm going inside and have a look around. I'll be right back."

I pointed to the cave, and the kids quietly followed. I started searching, under sleeping bags, inside packs, and behind rocks, but no Squishy. It didn't make any sense.

"Rusty, show me where you were standing when you threw Squishy."

Rusty strolled to the centre of the den and turned and faced me. "Now pretend you are holding Squishy, throw him just like you did."

Rusty raised his arm, then flung the invisible toy into the air. I looked up at the roof and sighed. There was a hole, which was large enough to show the soot and ashes floating in the air.

"Alright, I know where Squishy is. Let's go."

Once outside, I walked over to the edge of the ravine, suddenly remembering how high it was. We would have to wait until Taylor and Mai-Li returned as they had the ropes. We would have to wait to rescue Squishy and I hoped the ratty teddy bear hadn't been incinerated.

I gave the kids a sip of water and dried apples for a snack. I told them to stay outside, and to keep out of trouble.

The kettle was half full of water, so I started a fire. I watched the kids closely, and if one of them strayed too far, I called them back. The thought of a large animal being close unnerved me.

We worked for another hour; the boiled water had cooled enough for me to put it into our canister. I shook my head, hoping Taylor and Mai-Li managed to remove the rocks from the stream otherwise it would take us another two days to gather enough water to fill the canister. I realized the salvaged deer meat would need to be cooked, causing another delay. Taylor would not be happy.

The kids were hot and tired, and they came and sat next to me. I played a few guessing games, keeping them occupied. Just when I was running out of ideas, Taylor and Mai-Li appeared, each carrying a heavy gunny sack over their shoulder. They stumbled over to us and collapsed on the ground.

"Take a break, Willie," Taylor said. "We got the rocks moved and the water should start flowing a lot faster in a few minutes."

I poured water into a cup and handed it to Mai-Li. She drank and then handed it to Taylor.

"What's in the sack, Taylor?" Rusty asked as he started untying the rope.

"Just leave it, for now, Rusty, we'll show you later."

"Let's go inside," I suggested. "It's easier to breathe once we get away from the smoke and ash, and it's getting windy again. We'll check the stream in half an hour, we all need a break."

No one argued, and the kids raced up the slope, followed by Taylor and Mai-Li. I grabbed one of the gunny sacks, untied the rope, and peeked inside. It was full of meat, and Willie leaned over and grinned. "Yum, barbecue steaks."

We climbed the incline and entered the den. Taylor was hearing the whole story of

Squishy's predicament. "We'll rescue Squishy after I rest a bit. A few things need doing before we leave tomorrow, first, let's have something to eat."

Everyone got a swallow of water, and I opened a can of Spaghetti-o for the kids, and brown beans for the rest of us. Again, we just spooned out our share.

"What's the agenda for this afternoon?" Willie asked Taylor.

"First and most importantly, we rescue Squishy, and pray he survived his ordeal." All heads nodded in agreement, understanding the importance.

"The water should be running soon, and we'll fill the container. Try and find another jug or holder in our provisions where we can store water, would you Mai-Li?"

Taylor ran his fingers through his hair and continued. "While Carlie is bailing the water, I'm going to start a larger fire over there in the open to cook the meat. Willie, you can help me, and keep your gun handy. The smell of raw meat will travel a long way."

"You're still worrying about a large animal?" I asked.

Taylor turned and looked at Mai-Li and she nodded.

"We found fresh tracks around the deer; a large cat made it. It must have heard us coming and ran off."

My stomach lurched, and I took a deep breath. "Another cheetah?"

"No, bigger, maybe a lion, or a tiger," Taylor answered nonchalantly.

"Oh, only a lion or a tiger, wonderful, you had me worried for a moment," I countered.

Taylor grinned, then stood. "You kids stay inside with Mai-Li. Behave yourselves, she's worked hard today and needs a break."

Then he gestured for me and Willie to follow him outside. Just as we left the den, a voice called out. "Don't forget Squishy, please."

We groaned in unison. The stream was flowing faster, so I stoked the fire and finished boiling the water. I told Taylor about the shortage of firewood, hoping Willie was listening to what I was saying.

"I'll see if I can find any when I'm rescuing Squishy. I'll be right back."

I watched Taylor climb the side of the ravine without the aid of his rope. He was carrying his gun and was gone longer than it should have taken to rescue Squishy. I was beginning to wish we had never brought the stuffed bear with us, but immediately dismissed the thought. Squishy was Eddie's lifeline and provided him with comfort and support.

I knew how much Willie hated bailing water, so I asked him if he would like to start the new fire, and I would finish filling the canister. He readily agreed. Running into the den, he got the shovel and was soon digging a pit.

I finished boiling the water, then decided I would check upstream to see if I could find any wood. I told Willie where I was going, and he nodded without raising his head.

I removed my mask, which I sometimes did when I was away from the others. I knew Taylor wouldn't be happy if he knew. I walked for a short while, then rounded a bend and faced a field of bushes and sagebrush growing in the middle of the ravine, untouched by the flames. Rather than ploughing my way through, I walked over to the edge and looked up. At first, I wasn't sure what I was looking at, but then I realized it was a huge tree branch growing upward. I climbed the slope, grabbing twists of horsetail and shrubs for support. I dug my feet into the gravelly sand, grabbed the end of the branch, and pulled as hard as I could. All I managed to do was lose my footing, and I threw myself forward and grabbed the branch before I barrelled headfirst down the grade. There was no way I could move it, let alone carry it back to the den. I slowly inched my way down and wiped the dirt and soot from my jeans.

I heard rustling in the bushes and froze. Hastily, I grabbed the twigs and branches I had found earlier and quickly retraced my steps. A shadow fell across the ground, and I gazed up and spotted Turkey buzzards soaring high in the smoky sky. I thought of the animals that hadn't made it through the fire, their carcasses wouldn't last long from predators in the area.

I saw Taylor helping Willie with the fire and noticed Squishy propped on a rock, a bit grungier but intact.

"Carlie, are you alright, you're white as a ghost?" Taylor asked. "And where's your mask?"

I dropped the wood next to the fire and wiped the front of my jacket. "I'm fine," I answered, as I quickly grabbed my mask from my pocket and put it on. "Any trouble getting Squishy?"

He frowned and said nothing, I kept my head down waiting for him to start lecturing me.

"No," Taylor answered. "He was a good bear, although it took a few minutes for me to find him. He fell behind a rock."

I raised my head and forced a smile. "What a relief, I'll take him back to Eddie. What's it like up there?"

"Pretty bleak, and we have no choice, we must cross the scorched ground to get to the Foothills. It's hard to determine which direction the firestorm went; we'll have to see what happens."

"I'll let Mai-Li know and see if she's found another flask we can use for water. Oh, I found a tree branch growing out of the side of the ravine. I tried, but I'm not strong enough to pull it out. You're going to need your axe and ropes to retrieve it. It's just a short walk in that direction, next to a patch of weeds and brushes the fire missed."

"We'll look at it. If all goes well, we'll get out of here tomorrow."

I said nothing further, and Taylor frowned, then walked to his pack and removed his axe and rope. There wasn't much I could hide from him, and I'm sure he realized something was bothering me. I started up the incline approaching the den, then hesitated, my thoughts racing. Should I tell him what I thought I heard? What if there was nothing there at all and I imagined it. I already was in his bad books about taking off my mask, and creating a disturbance would just make matters worse. I shook my head, sighed, and entered the tunnel, Squishy dangling from my hand.

I chuckled when I heard the kids talking and playing. Mai-Li had an amazing ability in keeping them occupied and happy, which was a bonus for all of us.

Eddie was the first to see me, he jumped up and raced over, almost knocking me over in excitement.

"He's pretty dirty," I said as I handed him his beloved friend. "I won't be able to clean Squishy until we get away from all this soot and ash. And make sure you thank Taylor next time you see him, okay?"

Eddie nodded happily and returned to the others. The three kids began chattering at once. Rusty shook Squishy's hand, and

Debbie leaned over and kissed the sooty bear.

"Well, that's one more emergency solved," I said to Mai-Li. "Oh, did you find anything to put water in? I finished filling the canister."

Mai-Li nodded and went over to the supply pack. She removed a stack of pots and pans until she found what she was looking for. "We have this, it's the only thing I could find that might work."

I took the flask and laughed quietly. It was my old hip flask I used while living by myself on the streets. I had forgotten all about it. "Perfect. I'll fill this with water; I should finish around lunchtime. I'll come back and help you feed the kids."

Both guys were gone, so I started bailing on my own. Moving the rocks opened the obstruction and the water was flowing at a quicker pace, and soon I had the flask filled. It wouldn't hold as much as the broken canister, but it would do in a pinch.

What was keeping the guys, they should have removed the branch by now. I ran into the den and handed the water to Mai-Li. "Give the kids lots to drink, as much as they want to drink. Don't forget yourself. I can refill the flask before we go; we will be back on rations soon enough."

Mai-Li nodded, then I told her I was going to check on the guys, as they might need help carrying the wood.

"Carlie, be careful, do you have your knife?"

I nodded, then she went to her pack and returned with her cane. Saying nothing, I took it and tied it around my waist.

"I think Taylor's right, it's time I learned how to shoot," I muttered.

I slowly retraced my earlier steps. The silence was oppressive, and I sensed something was wrong. I came to the bend and peered around the corner; there was no one in sight. The tree branch was untouched, still intact.

I stood quietly, breathing slowly and deeply. Patience was not one of my virtues, it was not easy for me to stand motionless for any length of time. I slowly bent and removed my knife. I opened the cane and left it hanging at my waist.

Everything happened at once. I heard a scream, a loud shout, then two gunshots. I detected movement in the tall grass, then a tan shape hurled itself in my direction. I shook my head in astonishment, was that a lion?

The animal was severely injured, bleeding from a wound in its stomach. It was thin, its ribs protruding, its hide black with soot. It immediately detected me and moved slowly in my direction. I forced myself to remain calm, resisting the urge to run. When it was a few meters away, I flung my knife and embedded it deeply in its chest. It roared but remained standing.

I raised the cane and took a stance. *Okay, Mai-Li let's see if your lessons work*!

The lion was so close, I could smell its hot, pungent breath. It growled deep in its chest, then roared so loudly I felt the ground shake beneath my feet. Icy terror filled my body, then I remembered Mai-Li's instructions on staying calm and focused. I spun my body, lowered the staff, and struck the lion sharply on its nose. It roared in distress. I waited until it moved closer, then without hesitation, thrust the end of the staff as hard as I could into its eye. It growled, stopped in its tracks, swayed, and crashed to the ground.

Taylor raced into the open, took one look at the lion, and grabbed me tightly in his arms. I could hear his heart pounding. Suddenly my legs gave way, and I sank to the ground.

"Carlie," Taylor cried. "Are you hurt?"

I rose to my knees, placed my hands flat on the ground, then slowly raised my head and looked into his eyes. "I hate big cats, I *hate* them."

Taylor laughed, then helped me stand. "You can come on out now, Willie," he said. "The lion's dead."

Willie crept out of the reeds. At first, I was going to say something glib about his absence, when I noticed Taylor's hands covered in blood, but I couldn't see any injuries on his body. Willie was holding his arm tightly against his chest, the front of his shirt covered in blood.

He approached me, looked down at the lion, leaned over, pulled my knife from its chest, and handed it to me.

"Thanks," I said as I wiped the blade on a tuft of grass, then returned it to its case. "How bad is it?" I asked pointing to his wound.

I waited for him to shrug, but surprisingly he said. "Not too bad, it clawed my arm and shoulder, just as I shot him."

"You and Carlie saved the day," Taylor remarked, as he slowly approached Willie.

Willie quickly sidestepped, and almost bumped into me. "You're not goanna hug me or something like that, are you?"

Taylor grinned, then bent and picked up his gun lying next to Willie's foot. He had dropped it when he ran over to me.

I laughed, relieved everyone was alive, and except for Willie, uninjured.

"I thought I heard two shots," I stammered, looking first at Tylor, then at Willie.

Taylor's face reddened. "Yeah, I fell into a bloody hole and my gun went off. All it did was warn the lion. Good thing Willie was there with his gun."

"Let's get him back to the den, he's losing a lot of blood. Mai-Li can fix him up. With her herbs and medicine, she'll work her magic and have him better in no time."

"Sounds like a plan," Taylor said. "Carlie, you go with Willie, and I'll check the area to make sure the lion was on his own. Give me your knife, okay."

I hesitated, and Taylor looked at me curiously. "Is there something wrong?"

"We're not going to eat lion meat, are we?"

Taylor took my knife, and the last thing I heard as I turned to leave was him laughing. It wasn't until we reached the cave, I realized he hadn't answered.

Mai-Li patched up Willie's injury, first rubbing him down with deer fat. He protested vehemently because of the smell, but Mai-Li told him to behave, then explained to him deer salve was excellent for cuts and wounds and would help prevent infection.

"Willie, if you feel up to it," I said. "Why don't you tell the kids what happened, I'm going back to give Taylor a hand with the wood?"

It was as good a time as any for the kids to learn about the dangers we faced on our journey. I thanked Mai-Li for the use of her cane, then I told her I wouldn't have survived without it and promised I would clean it properly when I returned. I then thanked her profusely for taking the time to teach me how to use it.

As I turned to leave the den, I asked her if she could use any of the parts of the lion and she shook her head. She relied more on the plants and herbs she found along the trails in the forests and plains. I imagine lion was not something on her list of medical supplies or, for that matter, part of our cuisine.

It was dark by the time we completed our tasks. I helped Taylor cut and carry the wood, then he rigged up a spit and wrapped the deer meat around it while I kept an eye on the fire. He went and checked on Willie and Mai-Li mentioned she had given him a tea tincture and he was sleeping. It would be a few days before he had enough energy to put in a full day of walking, our progress hindered once again.

I had to remind Taylor delays happened. Interrupting me, he lifted my chin and kissed me lightly on my lips. This time I did not pull back. He said nothing, just held me for a few seconds then returned to his chores.

I cleared my throat, now was as good a time as any. "I was wondering if you would teach me to shoot."

Taylor was kneeling by the fire turning the meat. "What brought this on?" he asked, as he lifted his head.

"Two attacks by man-eating beasts."

He nodded, then returned to his chore. "I can teach you, once we get the opportunity, but not now, I don't want to announce our location to any unwanted company."

"Okay, so we'll wait until we get out of the Wastelands."

"We only have two guns, mine and Willie's, and limited ammo."

"You sound as if you don't want to teach me."

"No, there's nothing more I would like than to know you can protect yourself if you get into trouble again, and looking at your record, we both know there's a probability that will happen. Our guns used only as a final resort, we are low on ammunition and we need to be cautious. Today, you proved your knife and Mai-Li's cane are impressive weapons. Oh, and be sure to thank her for teaching you how to use it."

I stared at Taylor, and he chuckled. "The walls at the warehouse were paper thin. Everyone knew what you two were up to."

I shrugged my shoulders.

"But" Taylor continued, as he stood. "I would prefer teaching you archery."

"I had thought about it," I said. "But I don't think I have enough strength in my arms."

Taylor grinned, then stopped when he noticed the frown on my face. "I'm not making fun of you, but I've noticed what you are capable of doing, and although you're small, you're strong, flexible and fast, assets necessary to be an archer."

I mulled over what Taylor had just said. I did pick up Kung Fu quickly, so why should I have any problem learning archery?

"Okay, I'll do it."

"I'm not sure when we can start, but the first camp we make that looks safe, we'll give it a try."

"Thanks, Taylor," I said.

"Oh, that reminds me," he said. "When I checked on Willie, the kids and Mai-Li were drinking water by the cupful."

"Yes, I know. I told her to let them drink as much as they wanted, as we'll be rationing it in a few days anyway. I've been bailing and boiling water non-stop for two days and have refilled the canteen three times. I'll make sure both canisters are full when we leave."

Taylor stepped closer, took me in his arms, then kissed my forehead. "Beautiful and smart, I like it."

I rolled my eyes and pushed him away. "Here's a cup of water, drink all of it."

"Thanks, and you can sleep next to Eddie tonight."

Chapter Twenty-Two

We stayed an extra day, then Mai-Li announced Willie was healing, and we could leave the following morning. Taylor woke early, his bags already packed, while coffee brewed on the coals and a pot of porridge simmered on the fire. The kids slept late and woke up hungry. Willie was grumpy and moaning about his life-threatening injury, Eddie didn't pee the bed, and we were carrying full rations once again.

Climbing out of the ravine went without a hitch. We stood in a tight group, staring at the desolation as far as our eyes could see. The firestorm incinerated everything in its path. Heavy threatening clouds hung low in the sky, blotting out the sun. It was dark and depressing.

"Whoa," said Eddie.

"I think we all share the same sentiment Eddie," Mai-Li murmured.

"I'm sure everyone is tired of hearing this," I began. "But don't remove your masks, keep them on all the time."

"Good idea," Taylor said, looking directly at me. "Those clouds are the residue of the firestorm, and you don't want to inhale any, it could make you sick. Rusty, can I borrow your compass?"

"Um sorry, I lost it."

"What," I interjected. "Rusty, not again; you'd lose your head if it weren't attached."

Rusty, along with everyone else, was grinning from ear to ear.

That little monster, he got me again.

I grabbed him around his waist and tickled him. "Stop, Carlie, stop," he babbled. "It's right here, I was just kidding."

I set him down. "I'll never learn, will I Rusty?"

He shook his head, then handed the compass to Taylor, who smiled and winked at me.

Taylor opened the tarp and spread it on the ground. "I'm going to look around a bit, you stay here. Sit on the tarp, otherwise, you'll end up covered in ash and soot. Willie, I think you're strong enough to be in charge. You know the drill."

Willie nodded, then Taylor began walking, and soon he disappeared over a knoll.

"Where's Taylor going?" Eddie asked, always the first one to worry if one of us was absent.

"He's looking to see how far the fire burned," I answered. "We don't want to walk in the ashes, there might be embers still burning underneath."

"That would hurt, right?" Debbie asked.

Mai-Li hugged the young girl and said. "Yes, it would Debbie, so we have to be very careful where we walk and try to find the safest way."

Our answers pacified the kids. Worked well on Willie too, he was soon asleep, snoring loudly. I spotted his gun lying next to him, and since our guard was sleeping, I made a mental note to myself of its location in case needed.

We sat and talked for well over an hour, and Taylor hadn't returned. Each time he left on a solo excursion I worried, as there was always the possibility he could run into trouble.

"Carlie, I'm thirsty," Debbie said. Mai-Li looked at me and shook her head. I suppose now is suitable time as any to start water rationing.

"I'm sorry, but we must be careful and not drink too much water, at least until we get through the Wastelands. Can you wait a little longer?"

"Okay," Debbie said sadly. Eddie patted her back and handed her Squishy to hold.

I pulled the much-used books and comics from my pack; the boys each grabbed one, and I asked Debbie if she wanted me to read to her. We needed to keep her occupied because if she throws her ball one of us would have to walk on scorched land to retrieve it. Just as I turned a page, I looked up and spotted a figure in the distance.

"There's Taylor," I pointed. "I wonder what he found out."

I shook Willie awake, and after a few curses, he slowly sat up. He grimaced when he bent forward, and he quickly laid his arm across his chest. Mai-Li watched him closely, the last thing we needed was for him to get an infection.

Taylor's head was down, and he was making slow progress. When he arrived, he joined us on the tarp.

"You mind if I keep your compass for a while," Taylor asked, turning to Rusty. "Just until we get away from the path the fire made."

Rusty nodded.

"Thanks, bud. It's going to be difficult walking. We should go slowly and watch for holes and crevices where the fire is still burning."

No one said anything, we just looked at Taylor in dismay. He must have seen the looks on our faces. "It's a bit dangerous, but we've been through worse. I'm going to take a short rest, then we'll head out. Might as well have lunch now, we'll be walking until dark."

Which is what we did. After a quick bite, we put on our packs and headed out. The prairie grasses of wormwood and wild sage were still smouldering, scorched beyond recognition. We passed cracks in the soil where flames shot skyward. It was hot and dirty, unending, and exhausting.

"Look at the big birds, Carlie," Rusty said pointing in the distance.

"Those are Turkey buzzards."

"How come there's so many of them?"

"Well, they're eating the animals that died in the Firestorm. That is especially important as they keep the outdoors clean. Does that make sense?"

"I think so, because it would get pretty stinky if they didn't, right?"

"Exactly, every creature has a role to play on Earth, including man," I murmured more to myself than the others.

We pushed the kids, and Willie was having difficulty keeping up. I reached over and took the water container, he nodded, but said nothing.

We walked for hours, and as was the case, Debbie was having trouble breathing. The boys each grabbed the back of my shirt, as they had strict instructions to walk only where I stepped.

Taylor stopped at the top of a rise and pointed. In the distance, I saw a strip of brown earth. "Oh my God, is that open ground?" I asked excitedly, forgetting to breathe. I started to cough, my eyes watered, and I pulled down my mask. Taylor patted my back, then handed me the canteen.

"Take a sip," he said looking at all of us. "Make sure everyone gets one, and a granola bar, we'll need the energy."

After I took a small drink, I passed the canteen to Willie. Taylor spoke quietly to

Mai-Li and me. "That's the last of the granola bars and don't forget to put your mask back on, Carlie."

We waited until everyone ate, as we needed no distractions once we started walking. Without warning, Debbie dropped heavily to the ground, and Mai-Li couldn't get her to stand. I recognized Debbie's behavioural pattern when headed for a meltdown and so did Mai-Li, so she stopped pushing her and waited.

Taylor looked directly at Mai-Li. "We still have a long way to go."

I gathered the wraps of the granola bars I had stuffed in my pack and placed them in my pocket. Everyone took their places, except Debbie, who was now lying on the ground, covered in soot and ashes, but that was the least of our problems.

Mai-Li tried to coerce Debbie to stand, who was now whining and ready to have a total eruption. Frustration flashed across Taylor's face, but when he noticed me watching, he looked away.

"Oh no," I said, smacking the top of my head. "I have all these paper wrappers from the granola bars, and I don't know if I can carry them, there are so many of them."

Debbie stopped wailing and looked up. We always let her throw wrappers into our campfires, which for some reason she found hilarious. She slowly stood and put out her hand. "Can I have them?"

"I don't know, we are going to need them for our campfire tonight, and you're not coming."

"I can come," she said. Then she turned and looked at Willie "Can you carry me?"

"Debbie," Mai-Li said. "Willie is hurt and can't carry you right now."

Everyone held their breath. We all knew when Debbie stopped walking, it was either carry her or wait.

"It's alright," Willie said. "I can carry you a little bit, Debbie, but only for fifteen minutes, then you need to walk on your own. Is it a deal?"

"It's a deal." Debbie laughed.

Mai-Li and I looked at each other in amazement.

Debbie raised her arms, but Willie shook his head. "I can't pick you up, I'll have to piggyback you, is that okay?"

Everyone held their breath. Debbie hesitated for a few seconds, then ran behind Willie and I lifted her on his back.

"Put your arms around Willie's neck, and hang on tight," I said.

"You're next, Carlie?" Willie whispered.

I ground my teeth, picked up my pack, and said tiredly. "Cut it out, Willie."

Debbie leaned forward and looked into Willie's eyes. She raised her index finger and shaking it hard, commented. "Cut it out, Willie."

Mai-Li and I choked back our laughter, and the boys looked at us as if we were crazy.

"Okay, let's make tracks," Taylor ordered, as he stared angrily at Willie. "We've wasted enough time."

"No, Taylor, no," Debbie yowled. "Carlie has my wrappers."

I quickly handed them to her. Taylor rolled his eyes, turned, and began walking.

Our pace was slow as there were times we had to jump over embers and deep ruptures. My heart broke when I looked at the twins; their faces burned from the heat, their eyes glazed over, and it was clear we couldn't push them much farther.

Willie carried Debbie for well over an hour, not complaining once. It was Debbie who finally announced, "Okay Willie, you can put me down now. Our fifteen minutes are over."

I looked back at Rusty. I could almost hear him calculating the time in his head. I quickly covered his mask with my hand and shook my head. He sighed but said nothing.

"Thanks, guy," I whispered.

"That's okay," he whispered back. "I'll tell her later."

Hours passed, and the heavy cloud cover created dark shadows, making it difficult to see. Taylor guided the way, pausing periodically to check the compass.

Suddenly he stopped, Mai-Li was walking with her head down and bumped into him. Without turning, he reached back and steadied her. In a jubilant voice, he announced, "We made it."

The rest of us formed a line staring at the brown wilted scrublands, tufts of prairie grasses, and sage. I had never seen anything so beautiful and I'm sure the others felt the same.

"Do we stop here for the night?" Willie asked. "It's pretty open, if we start a fire, we'll be noticed."

"I know," Taylor said. "Let's walk a little longer."

The kids moaned. Unfortunately, we walked for another hour, and I was about to tell Taylor the boys were finished when Eddie tugged the back of my shirt; I turned and looked down at him.

"Is there a train around here?"

"I don't think so, Eddie?"

"Then what are those?"

"Taylor," I called, as I looked at the ground, "Come see what Eddie found."

"Carlie, we don't have time to look at bugs or rabbit scat."

"This is much more interesting. Come have a look."

Taylor walked over to us and pushed aside a tuft of grass.

"These are train tracks, and they're old. I remember reading an article in one of my history magazines, trains used to haul ore from the abandoned mine a few kilometres north of here. There were also passenger trains. Let's follow it for a short while, it should lead somewhere."

Taylor read the compass and then shook his head. "It's headed northeast, toward Sowaqua Creek. We won't make it there tonight, so we'll stop somewhere in a protected area, then keep going in the morning. The creek will provide water, and we can refill our canisters again, wash some clothes and take baths."

For some reason, the kids were no longer tired. The idea of following an old train track into the wilderness lifted their spirits.

"Speak softly, boys," I whispered, reminding the boys. "Remember your voices carry a long way."

Taylor turned on his flashlight, it was growing darker, and we had to be careful not to trip over rocks and holes, the last thing we needed was another injury.

We'd not gone far when Eddie stopped and asked. "What's that over there?"

"Just a shadow Eddie," I answered.

'No, it's a big box, look."

Taylor swung his flashlight around. It was an old train car, the sides covered with graffiti. It was sitting under a poplar tree, which had blackened over time.

"Everyone get down and be quiet. I'm going to have a look inside."

Then Taylor disappeared into the shadows. The rest of us lowered ourselves to the ground. He soon returned; our wait was not long.

"It doesn't look as if anyone's living in it," he reported. "We might as well set up our sleeping bags and sleep inside, then we can get an early start in the morning."

We followed Taylor around to the front of the railcar. One of the steps was missing, so we bodily lifted the kids and their packs inside. Taylor swung the beam of light into the corners and along the walls. At one time, it must have been a passenger car but the seats were damaged beyond use. Windows ran down both sides of the car; the glass panes in all of them smashed. Empty beer cans and discarded bones littered the floor.

"I don't know, Taylor," I remarked. "Someone stayed here at one time, what if they return?"

"I can't see that happening, this junk has been there for a long time."

"It's just I have this uneasy feeling in my stomach."

"Well, it's your call, if you want to leave, we will."

I hesitated, unsure of myself. "No, that's not fair to the kids, they're exhausted. We'll take a vote."

"Willie, Mai-Li?"

"Heck, I'm all for staying," Willie replied. "Better than sleeping outside."

Mai-Li looked into my eyes, hesitated before answering, then said quietly. "I think we should stay. We're tired and need to rest."

"Three to one, Carlie," Taylor said. "I guess we stay."

I nodded, then Mai-Li and I removed as much of the debris from the floor as we could. I gestured to the boys to set up their sleeping bags and I placed mine next to theirs.

"We should all take a sip of water, and have something to eat, we missed supper," I said. I looked inside the provision bag and took out the water flask, then handed around our shared cup of water.

"How are our supplies doing?" Taylor asked.

"Mai-Li knows better than me," I said, turning to her.

"There are still a few things left from the cache we found on Annacis Island, canned beans, that sort of thing, and we have a few crackers left, half a bag of flour, and half a box of sugar cubes, from your friends in Hope. Oh, and the chocolate mix. The apples and the granola bars are gone, but we have the deer meat. We should be okay until we get to the foothills if we ration carefully. I have some dried blueberries in my bag, and if we can camp somewhere and build a fire, I can make pancakes as a treat."

When the kids heard Mai-Li say 'blueberry' and 'pancakes' they jumped up and down and clapped their hands. Blueberry pancakes were my favourite breakfast, my dad always made them on Sunday morning for as long as I could remember. It's funny how memories tended to pop up when least expected.

We opened two cans of brown beans, and as we had no way of heating them, we ate them cold.

"Sleep with your clothes on," Taylor said. "Anyone has to go before I turn off the flashlight?"

I was so glad Taylor asked because he ended up taking the boys outside and Mai-Li took Debbie, who had to go again after Mai-Li lifted her into the car. Shortly, we were all settled in our sleeping bags, breathing sighs of exhaustion. When the flashlight went off, it was black as ink inside the car.

"Carlie, story?" Debbie asked.

"Aren't you tired?" I asked.

"Just a short story, okay?" Rusty muttered.

"Fine, I'll keep my voice low, Willie, Taylor, you guys okay with this?"

No answer, just snores.

I told about a family who lived in the mountains, and how they were friends with the animals, and I was just getting to the juicy part when Mai-Li interrupted. "They're all sleeping Carlie, thanks for the story. Night."

I rolled over and closed my eyes. I was almost asleep when I had that same feeling I had earlier. I heard a noise outside, a snap like someone stepping on a twig. What if there was a person instead of an animal out there? I knew I had to check it out or I would be awake all night.

I climbed out of my bag and crawled over to where Taylor was sleeping next to the door. I shook his shoulder, and he woke immediately.

"Finally," he whispered. "You've come to your senses."

"Shut up, Taylor, I thought I heard something outside."

"What did you hear?"

"A crack, like someone stepping on a twig."

"Okay, I'll have a look, you stay here."

I sensed movement as he climbed out of his sleeping bag. There was a shuffling sound as he searched through his pack. I knew he was getting his gun. He was so quiet I wasn't aware he had left.

The only sound in the car was light breathing, and Rusty talking in his sleep. I waited patiently, hoping Taylor would return soon.

Then I heard a gunshot and loud shouts, and I threw myself flat on the floor. Willie woke up cursing, the kids sat up in fear, their eyes big as saucers. Mai-Li talked softly, trying to calm them.

"Mai-Li," I whispered. "I'm over here by the door, I heard a noise and Taylor went to check it out. I don't know who fired the gun, but there's someone besides Taylor out there. Keep your heads down and be quiet."

I expected no answer from Mai-Li, she would know what to do.

"Willie, are you awake?"

"Yeah, what the hell is going on?"

"There's someone outside, and I don't know if it was Taylor or someone else who fired the shot. You have your gun?"

"Yeah, it's right here."

"Good, I'm going to see if I can find Taylor. Don't turn on your flashlights, you can't let anyone out there see us."

"You want to take my gun?"

I hesitated for a second before answering. "Thanks, Willie, but I'd shoot myself in the foot if I tried using it. You keep it, and crawl over to where the others are, okay."

I listened as Willie shuffled across the floor. I felt for the stairs and remembered, at the last second, there was a step missing. I almost took a nosedive but managed to grab the side of the car. I moved down the remaining two steps and crouched when I landed on the ground. Where was Taylor, was he hurt?

I removed my knife from the case, my hands were sweaty, and I wiped them on my jeans.

Time passed slowly, and I strained my ears for noises or movement. Suddenly, a hand covered my mouth, and I struggled to get loose.

"It's me, don't make a sound," I recognized Taylor's voice, and I relaxed.

He pushed me flat on the ground and lay next to me. Then he whispered in my ear. "I counted four, but there may be more. They're armed and took a shot at me."

I inhaled sharply, and he put his arm around my waist. "When I tell you to, get back inside the car, and keep low. I'll be right behind you."

I nodded, my heart pounding so fast, I found it difficult to breathe. I pulled my mask off, letting it hang around my neck.

I heard shuffling noises and saw beams of light approaching the car.

"Now," Taylor whispered urgently.

I found the bottom step, grabbed the edge of the floor, pulled myself up, and rolled to the side just as Taylor flung himself into the car and landed next to me. A shot fired and he threw himself over me. The bullet flew through the window and lodged in the back wall of the car.

"Everyone," Taylor whispered, "stay down and don't move. Willie, are you with them?"

"Yeah, I'm here, and I'm ready."

"Good man."

We waited, and again there was silence. Why were they shooting at us? It had to be one of the gangs Taylor told us about, and obviously, we were intruding on their territory.

"Taylor, what should we do?"

"I'm going to try talking to them."

I inhaled, praying we would get through this nightmare.

"Hey," Taylor yelled. "Can we talk about this before someone gets hurt?"

A booming voice answered. "You're trespassing."

"Look, we just wanted a place to stay for the night, we had no idea we were on anyone's turf."

"Your voice sounds familiar; you've been here before."

Taylor cleared his throat, then said. "No. We're just passing through the Wastelands but got caught in the firestorm."

Then we heard raised voices, then arguing. "You got anything to bargain with?"

"Shit," Taylor said quietly. Then he released me, handed me his gun, rose, and stood in the doorway. I reached up to pull him down. "No," he said sharply, turning to look down at me. "And don't let them see you."

"You armed?" one of the attackers asked.

Taylor remained quiet, and suddenly a beam of light shone directly into his eyes.

"I asked if you were armed?" the same commanding voice asked.

"Yeah, I got my bow and arrows."

"You alone?"

"No, I'm with a small group, look man, we're just passing through. I promise we're no threat to any of you."

"How many are in your group?"

"Three kids, and four older teens."

"Kids," a snickering voice asked. "Hey, you got any girls with yah?"

I inhaled, suddenly understanding why Taylor had given me his gun.

"Wrong question," Taylor said. Then he turned, threw himself on the floor, and grabbed the gun from my hand. He aimed and fired into the darkness. A sharp yelp and sounds of movement and cursing filled the air and shots fired back.

Taylor yelled, "Willie, get to one of the windows, use your gun, and shoot the bastards."

The whine of bullets passing through the car, and hitting the walls and floor was deafening. I covered my ears and slowly crawled over to the kids and Mai-Li. The boys were crying and huddled together, I grabbed one under each arm and held them tightly.

Suddenly the shooting stopped. I heard a noise behind me, and I swung my head around in time to see a muscular man balanced on the frame of one of the car windows. He was holding a gun and had it aimed directly at me. I reached for my dagger, took a deep breath, and threw it as hard as I could; it buried deep in his chest, just as he fired his weapon. He fell forward, landing with a heavy thud on the floor of the car.

Taylor saw what happened, then shouted outside. "Stop, before someone else gets wounded or dies. This is craziness, we have nothing to offer. Just let us go, otherwise, I use my weapons, and I never miss my target."

"We get one of you, that's why you're calling a truce?" It was the same whiney voice who earlier asked if there were any girls in our group.

"No, but we got one of yours. You can come to get him after we leave. Do we have a deal or not?"

There was no response for the longest time.

"I'm losing my patience, you have four seconds to answer," Taylor yelled. "Then I start shooting arrows, and as I just said, I'm damn good."

I watched him in amazement. He exhibited no fear during the entire conflict, and it was then I realized fighting was not new to him.

"Hell, now I know who you are," a deep voice said. "I thought your voice sounded familiar, only one I know who carries a bow is Taylor West?"

Taylor hesitated before answering. "Yeah, it's me, and I don't appreciate being attacked in the middle of the night; I'm giving you one chance to lay down your weapons and get out of here."

"Look man, if we'd known it was you, we would've welcomed you with open arms. Heard you were head of the Phantoms in Van, what are you doing out here?"

"What I just said, I'm passing through. I thought you Desert Rats were located further north?"

"At first, but with the firestorms and other gangs, we left. We found an abandoned mining town just over the tracks, and this train car was a real bonus for us when we...."

"When you what Lars?" Taylor asked as he waited for him to finish his sentence.

"Nothing, just shooting the breeze."

"Visiting time is over. Send two of your guys over here to collect your man."

"Yeah, you got it Chief. We're good right?" I sensed a trace of fear in Lar's voice.

"Yeah, we're good."

During the entire conversation, I never once took my eyes off Taylor. He stepped aside as two of their ruffians jumped into the car. They grabbed the arms of the dead assailant and dragged him across the floor to the exit.

Taylor stood rigidly, holding his gun, and just as they were ready to leave, he raised his index finger gesturing for them to stop. He grabbed the hilt of my knife and pulled it from the guy's chest, wiping the blade on the dead man's jeans.

"Let Lars know we plan on walking across the Wastelands, I know you'll be following us, but don't get too close. Unfortunately, this had to happen, but you had a choice, and you made the wrong one."

The two gang members nodded, then carrying their grisly burden, disappeared into the night.

I sighed in relief; Taylor got his flashlight and turned it on. He shone it on me, and his eyes opened in disbelief. I looked down at Rusty, his head turned facing the door. I tried to shake him awake, but his body went limp; it was then I noticed his shirt was covered with blood.

"Rusty," I said quietly as I shifted him in my lap. "Look at me."

There was no movement, and Mai-Li reached over and removed my arm. She put her hand on his neck, inhaled deeply, then turned and looked at Taylor, shaking her head sadly.

I shook Rusty again, begging him to wake up. Taylor bent down and took Rusty from my arms, laying him on his sleeping bag. Then he pulled me up, and I struggled angrily, but he wouldn't let me go. I pounded his chest, and he grabbed my wrists tightening his hold. He looked into my eyes.

"Carlie, he's gone."

All I felt at that moment was anger, deep, deep anger. "You told us everyone would be okay, you promised."

Taylor stiffened as if struck. Something shattered inside of me, and I whispered in his ear. "You lied." Then everything went dark.

Chapter Twenty-Three

"Carlie, open your eyes."

I heard sobs and frantic voices, something bad must have happened. Then someone was shaking my shoulders. "Please Carlie, open your eyes, and look at me."

I moaned and turned my face away. I recognized his voice; Taylor was calling me.

He whispered in my ear "You have to wake up."

I opened my eyes. Taylor was holding me tightly, and my head rested on his shoulder. Eddie was sitting on his sleeping bag, wringing his hands, sobbing inconsolably. Willie was standing next to the door his face white as a ghost, Mai-Li was kneeling on the floor, her body swaying back and forth, and Debbie sat next to her, her ball pressed against her face.

"Where's Rusty?" I asked. "Let me see him."

Taylor shook his head.

"Why won't you let me see him?"

Taylor held me tighter; he had been crying. I sat up and pushed him away. "No, don't touch me, stay away from me. You lied to me, you lied to all of us."

Taylor stiffened, saying nothing. I rose unsteadily. "Why can't I see Rusty, what's wrong?" I asked, swinging around to look at Mai-Li. Her face was wet with tears, and she looked away. I swayed, and Willie grabbed me before I fell to the floor.

"Who was screaming, was it Rusty?" I asked.

No-one answered. Why was everyone acting so weird? I reached out to Eddie, and he shrank back in fear, holding Squishy tightly.

"Eddie," I pleaded. "What's wrong?"

I walked over to him, and he flinched, then raced past me and threw himself into Taylor's arms.

Why was Eddie afraid of me? Why wasn't Rusty answering me? Why wouldn't anyone talk to me?

I approached Willie and reached for his hands. "What's wrong, why won't anyone tell me what's wrong?"

Willie stepped back, looked into my eyes, and said quietly. "It's Rusty, he was shot."

My throat felt raw, and I had trouble breathing.

Mai-Li slowly rose, handed Debbie over to Willie, and took me in her arms. "He died instantly."

"No," I screamed. "He's just a little boy, he's only ten years old."

Mai-Li was openly crying, and Eddie was clinging to Taylor's neck. When Debbie realized everyone was crying, she threw herself backward and Mai-Li rushed to her, catching her before she crashed to the floor. She tried to comfort the young girl but was not able to get her to understand what was happening.

I looked around the car and slowly walked over to the sleeping bags. I lowered myself to the floor, reached over, and pulled back the bag that covered Rusty's body. The bullet entered his chest, there was so much blood for such a little boy. His face was so serene, I touched it softly, then swept his hair away from his face. My Rusty, my heart, my soul.

I don't know how long I sat looking at him, but Mai-Li came and sat next to me. "It's almost dawn, Carlie, we have to get ready to leave."

"We can't leave him, Mai-Li, we can't leave him here."

"We're taking him with us, we'll find a peaceful resting place for him."

"It was the guy who came in the back window. He tried to shoot me, but I threw my knife at him, and his gun went off. Did he kill Rusty?"

Mai-Li nodded sadly. "Yes, it was him."

"It was my fault. If I hadn't thrown my knife at him, he would have shot me, and Rusty would still be alive?"

"Carlie don't say that. He would have killed all of us."

I rose, went to my sleeping bag, and rolled it up. "We better pack, we must leave soon. Give the kids a cookie, we'll eat later."

I waited, but no one moved. Eddie struggled out of Taylor's arms and walked over to me. He stood in front of me, saying nothing. I knelt and reached for him, but he stepped back, his face distorted in anger.

"Why did you let Rusty die?"

I felt like I was smashed by a jackhammer, Taylor's face froze in shock, then he ran over to Eddie and picked him up, shaking his head and talking to him quietly.

I don't remember anything after that, I felt as if I was drowning in hot liquid. I was floating in a bubble, it was safe, and the pain and loss could not touch me here.

I have no idea how long I left; I opened my eyes, I was lying in my sleeping bag, surrounded by shadows. I rolled over and realized I was holding something soft and smelly; it was Squishy.

"Mai-Li," I heard a voice say. "Carlie's awake. Why doesn't she say hi?"

"She will, Debbie, but let her return to us first."

I sat up, my head missing a rocky roof by a few centimetres. "Where is everyone?"

"I am right here," Mai-Li answered quietly. "And so are Debbie and Eddie. Taylor and Willie are hunting."

I heard crying, was it Eddie? Why was he crying, he never cried. I had to get to him, I had to comfort him.

I crawled out of my bag and looked around. Everything was strange. There was a fire burning near a rounded entrance. Mai-Li was stoking the coals, and Debbie was sitting next to her, holding her ball tightly in her hand. I smiled at her, and she shyly buried her head in Mai-Li's lap.

Eddie was sitting in his sleeping bag, between me and the fire. He rubbed his eyes and left a streak of dirt on his face. He lowered his head, refusing to look at me.

"Eddie, are you okay? Why are you crying?"

He sobbed louder, and a weight settled on my chest.

"Eddie, please answer me. You're scaring me. Is something wrong?"

Mai-Li reached over and touched his face. He stood, and slowly approached me.

"Here's Squishy, thanks for lending him to me?" Eddie reached over and took him. He was looking hard into my eyes and studied my face, as if I was a stranger.

"Eddie, why are you so angry with me?" I don't know why I asked him, but somehow, I knew I had to.

"Because you left me, you went away with Rusty."

Mai-Li inhaled sharply but said nothing. She handed a piece of paper to Debbie, who threw it into the ashes, clapping her hands when it caught on fire.

"Eddie, why would I leave with Rusty? I would never separate us, the three of us will always be together, and you know that."

His eyes lit up, and he whispered. "I know, Rusty said to tell you he's okay, and not to be sad."

My heart felt as if I had a knife shoved into it. As if in a trance, I stood and walked past the fire and stood at the entrance. We were facing a meadow, bordered by slim, willowy birches and aspens. The bushes and shrubs encircling the trunks of the trees were lush and healthy. I stepped outside and inhaled the clear air. Eddie followed me and I asked him quietly "Where are we?"

"In the Foothills, don't you remember?"

I shook my head. "How long have we been here?"

"A few days."

"So that's why Taylor and Willie are hunting?"

"Yeah, Taylor said there are lots of rabbits and pheasants here and if they catch some, we can cook them for supper."

I nodded, and walked down a small incline, heading into the heath; I sat down, then brushed my hands lightly over the blades of grass. I lay back and stared at the sky. Eddie watched me for the longest time, then lowered himself to the ground. I instinctively kept quiet, understanding he wasn't ready to talk to me.

The sun peeked around the fluffy clouds. The sky was deep blue, and I watched a pair of swallows diving and skimming for insects.

"Where's Rusty?" I asked.

Eddie flinched and clasped Squishy closer to his chest. He sat up and pointed to a solitary willow growing in the middle of the meadow.

"Is it okay if I go see him?"

Eddie nodded.

"Do you want to come with me?"

Eddie took my hand, and we rose and walked over to the graceful tree. He sat next to a mound of earth; with wildflowers planted on top. Someone cut two pieces of wood and tied them together to make a cross, and carved the words "Rusty Coleman, age 10."

Eddie reached over and placed his hand on the dirt. I hurt so much, I wished I were still inside my bubble, where there was no pain, only darkness.

Then he took my hand and placed it on the dirt next to his. Why couldn't I cry? Why couldn't I feel it?

I pulled back my hand, reached over, and pulled Eddie in my arms. He laid his head on my chest, although I sensed he was not ready yet to forgive me.

I spotted Taylor and Willie walking across the field; Taylor was carrying a pheasant and Willie a rabbit.

The guys noticed us under the tree and stopped a few centimetres away.

"Hey, Carlie," Willie said, then lifted his arm and showed me the rabbit.

I nodded. He shrugged, then headed in the direction of the den. Just as he reached the entrance, he shouted. "Honey, I'm home."

Taylor stared at me his face impassive. I knew he was waiting for me to speak first, but all I felt was anger and desolation. Eddie jumped up and ran to him. Taylor ruffled his hair, gave him the pheasant, and pointed in the direction of the cave. Eddie looked at me, then left.

Taylor remained silent, then crouched and looked at me. "Are you here to stay?"

My eyes filled with tears, and I fought them back. I knew what he meant.

"It's all right to cry, Carlie. We all have, we miss him fiercely."

"How long did it take us to walk across the Wastelands?" I asked, changing the topic.

"Two days, then we found this place. We let Eddie decide where we would bury Rusty."

I nodded and looked down at my hands. "Don't tell me," I said, "Debbie found the animal house."

Taylor nodded. "She has a talent that can't be denied."

I shook my head slowly, suddenly realizing he was carrying a rifle, and so was Willie. "Where did you get the rifles, I thought you only had guns?"

"We did, but after the Desert Rats left, I started thinking. Why was the passenger car so important to them, and why would they guard it with their lives? I discovered a hidden cache under the car. It was full of ammo — rifles, guns, bullets, and I decided they owed us, so I took a rifle for myself, one for Willie, and one for you. I thought you might prefer it to a handgun."

My thoughts were still in the Wastelands, and I turned and looked at him. "I thought Lars was your friend, he promised to let us go. Don't you trust him?"

"Never have, never will. I imagine the Desert Rats have discovered by now we found their weapon cache. Lars won't let it slide; he'll be tracking us and will find us."

"You make it sound like he has a personal vendetta against you. You told us you had never been in the Wastelands, but that wasn't true, was it? Lars knew you, and something happened between you two?"

Taylor sighed and sat down next to me. I stiffened, not sure I wanted to hear his account.

"I'm sorry I lied. A few years after the earthquake, it became evident our time was running out at Little Mountain. I was leading the Phantoms and I decided to check out other locations, so half of us went, and the rest stayed. We stumbled across the Wastelands, and we ran into the Desert Rats, who were living in an abandoned mining shaft. They took a few pot-shots at us; I don't think Lars wanted to take us on, as he was quite aware we outnumbered them and carried more weapons."

"So, did you leave?"

"Eventually, but when a gang challenges another gang, you never turn and leave."

"You mean, not if you were the Phantoms, I'm sure your reputation was well known, even in the Wastelands. When I lived on Little Mountain, everyone feared them, even the meanest hoodlums and it meant certain death if captured."

Taylor's face turned an angry red, and he clenched his jaw. "You shouldn't have believed everything you heard on the streets."

I would have responded to his remark, but I was still furious at him for not revealing he'd been in the Wastelands before and confronted the Desert Rats.

"Why did you leave the Phantoms?" I asked quietly.

"We'll talk later, Mai-Li needs help getting supper ready."

He was avoiding my question, and I refused to let the matter drop. "What will the Desert Rats do to us?"

"Nothing, if I have my way."

"We've found Paradise, but we cannot stay," I murmured.

"Carlie, we never intended to stay here, it's a healing place. We can't stay."

He stood and headed for the den. I watched as he walked across the field, I wasn't ready to forgive him, and I wasn't sure I ever would.

I returned to the cave, but I had no appetite for food. Eddie and Debbie played ball while I helped Mai-Li clean up. Taylor and Willie moved to the far corner of the cave and were talking animatedly. Willie raised his voice a few times, and Taylor waited for him to calm down. I knew they were talking about the Desert Rats.

Darkness slowly arrived, and the sunset was brilliant, lighting the sky and dropping golden orbs on the trees and flowers.

Mai-Li dowsed the fire, and Taylor turned the lamp to a low setting. Mai-Li got the kids ready for bed. I felt uncomfortable as if I was an interloper. They weren't ready to take me back just yet, everyone needed time to heal.

It was my fault Rusty was dead, and I felt hollow inside.

I realized Taylor wasn't the only one who was seeking forgiveness.

Chapter Twenty-Four

We left early the next morning and stopped at the gravesite for a final farewell. Eddie stayed close to Taylor, Mai-Li and Debbie followed, then me, alone, followed by Willie. We quietly crossed the meadow, then turned down an old animal trail.

I noticed Taylor had tied Rusty's compass around his neck. I was handed Rusty's backpack to carry as well as my own as everyone had their arms full.

We stopped around noon at top of a hill. In the distance I saw the mountains and was shocked to see snow in the upper reaches. The weather was noticeably colder the farther east we walked.

That night we camped next to a stream. I took over water duty, boiling, then refilling the canisters. Mai-Li and Taylor prepared supper, and I heard her laugh quietly. I watched them for a few seconds. Willie was sitting next to Debbie, whittling a piece of wood while she sang a song only Debbie could understand. He turned and looked at me, and he frowned when our eyes met. He must have noticed me watching Taylor and Mai-Li.

Debbie and Eddie went to bed shortly after sunset, Mai-Li read them a short story and tucked them in.

"Tomorrow you can read to them," she said to me when she returned to the fire. "I don't read as well as you, apparently Carlie's funner."

I nodded. I so missed spending time with the kids. I noticed Mai-Li and Taylor looking at each other. Why should I care if Taylor liked her?

Taylor spread his map on the ground. He pointed out our location, and the path we would be taking, following the creeks until we got to the mountains. With the erratic weather patterns, there was no way of knowing when, or how much snow would fall before we got there.

"It's getting colder at night; we need better shelter," Willie said. I looked skeptically in his direction. Willie making astute remarks was beyond my comprehension.

Taylor nodded in agreement, then folded the map and replaced it in his pocket. He turned and looked at me. "I imagine you have a lot of questions to ask since our clash with the Desert Rats. Is there anything you want to know?"

I sat astonished for a few seconds; his comment was unexpected. When I didn't respond, Mai-Li reached over and placed her hand on my arm. "What was the last thing you remembered Carlie?"

I began to tremble and lowered my head. "I remember killing that guy, and there was blood, Rusty's blood, and I couldn't get him to wake up. Then everything went dark."

Mai-Li nodded. "You remember nothing else until you woke in the den?"

"No, except sometimes I had dreams, but I can't remember them all. Someone was screaming, they wouldn't stop."

Mai-Li looked at Taylor but said nothing. Then she cleared her throat. "What did you dream about?"

"The three kids were running in a meadow, laughing and playing."

"Did you have that dream a lot?"

I shook my head. "Not a lot, just a few times, the last time was when I woke up. They were playing in the same meadow again, when suddenly, Rusty stopped. He took my hand and spoke. 'I'm leaving now. I love you, Carlie,' and then he disappeared."

"What a wonderful gift he gave you. He will always be with you in your heart, you know?"

"Nothing will bring him back. My dear sweet Rusty, why did this have to happen to him?"

Then I started to cry, deep-wracking sobs. Mai-Li gathered me in her arms, shaking her head at Taylor when he stood. When I had exhausted myself, I pulled away. Willie and Taylor were gone.

"I'm sorry Mai-Li," I whispered. "I never cry."

"I know, and that's your problem. Come, we should get some sleep, Taylor wants to leave early."

I nodded, helped Mai-Li put out the fire, then followed her to the tent. She went inside gesturing for me to join her.

"Did I sleep in here with you guys when we left the Wastelands?"

Mai-Li did not answer, and I turned and looked in her direction.

"Mai-Li?"

"You slept with Taylor; he was the only one who could control you. You would wake up screaming and crying."

"Where did Willie sleep?"

"Here with us, you and Taylor slept in the small tent."

"Why can't I remember any of this, Mai-Li? It's like a huge chunk of my memory has disappeared."

"In a way it has, it may return, and it may not, it'll be up to you."

"Eddie said we walked for two days before finding the meadow. How did I get here?"

"You walked on your own, carrying both your pack and Rusty's. You never said a word to anyone. You scared us, your eyes were unfocused, and you wouldn't eat. Taylor would force water and food down your throat. I don't think you were with us, and I know he feared you would never come back."

"He does so much for us Mai-Li, but I don't trust him, he lied to us, about the

Phantoms, and being in the Wastelands and confronting the Desert Rats."

"We have all done something in our lives that needs forgiving, none of us are perfect, and when Taylor joined us, he took on the responsibility of protecting all of us, even Willie. Weren't you the one who called him our Protector?"

"To keep Willie under control, at the time I thought it was a perfect solution."

Mai-Li laughed, climbed inside her sleeping bag, and closed her eyes.

I don't know how long I slept when I awoke from a disturbance. Mai-Li and Taylor were standing outside the tent, they were whispering, their voices strained.

"I'm going to find him," Taylor said. "Don't let Carlie know."

I looked at Eddie's sleeping bag, it was empty, and Squishy was gone. I frantically crawled out of the tent and heard Taylor swear under his breath when he saw me.

"Where's Eddie?" I asked, my heart pounding so fast I had to take a deep breath.

Taylor ran his fingers through his hair, saying nothing.

"He's gone," Mai-Li answered. "Taylor thinks he's going back to the meadow, to Rusty's grave."

"Alone, out there in the dark? Taylor, please find him. I can't lose him too."

Taylor nodded and touched my arm lightly.

He went to his tent and grabbed his bow and arrows and rifle. "Willie," he hollered. "Wake up, you're in charge."

He turned and looked at me, then disappeared into the darkness.

We heard Willie grumble, then he poked his head out of the tent. He spotted Mai-Li and me and scratched his head. "Is it morning already?"

We explained what happened. Willie retrieved his rifle, then came and squatted next to our tent. Mai-Li and I went back inside; the noise woke Debbie, and when she saw Mai-Li, she smiled and went back to sleep.

"Mai-Li," I whispered. "How could he get away, I heard nothing, and he was right next to me?"

"I heard nothing myself. He must have been planning this for a while."

"What if something happens to him?"

"Taylor will find him and bring him back."

I lay down on top of my sleeping bag, staring into the darkness. I put my hand on Eddie's sleeping bag and closed my eyes.

I woke with a jolt; Eddie's legs wrapped around my waist and Squishy under my neck. The sun was shining, and I realized it was morning.

Eddie opened his eyes and looked at me. There were no words, we just hugged each other, and I held him until he fell back to sleep.

Mai-Li was talking quietly to Debbie, and they both left the tent. I dressed quickly and joined them. Taylor and Willie were sitting around the campfire, drinking coffee, and talking quietly. We walked over and sat down.

I found it difficult to look at anyone, I was ashamed and wondered how I could have fallen asleep when my world was in shatters.

"Don't beat yourself up," Taylor said tiredly, looking at me. "He was wandering in circles, scared but determined to return to his brother. We had a long talk, and he cried for a long time. Then he told me he was ready to come back and was sorry he ran away."

"Thank you, Taylor, thank you so much; I've been so wrapped up in my grief I forgot about Eddie."

"We all forgot about him, but that's going to change. The kids are our number one priority, and if it takes a year to get to Princeton, so be it."

I smiled, as did Mai-Li. Debbie grinned, although she wasn't aware of what happened. If Eddie wanted her to know, he would tell her; she always understood him.

"A year?" Willie sputtered. Then he filled his plate with beans and took a handful of crackers.

"By the way, the sooner we get to a stream," I said, "The sooner Squishy gets a bath. He's starting to smell like a real bear."

The End

BWL Author
Shirley Bigelow
DeKelver

Shirley Bigelow DeKelver is the author of four novels: *The Trouble with Mandy, Lilacs & Bifocals, Child of the Ancients,* and *Climate of Fire* series as well as two short stories, *Nature's Precious Gift,* and *Ziggy's Revenge.* She was born in Calgary, Alberta, and after working for over forty years in law firms as an administrator and paralegal, she and her husband Don retired to their cabin at White Lake, located in the British Columbia Interior. She is an avid photographer and many of her photos were published in books and anthologies. She enjoys acrylic painting and birdwatching. You can visit her website at: www.shirleydekelver.com.

BWL Publishing

BWL

bwlpublishing.ca